AREION FURY MC

ZACK

"Zack" Areion Fury MC #1
By Esther E. Schmidt

Dedication

This one is for two people who not only made a huge change in my life, but I honestly can't even imagine my life without them anymore.

They are a huge part in my everyday life and in my heart. Support, motivation and kicking my ass, they are always there. A fine road between laughter and guidance. They are the very reason I started writing this book and have been there every step of the way.

Without the both of them, Zack wouldn't exist.
So this one is for you two:
Christi Durbin & Fran Gray.

I love you both...you fucking bitches.

Chapter 1

"These two buildings just might work. Well, at least one of them doesn't seem to be such a bad deal and it would be perfect for a gym. We've got to get this property. Seems like a good investment for the club. What do you think?"

I look back at Dams. His back is facing me and he's looking out the window. I've no idea what's caught his attention, but I'm pretty sure it's not me.

"Hey, I didn't spend yesterday going from one property to the next for nothing, dude. We have to decide today, since they're auctioning off the property tomorrow."

Still my Vice President doesn't move or indicate that he's even heard me. I turn in my chair and it squeaks under my weight. I know the damn thing is old, but my dad sat in this chair. He fucking died in it just a little over ten months ago, leaving me to step up and take his place as President. His heart gave out, just like this chair will any damn time now. So call me sentimental, I don't care, and I won't replace it until it breaks.

"Making money, club business, you and me asshole... Decision time... Hey, talk to me, stupid." I throw the files on the table landing with a loud smack. Papers and photographs slide out of the folders, off the table and on to the floor.

"Fuck, dude! Am I having this conversation with the walls or what?"

Nothing, no reaction at all. His eyes are still glued to the window which has a clear view of the main room in the club. He's holding the blinds down with two fingers.

"Hey, eyes here." I'm starting to get really pissed off and slam my fist on the table. At the exact same time loud music starts playing. It's coming from the main room of the clubhouse.

"What idiot pumps up music, that loud, and at this time of day?"

Without turning Dams signals his hand for me to calm down. What. The. Fuck?

"Just calm down, man," he says to go with it.

The song "Footloose" by Kenny Loggins is blasting through the speakers.

For real? I grumble out my thoughts. "Jesus, who the fuck listens to this '80's shit?"

Dams gives me an angry and irritated look.

Exactly dude, that's how I feel. Now that my curiosity's spiked, I walk to the window to see what the jerk is so damned focused on. As soon as my eyes meet the object of his attention all the blood drains from my body. Well, not from my body, more like a one way trip south, ready for some serious action.

"Fuck." I didn't think anything could get me rock hard from just one look. "What the…. Who is… She can't… fuck. Does she know where the hell she is?" I fucking trip over my own goddamned words.

Dams, the fucker, can't hold himself back. He shakes his head and barks out a laugh.

Down in the main room of the club there's a chick tapping her foot to the rhythm of the music. Her hips start to sway. She's putting something back in the front pocket of her jeans. She slowly moves to the rhythm of the music while taking off her leather jacket.

"Jesus. Did somebody order a stripper? That's gotta be it. Damn. Doesn't she know she's in the middle of a biker club filled with horny dudes?" My voice is laced with a hint of anger.

Dams' grin seems to grow. "Like putting honey on a horny bear." He finishes the sentence on a moan.

I whack him on the back of his head with my hand and grab the door handle. I've got to put a stop to this before one of my men spot her.

Dams grabs a hold of my arm. "Just wait, Prez. Really, she did the same thing yesterday. Pokey grabbed her ass and she had him on his knees in less than a second."

"Pokey? On his knees?" I give him a dazed look, since Pokey's like a tank on steroids. How the hell can this chick handle that kind of muscle?

"Yeah. On. His. Knees. Believe me, this chick can do whatever and wherever. Relax and enjoy buddy." The jerk even throws me a wink.

My hand slips off the door handle and my eyes slide back to the woman. She walks to the bar and throws her leather jacket down. Her body is pure perfection. Curves right where they should be; perfect ass and hips to hold on to.

When she turns I see the ideal tits to keep that ass in balance. Her blonde hair with streaks of bright blue falls in curly waves over those damn fine ass tits.

"Blue hair?" I shake my head. I mean, come the fuck on. Who the hell has blue hair? Okay, so it's only the last 4 inches and the rest of it is white. But with this chick, it just adds to the hot vibe she's got going on. Our eyes follow her until she walks into the storage room and out of sight. We both release the breath we're holding.

"That's one hot piece of ass I wouldn't mind sticking my dick in." My VP gives me a shoulder bump. "Right?"

My eyes are still fixed on the storage room, ignoring the jerk like he was ignoring me a few minutes ago.

"I call dibs on this one," Dams' annoying voice slices through the air.

No way am I ignoring that. "The fuck you ain't." Turning to look one another in the eye, I go on, "I'm President, I own every pussy in this joint. First dibs or not, that piece of ass is mine."

Dams is about to fight me on this, when Heineken crates start to slide over the floor and out of the storage room. The chick walks out with an empty crate in each hand. She puts the crates on top of each other. Turning her head to the window, she gives a small smile while her body is still moving to the rhythm of the music. She shakes her head, takes a crate and begins to collect the empty bottles off the tables.

Last night's party left all the tables and bar filled with empty bottles and glasses everywhere. The song ends and another one comes on.

Shit. I need to know more about this one. "From 1980's to 2014 punk rock, this chick has some weird choice in music. Who is she, Dams? Any idea?"

Again, no answer. I jam him in the side with my elbow.

"What?" Dams' eyes are still locked on the window.

"Who. Is. She?"

He releases his breath with a whistle. "I have no idea. I think she's a friend of Lynn's. Lynn is sick so she asked this chick to fill in for her."

"I know all my sister's friends. Believe me when I say I've never met this one." I throw the words back at him because I, for damn sure, know all her friends.

Meanwhile all the tables get cleared except the one in front of the window. I'm checking out her perfect body while she's swaying to the beat walking straight to our window. Faded jeans, black Harley Davidson top with a rhinestone skull cross graphic on it. She's put her hair up in a bun, some strands have fallen into her face. She bends over the table to grab a bottle, giving us the perfect view of her rack, tits almost spilling on the fucking table. Her head comes up and with the brightest blue eyes she stares straight at us.

"Woahhh!" Dams sucks in a breath.

I don't realize the low moan I'm hearing is coming from my throat. Those eyes, that face. She reminds me of someone, but who?

"Oh, hell no!"

Belle

I shake my head and laugh. Guys are so easy to distract. Give them a pair of tits to look at and you can shove a bucket underneath them to catch all the drool coming out of their mouth. I know my twins look good; more than a big handful and they've come in handy several times.

They used to bother me during kickboxing matches but seeing how I stopped competing three years ago, that's off the table and no longer matters. But as I lean over this table...

yeah, I'm working it to my advantage.

I clear the last of the beer bottles. It's time to shove the full crates back in the storage room. Walking back out, I grab my iPhone and change the song. I just love this new app, it allows me to change songs and volume. Saves me from having to walk back and forth to the sound system behind the bar.

"Bluetooth rules," I mumble to myself while placing a bucket beneath the running hot water.

I glance at my watch, just forty-five more minutes before I have to open up the shop. My first client is scheduled to come in a half hour after I open. So, I don't mind taking this shift for my best and only friend.

Bikers don't scare me. My dad was a multiple time world kickboxing champion in his early days. He spent years coaching guys in his own gym. He even trained me as I followed in his footsteps to become a world champion. So I was raised to ignore rough guys and taught how to handle them if they got stupid.

Besides, we used to live right next to the president of this club until my dad took my brother and me away to Japan. I shake my head at the memory. That was over 3 years ago. Now I've been back in my hometown for three weeks and I need to focus on the task at hand and that's cleaning the clubhouse of Areion Fury MC. As I walk to the first table with a bucket in my hand, my eye catches something white on the floor.

"Oh, that's just nasty." There's a condom that looks like it was ripped off a dick and smacked down on the floor.

Good thing Lynn already warned me it would be a fucking mess. Didn't think it would be that literal. After I wipe down all the tables and use a broom, the place looks better than it did an hour ago. Walking behind the bar, I look inside the fridge.

"Figures." You can tell a lot about someone by looking in their fridge.

These people have a who-needs-soda-when-all-we-need-is-alcohol mentality. Okay, I'm really thirsty and I could go for a beer right now. Looking around, not seeing a bottle opener, I put the cap on the side of the bar and give it a whack with my other hand. The cap pops and I bring the bottle to my mouth.

Zack

"Holy fuck that was hot." I can't believe my eyes.

Wiping a hand down my face I hear Dams. "Tell your sister to stick with her day job. We're keeping this one." He bumps my shoulder. "Right?"

I can't respond due to the shouting coming from the main room. I see Dell burst through the door with Jack behind him.

The shouting continues as Pokey enters, roaring at the top of his lungs. "You motherfucking idiot! I can't believe… you... Fuck. That hurt man. Jesus, I'm in pain."

Halfway through his screams the music comes to an end. The chick walks to the guys, tucking her phone back into her jeans. Pokey hops up on a table. Blood is dripping down his boot and on to the floor. He points to the prospect that's hiding behind Jack.

"You. You, idiot. You fucking shot me." His voice indicates murder will be next on his list as payback.

I grab the first aid kit as Dams and I walk toward the guys, just in time to see the chick grab a hold of Pokey's thigh and rip open the bloody tear in his jeans.

"Oh, yeah babe. You can rip off my clothes any day." Pokey's voice has my hand clenching into a fist.

Before I can shut him up I hear him scream again.

"You fucking bitch, you did that on purpose. Get your fucking hands off me," Pokey growls out.

I need to shut the fucker up. "Shut it, Pokey. Here's the first aid kit."

Without looking she reaches for the first aid kit and grabs a hold of my hand. I see her hold her breath as a shiver runs through the both of us. She turns her head to look and the most intense blue eyes stare back at me. Belle... It's fucking Jazzebelle.

The girl next door, my first love. Who am I kidding? My only love.

Until she took my heart with her, the day her father took Belle and her brother to Japan. I can't believe she is standing right in front of me.

"Belle?" Yeah, her name stumbles from my lips as a question.

"Sally." Belle jumps straight at me, wrapping her arms around my neck.

Dropping the first aid kit, I hug her tight. I can't believe I'm holding her in my fucking arms. Her body fits perfectly against mine. With her head tucked in the crook of my neck, I bring my lips close. I can't help myself as I brush my nose along her soft skin and inhale her sweet scent. My hands slide down her back and grip her ass as my mouth feathers up her neck.

"Are you seriously grabbing ass while I'm dying here, Prez?" Pokey's voice is laced with annoyance and a little jealousy.

I hear Belle chuckle while she slides down my body. "You're not dying, you pussy. The bullet barely grazed you." She opens the first aid kit, puts on rubber gloves and starts cleaning Pokey's wound.

"Sooooo. Sally, was it? You weren't kidding when you said that ass is mine." Dams' voice comes up from behind me.

Swinging my head back, I look him straight in the eye. "No one calls me Sally, you dick. It's Prez, Dams."

Raising my voice, so everyone is on the same page, I add, "And no one touches her, got me?"

Dams chuckles and I hear the guys agree.

"Be sure to spread the word so they all know." There, now all hell will break loose if some dipshit fucks up.

When I look at Dams he has a huge grin on his face when he says, "Sure, Prez."

I nod and look back at Belle who's just finished dressing up Pokey's wounded leg.

"There, all done, you big pussy." She turns and walks to the sink, throws the rubber gloves into the bin beneath it, and washes her hands.

*** Belle***

Watching the soap wash away, my mind goes back to Zack. I can't believe I threw myself at him. But the sound of his voice when he called me by the nickname he gave me all those years ago... Damn, I need to keep my distance. Everything seems to fall away when we touch. His breath on my neck, his hands sliding down my back... I shake my head and hands. Wiping them off on my jeans, I grab my jacket and head for the exit.

"See you guys later!" And I'm out the door.

Pulling the keys out of my jeans, I swing my leg across my blue Fat Boy Lo.

"Hey, wait up." I lift my head as I see Zack walking up to me. "So, you finally got your bike, yeah?"

A huge grin spreads my face, he remembered. "Yeah...I got her three weeks ago, the second I got off the plane. Since my dad ain't around anymore."

My eyes hit the ground. I shouldn't have mentioned that last bit, because I dread the following question he's going to ask.

"He's still in Japan with your brother?" he asks, surprise clear in his voice.

I can't do this right now. I start my bike and raise my voice. "Nah, they're both dead."

I leave him standing there, eyes on me, as I ride off.

Chapter 2

Belle

I park my bike right in front of the shop. The sign says "Open" which is weird, because I'm the one who should be opening today.

As I walk inside I see Brandlee standing behind the counter, eyes on his phone. "Hey, Lee."

"Hey, Jazz," he greets back without even taking his eyes off his phone.

"I thought I was opening this morning?"

Now he lifts his head and smiles. "You were, but you're fifteen minutes late."

I check my watch and see he's right. "Damn!"

I walk behind the counter and start preparing for my client. I pull out the design I've been working on for my first client of the day. It's a key with a snake behind it. The tail will wrap around, while the mouth of the snake is open and ready to eat the key and swallow it whole.

"You okay there, Sugar?" I look up to see Brandlee staring at me.

"Yeah, sure," I answer mindlessly.

He gives me a smile and his eyes twinkle. "Want me to pierce your nipple? I've got time and you've got...what, fifteen minutes, give or take?"

Now it's my turn to smile. I think back and remember Zack's lip piercing. Oh, what the hell...why not?

"Sure. I've got fifteen minutes to kill, so why don't I let ya kill my nipple. Right?"

He barks out a laugh. "Seriously? You're gonna let me?"

"Hell yeah, let's do this." My voice is solid.

Brandlee stretches his arm out toward his room, and follows me in as I sit down in his chair.

"Left, right or both?" He wiggles his eyebrows.

"Left?" I throw back at him.

He puts on his gloves as he prepares everything else.

"Right," he says.

Wait, what? "No. I said left, right?"

"Right, I heard you the first time, Sugar," he adds, followed by a chuckle.

Fuck me, I can't believe this guy and I can't believe I'm doing this. "Just the left one, Lee, don't fuck with me on this."

I chew my gum and stretch it out against the front of my upper row of teeth and to the back of my lower row of teeth. I suck in air through the gum, hearing four loud pops as a result.

"Cut that shit out," Brandlee snaps. "Now show me your tit."

I roll my eyes and stroll over to the trashcan, spitting out my gum before I walk back. "Smooth, Lee, real smooth."

"What? You'd rather have me ask to see your nipple? Still the same thing, Sugar. Now, bring that round piece of goodness into the daylight."

I shake my head and lower my tank, popping out my left breast. "Jesus, woman! Would you let someone pop it out when you need to tattoo a tit? I mean, if you want me to suck it, okay. That's the fastest way. Seriously...take the tank and bra off."

Okay, he's probably right. Either that, or he just wants a very good look at my tits. I take a deep breath and pull off my tank and bra.

"Right," Lee mumbles to himself.

"Stop saying that. Freaks me out thinking you're gonna pierce the right one instead of the left," I grumble.

He just fucking winks at me. "No worries, Sugar, I'll just pierce the other one next so they're both just right."

"Ah hell, just do it already, you idiot!" I huff and roll my eyes at said idiot.

He cleans my nipple and puts something that looks like some sort of tweezer on there. I know Lynn told me it's called a forcep septum, but it looks like a tweezer. He grabs a huge needle and, oh fuck. I can't watch this.

My nipple is hurting just at the thought of him pushing that huge thing through it. Or is it because he's squeezing the hell out of it with those? Fuck. Through my nipple. What. The. Hell. Am. I. Doing? It feels so weird; something clamping down hard on my nipple. He wiggles it left and right like he's checking to see if he's holding it right.

Hot, flaming heat surges through me. I bite my tongue, close my eyes and try not to scream, pushing the pain away... Fuck that hurt.

"Dude, for a woman, the greatest pain is having a baby, but this? Fuck. Close buddy. Fucking high up on the pain list." I suck my bottom lip in and hold it between my teeth.

"There, almost done," Brandlee assures me.

I open my eyes and try to look down at my nipple.

"You got kids, Sugar?" He grabs the ring and sticks it through.

"Nah, just a vivid imagination." I feel slightly nauseous and swallow down the guilt.

My hand reaches for the pendant I keep around my neck and I hold on to it.

Lee closes the nipple ring. "That looks hot. Want me to do the other one?"

I shake my head. "The hell no."

"Lip?"

"Fuck no," I growl.

He tilts his head. "Lady parts?"

"Lee," I gasp out his name. "How can you jump from that to my VG? I mean, you could have said tongue or navel. So not cool."

The idiot chuckles. "Sugar, you're gonna come back for more. Besides, you're the one bringing up lady parts in the first place."

"Not any time soon Lee." Shaking my head, I repeat, "Not any time soon."

"Yeah we'll see," Brandlee answers with a smug grin on his face.

I put my things back on as I hear my client walk into the store. "Thanks Lee. If you want me to ink something, lemme know."

With a nod of gratitude, he adds, "I'll keep that in mind."

As I walk out, I signal the client without looking, to follow me to my room. I pick up the design on the counter and flip on the lights. "Have a seat."

Turning around, I look at my client and recognize him as one of the bikers I just saw at the clubhouse. My eyes slip to his patch and see the abbreviation VP. Damn, gonna be one of those days.

He smiles when he sees I recognize him. "Belle, we meet again."

My smile falls. Only one person can call me that and even then it annoys me every time. That is the very reason I call that person by a girly name in response. So when Zack uses it, I use Sally.

My voice is firm when I say, "My name is Jazzebelle, or Jazz for short. Here, this is the design I've been working on. Hope I got all the details you mentioned on the phone right."

He takes the piece of paper from me while he stares at the design while I continue walking around my room setting things up.

"I'm Dams by the way, and this is…this is just…wow. You drew this with just one phone call? Damn woman, you're good." Approval and awe are heavy in his voice.

He makes me smile. Yeah, I know my drawing skills are perfect and even better when I'm tattooing. This is the very reason I quit my internship at the hospital, even though I invested all my time and devotion. I wanted to become a surgeon, just like my mom. But this… This is where my passion is, and what I want to do for the rest of my life.

"Thanks, I'm glad you like it. Where on your stomach did you want it?"

He takes off his cut and places it on a chair in the corner. Turning around, he reaches down and grabs the hem of his shirt. He pulls it over his head, leaving it at the back of his neck with the sleeves still in place. That's the moment I stop breathing.

His abs are rock hard. His broad chest is already covered with a huge tattoo. Left and right the same design of a horse at full speed running through flames. Since the design on the back of his cut is only the head and wings of the horse, this looks like an extended version of their patch. Areion Fury MC; Areion as in an extremely swift immortal horse. He steps closer to me, his biceps flex and I'm lost.

My nipple throbs like crazy and my head's spinning. Damn that beer and no food. Black spots appear in my vision. My feet start to sway as I feel two strong arms wrap around, holding me.

"You okay there, J?" His voice is soft and close to my ear.

"Yeah just got my nipple pierced, that's all. Oh, and you're hot," I mutter.

Wait, what? I groan as I realize I just said that out loud. A soft chuckle leaves his mouth and I feel it in his chest, which is still very close to my nipples.

"No shit, J? Can I see?" he rumbles.

Feeling my cheeks heat and my head still spinning, I step back. I walk to the fridge and take out a bottle of water. Downing half the bottle, I reach in my desk for the chocolate bar I've got in there. Tearing it open, I put a piece in my mouth, groaning at the sweetness that hits my tongue.

I open my eyes and see him staring at me with a hungry look in his eyes and I'm pretty sure it's not the chocolate he wants to eat.

"Want a piece?" I offer.

His eyebrows rise just as the corner of his mouth heads in the same direction. "Hell yeah, but not chocolate though."

Well damn, I should have seen that one coming. I put the chocolate down, grab a piece of gum and put it in my mouth. "Okay, time to get to work. Where did you want the design?"

He steps closer to me and flips the button on his jeans and pulls them a bit lower. He points to his left side, right along the line of the V that now shows a hint of black curls. Pretty sure this guy isn't wearing any underwear.

"Right here," he points out.

I take the design and drop to my knees. Putting the design in place, I look up. "Like this?"

The look of hunger is back in his eyes and I suddenly realize I'm in the exact position for a blow job.

"You're making this too damn easy for me, J." His voice is laced with a husky vibe.

I hear the front door open and turn my head even before I hear a voice loud and booming filling up the shop. "Get. Away. From. His. Dick. Belle."

Each word is spit out with a lot of anger and authority. I look in front of me, to see the huge jeans covered dick he's talking about, and then look up. Dams is grinning like an idiot and turns to look at Zack who's now standing next to us.

"Hey, Prez. She needs to be near my dick to do her job." He looks back at me and winks.

I hold up the design for Zack to see.

"You're the tattoo artist? You were a fucking intern when you left here! What happened to your dream of becoming a surgeon?" Zack growls.

I take a deep breath and close my eyes to the memory. That was my mom's dream for me. When I open my eyes I see his hard stare demanding an explanation.

I shrug my shoulders. "Well, things change. I decided I liked working with different kinds of needles. So yeah, I'm the artist and he's getting this tattoo."

He takes another step closer and looks at Dams. "A piercing isn't enough, you need ink on your dick too?"

Holy fuck. My head shakes back and forth from Zack to Dams. "Your dick is pierced? No shit. Can I see?"

Before my eyes reach the place between his legs I'm lifted off the ground. Zack has his arm around my waist and my back against his rock hard body.

"No way are you going anywhere near his dick, Belle." He grumbles his words on a hot breath through my hair.

I stretch out my gum and suck hard, making three loud pops while the fourth is smothered and that just pisses me off more. "Let me go Sally, I need to do my job and that means my hands will be near his dick."

Dams is clearly enjoying this.

"You can see, J, as long as I can see yours after I show you mine." He wiggles his eyebrows.

"Out, out, out. Now!" Zack barks.

Dams walks out of the room with his hands up.

Zack turns to shut the door and flips the lock. "You got a piercing?"

Okay, so not the question I was expecting.

"Yeah, as of 20 minutes ago. Freaking thing is throbbing like crazy." I look down at my boob.

"Christ, you got your nipple pierced?" his voice cracks.

My cheeks burn and I'm sure they're flaming red by now. My room is getting too damn small and he's getting too close. His smell is everywhere. Rough and spicy...all male... all Zack. Just so different from the Zack I remember from three years ago.

I can't breathe, can't be alone with him right now. And I can't believe I'm still calling him by that girly nickname, while he looks like a giant alpha man hunk. Taking a few quick steps to the door I flip the lock back open. Before I can reach for the door knob he reaches my face with his big hand.

His fingertips go to the back of my neck, his thumb caressing my cheek as his face inches closer to mine. "I've missed you so much."

His touch shoots hot vibes through my body and I feel the need to grab his shirt and slam my lips down on his.

I move to do just that when Dams knocks on the door. "Hurry up already, you two are on my damn time."

I can't help but laugh. "He's right, except it's my damn time."

Giving Zack a smile, I step away from his hand and feel the loss of his warmth. I open the door for Dams.

"Have a seat." I walk in front of him and pick up my gloves.

Zack's phone rings. Looking at the display he swipes his phone and answers. "Lynn."

I'm curious what the call is about. He's talking to my best friend, with whom I'm currently living with. So, I wait and look at him.

"Yeah sis, I'll get it for ya. No prob. Dams is getting new ink and we're in one car because we had to drop off some shit..." His eyes roll, clearly frustrated by his sister who

30

dares to interrupt him. "Hold on to your..."

I've had enough. Before he can finish his sentence I've got his phone in my hand. "Hey Lynn, what's up, bitch."

Lynn's voice cracks. "Hey. If it isn't my favorite lifesaving bitch from hell. The television isn't working. Neither is the DVD player or, oh hell...I dunno what the problem is. But I do know it's not fucking working at all. Oh and we're out of toast. I'm keeping the soup and the last of the toast down so I need more toast."

A giggle escapes me. I can't help it. I'm so glad to hear my friend is feeling better. While my favorite word is fuck, hers is bitch. She hates, and I mean truly hates the word cunt. Not so much coming from her own mouth, only when she's really pissed off. But call her a cunt? Yeah, you'd better pack your bags and leave the country. "He'll be right there, Honey."

"Thanks girl, see ya tonight." Her tone indicates she's happy help is on its way.

"Tonight," I promise her.

I give the phone back to an angry Zack, my smile still in place. "She needs toast and you've gotta fix the TV thing."

"I'm staying right here. She can wait," Zack growls.

I shake my head. "Yeah right, Lynn doesn't wait. You know how she gets. Oh and if it's the ride you're worried about, leave the keys for Dams and you can take my ride. Or Dams can take my ride, I don't mind."

"I'll take your..."

One look from Zack and Dams' voice disappears before he can finish that sentence.

Zack stands up and towers over me. "Gimme your fucking keys, Belle."

I'm chewing my gum furiously because I'm so annoyed.

Just before I can pop it Zack shakes his head. "Do not pop that gum."

I know it's like a five year old sticking out her tongue, I can't help myself and I pop it. Three loud ones, very fast. Giving him a satisfied smile, I reach inside my pocket and hand him my keys.

"Just a reminder, Dams, if she's annoyed, angry or nervous…she pops her gum." His head slightly turns as if he's remembering something. "Come to think about it. Right after those pops, didn't you used to hit people? Or anything else that got in your way? Did you get some anger management classes to work that shit out?"

I walk to the trashcan and spit out my gum, smile and blow him a kiss using my middle finger.

The left side of his mouth twitches as he looks down at the keys he's holding and growls. "Christ, seriously?"

He's holding the fluffy pink unicorn keychain that's attached to the keys of my bike. "What? It's cute and fluffy. Nothing's cute and fluffy about my ride. There needed to be some balance. Suck it up, buttercup and don't you dare scratch my ride."

Now he actually snorts. "Scratch your bike. I ain't no damn rookie."

He shakes his head and mutters some more curse words.

"Don't forget the toast!" I yell.

Without looking back he sticks up his arm. It looks like he's waving but I see that one finger pointing up in the air.

"Asshole," I bellow through the shop.

I hear him laughing as he walks out the door.

Locking eyes with Dams, I nod. "Okay, pretty boy, let's do this."

Dams' eyes are on my breasts. "You think I'm pretty?"

Giving him an eye roll, I stroll toward my desk and grab myself a new piece of gum. "Shut up and lie down so I can start."

Chapter 3

Zack

I park Belle's bike in my sister's driveway. Getting off the bike, I grab the keys out of the ignition and look at the fluffy unicorn. My cheeks ache from the huge smile on my face. Damn that girl, I'm so glad she's back. Now I just need to get her back into my bed and all will be right again.

Putting away the keys, and damn well making sure the unicorn is tucked in my pocket, I grab my own keyring. I open the door to my sister's house and step inside. Lynn is lying on the couch. Silently I close the door and walk into the kitchen to put the toast on the counter. I stroll back to the couch and inch close to her sleeping face.

I bark, "Wake up!"

She jolts awake with a scream.

"Why in the hell didn't you tell me she was back, you evil twat?" I can't hide my anger.

She rubs her hands over her face. "You're the evil one here. I'm sick and you scared the shit out of me."

"Yeah, you're sick alright." I shake my head. "Why keep it from me that she's back in the states? In. Fucking. Town. Lynn."

Her hands leave her face and she's trying to give me an evil glare. Gotta give her some credit, she's making an effort.

"Why should I have told you? Three years ago her father dragged Belle and her brother out of the country, the day her mom was killed. When her plane took off, so did you. Only to come out of the Army two years later. You knew Belle and I stayed in touch. You never asked me. So why in the hell would I mention after three years that my friend is back?" She crosses her arms in front of her chest. "Did you bring me toast, or did you forget?"

Anger still flows through my veins, but I know she has a point. "Yeah, I put it on the kitchen table. Now what's wrong with the television?"

"I don't know, I wanted to watch a movie but there's no sound." She releases a huff in frustration.

Walking over to the TV, I check the back and see a cable hanging loose. I put it back in place and turn the television, and the DVD player on to check if that was the problem.

"She's got a lot of demons to fight from her past, Zack. Old ones and a few new ones. Leave her alone, she's barely hanging on as it is," Lynn presses.

I shake my head. "Not happening, she's mine and you know it. Hell, I bet deep down even she knows it."

Sound bursts through the speakers as I switch to the DVD channel, so I turn it down fast and toss the remote in her lap. "There, problem solved, sis."

"Her father and brother died in a car accident three weeks ago. She's a mess, Zack. She doesn't have any family left. That's why she came back here. To me. Not to get back

35

with you. Leave her be, Zack. She doesn't need your alpha caveman biker shit. Stay away." That last part is clearly filled with a warning tone in her voice.

I run my hand through my hair, only to have it fall right back into my eyes again. "Fuck. That's just... Fuck. That's fucked up. Her mom killed; shot to death right in front of her dad. Then, three years later losing her father and brother in an accident? Fuck."

"Like I said. Leave her be, she's got enough demons to fight." She shakes her head, thinking about all the things life has thrown into Belle's path. "Not your fight, Zack, she's my friend and I say you need to back the fuck off."

As I walk to the couch, I grab her legs and swing them off the couch so I can sit down. "Not happening, evil twat. So what DVD did you put in?"

Hearing her mutter a few curses, she pulls her feet beneath her ass and brings her eyes to the television. "World War II documentary."

No surprise there. I don't even think she owns a normal movie. Every DVD she has is a documentary of some kind. And her book collection? There's a huge bookcase next to the television filled with smut. My eye spots her phone on the table in front of her.

Without thinking I get up. "Want something to drink? Some tea with toast?"

She gives me a strange look. "Sucking up won't make me help you get her back."

"Don't need your help. She's already back." I give her a wink, and as I walk past her, I grab her phone without her noticing.

Strolling into the kitchen, I swipe my finger across the screen and search for the number I need. I pull my own phone out of my pocket and insert Belle's number. While making tea and toast, I think about the message I want to send. A chuckle escapes as I type.

Me: Nipple still throbbing?

Belle: WTF? Sally?

Me: It's me, tryin to ring my ....

Belle: Not yours to ring, besides...my ring = throbbing ;) :P

Belle: & WTH did your sister give you my nr! She all better? Cause I need to kill her!

Me: Stole her phone & your nr. Need me to ease the throbbing?

Belle: U R evil & I'm working on Mr. JewelDick.

Me: Stay away from his dick.

Belle: His piercing might be throbbing too ;)

Me: Don't fuck with me, Blue.

Pressing send, I throw my phone on the counter. My blood reaches the same boiling point as the water in the kettle that's screaming. Grabbing it and pouring it into a cup, I can hear my phone buzz with an incoming message. As I put the kettle down I reach for my phone with my other hand.

Belle: I'm not gonna fuck with you. Blue?

Me: Your hair & my balls. Do you want your bike back in one piece? Stay. Away. From. His. Dick.

Putting my phone in my front pocket, I grab the cup of tea and the toast and head back into the living room. Lynn is holding her hands out to take the tea and toast. As I sit down my phone vibrates in my pants, making my dick throb knowing it's Blue.

Didn't even think about giving her a new name, but it suits her perfectly. The shit that's surrounding her, bet that's why she's got the ends of her hair bright blue. She always was a sucker for that sentimental shit. Like that song that Chris Isaak dude sang "Forever Blue", bet she still listens to it when she's alone. Pulling my phone out I read the message and can't help but smile.

Belle: What dick?

Me: Good girl.

Belle: Dick.

God I missed her. When I look at my sister I see her hugging the cup of tea while blowing over it. Her eyes looking straight at me.

"I meant what I said, she doesn't need you complicating things right now. It's all a mess. I mean..." She puts the cup on the table and turns her body facing me. "She couldn't even hug me, Zack. I held her tight in my arms when I picked her up at the airport. Her hands were molded to her body. Then she just patted my back. Patted!"

Can't help but fucking smile. Big.

"Jesus, you're scary. What's there to smile about, dick?" Lynn frowns at me.

Still smiling, I shake my head in disbelief and remember what happened a few hours ago. The hard slap on my bicep brings me back to look at my sister.

Her head is bright red and her hand is going to hit my bicep again. "I said. What. The. Fuck. Are you smiling about?"

"Just remembering me catching her when she launched herself at me a few hours ago. Hugged me tight, like really tight. Felt boobs and legs wrapped snug around me."

She fucking hits me again.

"Oh no she didn't, we agreed you were on the things to avoid list. That little cunt," she seethes.

Now it's time for me to slap her. So I do, giving her a little tap on the back of her head. I know how much Lynn hates the word cunt, so for her to use it. Yeah, she's pissed off.

I snap out my words, "Don't call her that, you conniving little twat."

Lynn rubs the back of her head, grabs her tea from the table and sits back down as her eyes go back to the television. She mutters some curses, and I swear I hear the word cunt at least three more times. Can't help but smile.

Belle

As I spray and wipe at the new ink I just finished, that proud feeling hits me. It's kind of like a drug for me. To create something epic on a person's skin. "Have a look."

Dams gets up and walks to the mirror. "That's wicked. Great job there, J."

Yeah, another vibe goes through me. Never one ounce of remorse. Best thing I ever did was quit my job and become a full-time tattoo artist. When I called Lynn after the accident that killed my father and brother she asked me to come work for her. It took me a few days to finish things up in Japan so I could come back to live here again. Best choice ever.

"I wanna make a new appointment to do other side." Dams points at a spot on his stomach. "Gonna need a lock and an eagle this time."

Dams seems to have this thing for hidden meanings for his ink and that's something I've always appreciated.

"We can do that. I'll need some time to sketch, so how about three weeks from now?" I grab my phone and check my agenda. "How about..."

"Any date or time is fine with me," he states.

I look up and find him staring at me with that hungry look in his eyes again. "You sure about that, Buddy?"

Dams chuckles. "Yeah, I'm sure. Put my number in your phone and send me the details later."

He rattles off the number and I've just about put it in my phone as he starts to pull his shirt over his head. I wanna cry just at the thought of him covering up those muscles and abs. Not to mention his V that leads to. Oh. My. God. I need to stop thinking about his dick. Or his piercing.

"No, don't cover that shit up with your shirt," I snap the words at him.

Sliding the shirt back to his neck, he takes a few steps closer to me. "Thinking about my piercing or my dick? Or both?"

My eyes slide up to meet his. Yes, I had my eyes on his dick, so denying isn't an option. "Well it's hard to think about just the one without the other."

His deep chuckle gives me goose bumps and makes my nipple throb that much harder. "Oh it's hard alright."

It's been too damn long since I've had a dick in me. The last one being the first one and all. A real one that is.

41

I mean, I have my fair share of toys, who needs a real one right? With a piercing. Oh God, I need it. Hey, maybe I can pierce one of my toys, would that work?

"Are you daydreaming about it already? If so, I could make it reality." His hands go to his zipper and I'm seriously waiting to see.

Control, I need it and with a dick in front of me there is no way I'm gonna be able to resist. "Keep it locked, Mr. JewelDick. Now come here so I can wrap up the ink and send you on your way."

He sticks out his lip and actually pouts. He looks adorable and my heart skips a beat. I work fast, eager to get him out of my shop. He's too cute and I'm too horny. I need some of my toys to play with so I can have some of my control back. Pretty sure my nipple piercing set it off. Maybe I do need to get my other one done, just to balance things out. I snicker at my own train of thought.

"There, all done." I nod and step away. "I'll send ya a message about the where and when, okay? Take good care of it."

Now he puts his shirt and cut back on. "We should go out to dinner."

My mouth falls open. I shut it just as fast, trying not to look like a fish on dry land. "Yeah, we really shouldn't."

I tug at his arm to spin him around a bit and give him a slight shove on his back.

"Your Prez threatened my bike while mentioning your dick. Until I get my bike back I'm playing nice."

He turns and grabs hold of the doorway. "So it's dinner after you get your bike back."

"Yeah... I don't think so." I look at the waiting area and see my next client. It's a back piece I have to finish. "Come on in, Joe."

I look back at Dams. "Till next time, Mr. JewelDick"

He grabs his dick and gives it a squeeze. "Till next time."

He winks and I swear I need a fresh set of panties since mine just got wet. I grab my phone and shoot a quick text to Lynn.

Me: Fucking Dams would be bad, right?

I haven't even put my phone back in my front pocket when it vibrates in my hand.

Lynn: Piercing and a huge dick... BAD! Stick with toys.

Me: You knew about the piercing? Huge as in?

Me: Can you pierce a toy?

Lynn: Hell yeah, that's how I learned. Bahaha and huge as in HUGE space between finger and thumb huge ;-)

Me: Personal experience? And u r so gonna pierce my toy!

Lynn: No way! Saw his junk at the clubhouse, trying to stick it in a ho's mouth. Consider your toy pierced.

Me: Glad to see you're feeling better. Yay toy!

Lynn: :-)

By the time I'm finished with Joe, my eyes are burning and my stomach rumbles. Since I already finished off the chocolate bar, I grab a piece of gum out of my bag and throw it into my mouth as I walk over to Lee's room. He's cleaning up for the night.

"Got time for one more?" My voice catches his attention.

His gaze hits mine and his eyes twinkle. "VG?"

I snort a non-female sound. "No way. But you can make a hole in my other nipple if you want."

"Sit, and expose that pretty titty."

With a big smile—I'm sure that will disappear within seconds—I sit down and expose my boob. Lee comes up in front of me and holds up the trashcan in front of my face.

"Spit, woman." I glare at him but spit out my gum anyway.

"Glare all you like, that popping is annoying the hell out of me," he grumbles.

"Just hurry the hell up already." Oh yeah, bring the freaking pain.

Now it's his turn to glare at me. Knowing what's coming, I just close my eyes and block everything out. Before I can think about it I'm done and we're closing the shop for the day.

As I put my keys away and turn around, I see Zack standing in front of my bike with the keys in his hands. His own bike right next to mine.

My eyebrows shoot up. "You let someone else ride my bike?"

He steps away from the bike and hands me the keys. "Nope, I had a prospect drop off my bike. Before you ask, no he didn't ride mine either. He used the trailer. Nobody rides my bike."

I grab my keys and see a new keychain dangling from it. Bright red and orange flames shine from a metal, round shape. I can't help but frown at him because I know what he's trying to pull.

My unicorn is similar to a horse and with the flame keychain it becomes a direct link to his club patch. "Cute, Sally, real smooth."

He just gives me a smile and gives my nose a tap with his finger.

Walking back to the bike I watch as he straddles his. "Get your ass on the bike, Blue."

I already have a goddamned name, even a fucking nickname. What's up with calling me Blue all of a sudden?

"Get used to it, baby, that's you from now on," Zack states.

Fuck, I'm so tired. I can't believe I said that shit out loud.

45

"Go home, Sally," I shout, so he hears me loud and clear above the rumbling of the two bikes.

"Not a chance, Blue, I'm right behind ya," he throws back.

Giving him a lovely wave with my favorite finger I hit the throttle and leave him standing there.

Walking the bike into Lynn's garage I turn just in time to see Zack pull into the driveway. "Getting kinda slow there, Prez."

The way he jumps off his bike I just know he's mad as hell. "This isn't a fucking game, Blue. What's up with driving like a fucking bitch from hell with a unicorn on wheels?"

I laugh at the phrase since it's exactly how my bike feels when I ride it. "Spot on, Prez. Bitch from hell with wheels."

Minus the fucking, but this time I make sure that part doesn't leave my mouth. Turning toward the door, I only get three steps in before I'm turned around and my back hits the door. He's holding both of my shoulders with his hands. My eyes are huge since his face is only a few inches from mine.

"It takes a split second for something to happen and you die, Blue," he snaps his fingers right next to my ear, "Just. Like. That," taking a dramatic pause between each word.

I know where he stands, it's not that I don't value life. I just lost my father and brother in a car crash. It only takes a second, a fragment of life to lose it. But that thrill makes me feel more alive because of it. Reckless, I know, but I need this.

"I don't need your lecture, Sally. I'm very aware of what might happen on the road." I stare him down while he connects the dots.

"Fuck, Blue. I'm sorry." His hand leaves my shoulder and strokes my arm as his other hand goes around my neck pulling me into his hard chest.

"Ouch," I gasp.

Pushing him away, he looks at me with a smirk on his face. "Need me to put your nipple in my mouth to make the pain go away?"

"Not unless you have two mouths," I snap.

"Oh fuck, you didn't." Desire swirls in his eyes.

"Um... yeah Lee did it before we closed the shop." His hand goes into the direction of my boob. "No touching."

He shakes his head. "Oh, Honeybump, there will be touching. Maybe not right this second, but there will be... soon." His hands go down, pulling the keys out of his pocket, and opens the door.

I stroll into the living room as Zack closes up for the evening I notice Lynn has fallen asleep on the couch with a blanket tucked beneath her chin. She looks so cute.

I turn the television and the lights in the living room off. The soft light coming from the kitchen is giving me enough to walk safely without bumping into things. Zack pulls something out of the freezer and closes the door. He turns and walks right to me reaching for my shirt and pulling it down so my pink bra is showing.

"What the hell, Zack?" I try to smack his hands away but am failing drastically.

"Stop it, Blue. I'm only trying to help you out here." He pulls my bra down.

When I see the ice cube between his fingers, it's too late. The cold hits the skin around my piercing and sucking in a breath I manage to swallow back a moan just in time. Fuck. He's like a hot fireman rescuing a puppy out of a burning house and all I wanna do is climb his firehose. This time I can't help the moan that slips my lips.

"Make another sound like that, and the next one will be from me shoving my dick into your tight little body." His voice carries a promise.

I slam my hand over my own mouth. Because there is no way I'm trusting it right now. It's been three years, but what happened still feels so raw and fresh.

When I look in his eyes, I can see he's not the boy who took my virginity. He's the man the boy turned into. The sex back then was sweet and although it hurt at first, he made it perfect. I'm betting his dick grew up too. Judging by his appearance and with him being the president of a motorcycle club, yeah I guarantee the sex would be different this time.

A strangled noise slips beneath my fingers and his eyes go wide. "No, no, no! That wasn't..."

His hands leave one breast as he reaches over to the other so he can put out that fire too. He sucks on his own lip ring as my eyes enjoy the movement. Meanwhile it's taking great restraint to hold back any noises that might slip out of my mouth.

Still watching his mouth while deep in my wicked thoughts I see his lips move, bringing me out of my day-dream. "What?"

He gives me a smirk and repeats himself. "Wanna see my piercing?"

"I was just looking at it before you interrupted," I mumble.

Zack shakes his head either of my remark or, fuck. "You got more than the one in the lip?"

With a stern nod my eyes go south and a moan of frustration rumbles deep in my throat.

"Oh now you want me balls deep." A husky chuckle falls from his pierced lips.

With a loud gasp I give him a shove in the chest. "Dick."

He steps closer and puts his hand on my hip and nods. "Now that we've got that settled."

His hands are unbuttoning my jeans. His eyes trail down and land on my bright blue thong.

Raising one eyebrow he smiles. "Pink bra, blue panties? Ain't you a colorful one."

Before I can form any words, his tattooed hand slides in my jeans while the other one goes around to stroke my back. My head falls to his chest as he pushes two fingers inside me.

"You'd enjoy my hardware. This tight pussy of yours would eat it up. Fuck. Wouldn't have any problem sliding in there in one stroke. Balls-fucking-deep. Pull out and tunnel right back in till my piercing hits your cervix. You'd like that, Blue. Am I right? Say it, Blue."

Jesus, does he ever shut up? He never used to talk and now his mouth is like a hose. Just like my VG, because I'm so aroused by those very words, he has no problem sliding and curling his fingers inside me. Pressing his thumb against my clit, he makes a few circles and I'm lost the second he pulls my hair back and bites my neck.

Bright dots and tingles all over my body, while shooting hot fire for the longest moment. Don't think I'd ever get that feeling using my toys. When I start to open my eyes I see him staring back at me with hooded eyes.

"You need to do that again, Honeybump, right now." His thumb applies more pressure and my body seems to recognize him as its master. How fucked up is that?

"I can't, you just..." I wiggle my hips, he needs to stop, I can't take it. It's such an intense feeling. "You can't order me to orgasm on command." I'm proud that I was even able to get that sentence out in one breath. I'm still wiggling to get away from his thumb that's still applying pressure while he adds a third finger.

"I can, and you will. Now come for me. Throw that head back, open those fucking perfect suck me off lips and make that noise again... for me," Zack growls.

I can only gasp as he grabs my left leg by the knee and lifts it up so he can slide his fingers in deeper.

His grip is almost painful as he digs his fingers into my flesh.

Zack's lips touch my ear as he blows out the words on one breath, "Now Blue, fucking obey me."

At his teeth sinking in my earlobe, my body obeys. My VG grabs his fingers so hard I think it's payback for him being the arrogant fuck that he is. A mind-blowing orgasm has filled my body with heat. I'm trying to keep myself up and get a hold of my need for oxygen.

"Fuck me." I have no other words.

Shit. I run for forty-five minutes, twice every fucking day. I hate cardio but need it to keep my mind at ease and my body in shape. I should be able to stand on my own two feet.

"Oh, I intend to." When my gaze finds his, I see the twinkle in there.

He knew I didn't mean it that way but he just couldn't resist.

"Are you two done?" Looking over Zack's shoulder I see Lynn standing there. "I was feeling better but with the noise and view, now I need to puke. But I need a bottle of water first, so hand me one and go fuck in a room. With a door. And a lock. And for fuck's sake be fucking quiet already."

Zack holds out a bottle of water to her. "Sleep it off, twat. You're just jealous I'm getting all the hugs."

"Christ brother, if you declare that hugs. Please stop being friendly." She turns and walks back into the living room.

"Yeah I need to go to bed. Sleep. Alone. Up early and stuff like that." Stepping around him I feel his hand around my wrist.

"Aren't you forgetting something?" My eyes drop south.

His dick twitches in his jeans, which to me looks like a personal wave. His hand leaves my wrist and goes under my chin to lift my head up.

"A kiss, Blue, just a goodnight kiss." His lips find mine and the delicate touch together with the hard brush of his lip ring against my lips make me moan into his mouth.

He touches his forehead to mine. "Goodnight, Blue."

Zack steps around me and walks out the front door.

Chapter 4

Zack

Fuck, I'm late. With only a few hours of sleep, my head is pounding and my eyes are burning. I can't believe I managed to walk away after giving my Blue two orgasms. My dick is still up, looking around to find that sweet pussy he missed out on last night.

With great pain, both mental and physical, I tuck him away. I hope the zipper doesn't pop because I never bother with underwear. I pull on my boots, run my hands through my hair and I'm good to go.

Dams is picking me up so we can go to the auction. We need this investment. The club has been slowly crawling its way out of debt. This could be the break we need to finally make some fucking money. There's an apartment above the gym, but that doesn't mean shit to me. Maybe we can rent it out to the brother who will be managing the place for most of the days.

Damn, I'm already jumping the gun and making plans on how I want to run the place, and we haven't even bought it yet. I just hope there aren't too many others as interested as we are. It's an old building and located right next to the tattoo shop my sister co-owns with Brandlee. The shop Blue works at now too.

Great, now I'm really starting to feel that zipper. Loud knocking on my door pulls me out of my discomfort. Pulling on my cut, I grab my keys and open the door.

"You ready for this, man?" Dams throws the question at me.

I walk past him and close the door. "Yeah, let's go buy it already so we can finally start making some money around here."

We walk out of the clubhouse straight to our bikes. For a split second I think about our appearances. Then the moment is gone. Our money is good, and the same color as the rest of the investors. They should be happy we're the ones that wanna take it off their hands as it is.

When Dams and I pull into the parking lot I'm surprised by the amount of cars. A lot more than I expected and a few high-class cars right in front of the building.

"Feel that chill on the back of your neck?" Dams mumbles.

Shit, he's thinking the same thing. "Are you giving up already? We haven't even stepped inside the fucking building, you fuck."

He chuckles as we walk toward the doors. A woman wearing sky high heels, a tight black dress, and gray hair walks in front of me. She looks back and her face turns into one of disgust.

My gaze shifts to Dams. In all honesty I ask, "Did you not wash your face this morning, Dams?"

Dams shakes his head, laughing at my question. "Nah man, I had caviar shoved up my ass so high, I had to puke it out. Is there still some on my face?"

He touches his face as if he's serious about his appearance. The woman visibly gags as if she's about to puke and runs away as fast as those heels will carry her.

I shake my head when I say, "Christ, this shit is going to be bad. Why the fuck are all those people here?"

"Yeah man, my thoughts exactly," Dams replies.

Hearing heels behind me I turn. I didn't spin fast enough, and only see the back of a woman with marine blue heels beneath killer legs, and a tight marine blue skirt. There's a very light blue blouse above it and her white hair is pinned up tight on her head. Her perfume travels behind her, vanilla with a hint of cinnamon.

"Sweet Jesus, I need to nail that one," Dams states.

We both watch that tight ass as she takes a seat in one of the front rows. Walking toward the chairs, we find our seats. My eyes go back to the woman who is sitting two rows in front of us. I want to see her face but I don't get to because the auction is about to begin.

I grab the list we got from our chair and see the first up will be the property we want to buy. Fuck that, *need to buy*. The announcement has been made and the auction begins. I wait as a guy in front raises his hand for the first bid. The woman with the light blue blouse raises her hand too. This goes back and forth three more times.

The guy in front looks behind him. Spotting the lady, a sense of recognition flashes over his face. He smiles and signals his hand as if he's giving her the property to bid on freely. Yeah not happening, dude. I raise my hand and take the lead bid. Only for a second because the lady raises the bid.

We go back and forth eight more times and Dams is hitting me in the shoulder. "You need to stop. It's not worth that much. Think, bro."

Yeah he's right, but it pisses me off. I wanted that property, it's perfect. And what the fuck does that high-class piece of ass want with a gym anyway? My mind takes too long to process because I hear a loud knock and Dams' curses. We lost the fucking property.

I get my ass off the seat and grab Dams, pushing him in front of me. A dick move but I'm pissed and I want to get out of here. Dams curses some more but keeps moving out of the room.

Standing in the hall, Dams turns to face me. "Well that went fucking great!"

"Shut it, VP. I need to know who bought it, and I need to know now." I hear heels clicking behind me and watch as they pass.

Looking up those legs and ass I see her hands go into that white hair and pull the clip out. The white strands fall down reveling blue ends. Fuck. Me.

"Blue?" My voice is like a rough growl as her new name leaves my mouth and she turns around in shock.

"Zack. What are you doing here? Dams." She nods to my VP.

I don't have time for this shit. "Eyes here. Now answer me. What the fuck are you doing here and why the fuck did you just buy that fucking property?"

Her face turns angry, resembling the same look I must have on my face. I could have made an effort to soften my face and chose different words when I asked her that question, but I don't fucking care. She's about to give me hell, when a guy steps in front of her.

He takes her hand and brings it to his mouth kissing her knuckles. "Jazzebelle, I'm so pleased to see you."

She gives him a shy smile in return. "Frederick, I didn't know you'd be here. Aren't you supposed to be in Japan?"

He's shaking his head and stepping closer to my woman. "I tend to go where my business takes me. I'd gladly handed over the property for you to take. You've got a good investment there. Are you going to train fighters, like your father?"

Shit, how come I didn't think of that, and how does this dickhead know about her father?

"Well now, that's just something you just have to wait and see." She gives the fucker a shy smile.

That's my girl, keep dickhead out of the loop.

"Hmm, that's not the only thing I want to see. How about that second date, Jazzebelle?" the guy croons.

Oh, fuck no. I step between them and pull Blue behind me. "There will be no dating Blue. She's mine and I don't share. So get that thought out of your fucking head and then take your smooth talking ass out of here."

Dams crosses his arms as he stands next to me. With his inked sleeves and muscles he's quite impressive. This fucker doesn't seem to be intimidated though.

He takes a step closer with a big smirk on his face. "Blue? That's Jazzebelle and she doesn't seem to have a leash on. So the lady can date whoever she wants."

I jab my finger in his chest as I feel Blue stepping up next to me to grab my bicep. She looks at me. Her eyes slide to my finger that's pressing into his chest and then back to my eyes. A flash of heat flares in her eyes. It's there for a second before it's gone, and I know she just got a reminder where my fingers were last night.

The smirk now settles on my face as Blue sees in my eyes what I'm about to say. "Listen up, buddy. I can shove my fingers up your nose and let you take a whiff as to where they were only a few hours ago. That's how close you'll ever come to her pussy."

With that said, I take Blue's hand, bend my knee and place my shoulder in her belly, to pick her up and carry her away fireman style. By this time Blue is screaming bloody murder. I walk out with Dams behind me, laughing his ass off.

I put her down next to my bike and she punches me in the stomach. Getting the breath knocked out of you by a girl is kinda amazing. But right now I'm in pain and I'm trying to catch my breath while Dams is still laughing. I can't do anything but endure the fury that is now pouring out of her mouth.

"You fucking no filter, dirty mouth caveman with a peanut for a brain. How dare you talk to him like that? Dragging me off like a helpless sheep without a choice to follow. I should kick your ass, you dick!"

Still struggling with a bite of pain from the punch, I straighten myself so I can look her in the eye. "You're mine, Blue. He needed to be set straight."

She takes a step closer to me and jabs three fingers in my chest. Looking at those fingers and back into her eyes, I can't help but be reminded of the three I had in her tight pussy.

Her eyes narrow and her eyebrows go down. "Pushing three fingers in my VG doesn't give you ownership. Maybe, and that's a tiny maybe buddy, you owned those two orgasms you gave me, but that's fucking it! You don't own me and I can date who the hell I want."

I like this feisty side of her and my dick is giving her a painful wave behind my zipper.

"That guy in there is the son of an old business associate of my dad. He helped me out with handling a few things after the accident. He didn't have to. Because we just fucking met a few hours before the accident. That night would have been our first date. But he did, he was there for me. So. Fuck. Off. You don't know shit, and you don't own shit," Blue seethes.

She walks off and I can only stare at her tight as hell ass in those killer heels while her words settle.

"That was quite the punch she threw." Dams smiles at me. "You okay there, Prez?"

Rubbing a hand over my abs, I still feel a slight sting.

"Oh, I didn't mean the gut punch. I meant the verbal punch with Mr. Slick being her night in fucking sparkling armor." He slaps me on the back. "Let's go back and call church. We need to talk about how the fuck we're going to find a new investment."

"It's shining Dams, knight in shining armor," I grumble.

Dams shakes his head. "Nah man, that guy is dirty. My gut is never wrong about these things."

Giving him a nod, I know Dams is right. That guy is too slick and I can't help but have a bad feeling. Why the fuck did this guy show up here? Traveling after my girl, acting like it was a fucking coincidence.

"Coincidence my ass," I mumble.

"That's what I'm sayin' bro, that's what I'm sayin'," Dams agrees.

We head off to the clubhouse.

Belle

I throw my keys on the table near the door. "Your brother is a dick, you know that, right?"

Walking into the living room I see Lynn smiling as she looks up from her book. "Yeah he is, but you already knew this. We talked about it, and I did warn your booty squatting ass."

My friend always makes me smile. Besides, she's right. We did talk about it and I remember her exact words were; stay away from that dick.

"Okay, let's have it. What did that dick do now? Spill. Well except if it actually involves his dick, cause then I don't wanna know, him being my brother and all. Oh God, that's just nasty." She shakes her head and holds up her hand in a stop sign. "No sex talk. Hearing you guys and seeing him pressed against you, even with clothes on. Yeah, let's never talk about that stuff, okay."

I sit beside her on the couch and she puts the book down.

"Believe me, no hands down pants, no dick in my body will he ever stick…again," I grumble.

"Ha! That sounds so poetic, just like freaking Shakespeare. Well except for the again part, but I'm sure we both know that's a lie. So let's hear it." Her voice is filled with laughter and mock.

My head falls back and I look at the ceiling. "I bought a property today since I wanted the apartment that was attached to it. The guy who I went out with once back in Japan was there. As were Zack and Dams."

"The guy who helped you out with the funerals and everything?" Lynn questions.

"Yeah." Nodding my head, I remember Zack talking to the guy. "Your dick of a brother told him, and I quote 'I can shove my fingers up your nose and let you take a whiff as to where they were only a few hours ago. That's how close you'll ever come to her pussy.' Then he told him I was his."

I turn my head and see her staring at me with her eyes wide and her mouth open.

"He did not!" she gasps, shock clearly in her voice.

"Yeah he did."

"Fuck me, that's just…oh my fucking God. What happened next?" She turns to me and lifts her knee up on the couch and almost bounces from excitement.

I roll my eyes. "Then he put me over his shoulder and dragged me out of there. Fireman style."

She laughs so loud the intake of breath in between come out in snorts.

I point a finger in her direction. "Stop laughing. It's not funny. I'm so mad, I threw a punch in his gut and he doubled over. I told him off and walked away."

Now she's falling off the couch and rolling on the floor, making sounds I can only relate to the bulldog my grandfather used to own. "Are you dying on me? Jesus woman, show some support here."

Lynn wipes her eyes and tries to stand up while suppressing her laughter, failing miserably, and still barks out a laugh while she settles back on the couch.

When she finally catches her breath she says, "I hope you hit him hard. Hey, what property did you buy? I was kinda hoping you'd stay here, with me."

I give her a sad smile, knowing I'd hurt her feelings. "I know, and I would love nothing more. But this is just something I need to do and it was too good to pass up. I bought the building that's right next to the shop. It's a gym that has a huge apartment above it."

I watch as her face pales. Her eyes go wide and her mouth falls open. All I hear are loud strangled noises come out... again.

"What?" I question, because her reaction is starting to freak me out.

"You didn't," she gasps.

"I did and it's mine," I state.

"Fuck. The club needed that," she says with panic clearly in her voice.

"Say what?" Now my eyes are wide.

"Yeah, they needed that investment as a money cow so they could finally make money with something they like. Oh boy, are they gonna be pissed. They know you have it, right?" Her gaze is locked with mine.

I give her a nod while I think things over. "Um, yeah. But it kinda didn't come up with the whole who's got a bigger dick and who owns me discussion."

She stands up from the couch and starts walking back and forth. "I'm happy for ya, really. But now I'm kinda worried about the boys."

An idea comes to mind and I stand up. "Don't worry, I know what to do."

I grab my keys as I hear her ask where I'm going. I'm still pissed at Zack, but this idea I have might just work for all of us.

Opening the door I turn. "Hey, did you pierce my toy yet?"

She holds up her hand. "You owe me forty-five bucks. I bought a new one and pierced it for ya."

"Thanks! I owe ya." I can't help but smile. Lynn is a bit of a germaphobe.

"Yeah, forty-five bucks." She winks and gives me a huge smile. I laugh and shut the door behind me.

******

Driving into the parking lot, I pull up right next to a row of bikes. Seems like almost all of them are here. I walk inside the clubhouse, it's empty except for the few prospects.

"Where are they?" I ask the prospect behind the bar.

He points to the door next to the window with the blinds, reminding me how they were watching me the other day.

I smile and mumble, "Thanks."

As I start to walk toward the door, I hear all of them yelling how I'm not allowed in there. I'm not stupid, I know club rules. This is just an exception and they have to suck it up. Walking a little bit faster, I reach the door before they can stop me, and open it.

The first thing I see is Zack sitting at the head of a very large table filled with bikers. A tingly feeling starts in my belly to see him like this.

I can't take my eyes off him as I hear Dams and others say, "You're not allowed in here."

Apologies come from behind me as I turn to shove the prospects back. "You heard them, y'all aren't allowed in here." Shoving the door in their faces I turn back to the table.

A few of them laugh while Dams shakes his head.

"You too, Blue, out!" Zack says as he's ready to stand up.

I walk up to him and say, "Sit, I need to talk to all of you. Business, the investment kind, so suck up the not allowed part. Otherwise you'll be dropping to your knees and begging me to change my mind as I walk out that door."

"I'd drop to my knees for you anytime, pretty girl."

My head turns as my eyes search to see who said that as I hear Zack growl, "She's off limits, Sico."

Sico's got a full beard and green eyes. Long hair pulled up in a bun and tunnels in his ears. He's got a septum piercing. My mind trails off and wonders how that might work if he has a cold. Or in wintertime, will there be a snot icicle dangling from it? I laugh to myself as my eyes travel down to his lips. He's got such a sweet face I can't help but give him a smile.

"Blue." Jesus, that sounded more like a bark then this stupid nickname he keeps using for me.

"What?" I throw back in a bark.

Looking back at Zack, I see his eyes turn soft. "What did you want to talk about?"

"Right. Well, you know I bought that property this morning." My voice carries a hint of an apology.

He nods and I hear frustrating sounds all around the table.

I throw my shoulders back in defense. "Your sister just mentioned to me that you guys wanted to buy it. I swear, I didn't know."

"Yeah, we figured as much," Zack mumbles.

I take a deep breath for what I'm about to say. "Well, I bought it because I wanted the apartment and a place to work out. So, how about a partnership? Fifty-one percent for me, forty-nine percent you guys. I take the apartment, you guys the gym. Interested?"

It's so quiet that I can hear my own heartbeat.

They all look shocked so I continue. "And the price is forty-five bucks which I'm gonna need right now and in cash. My lawyer will draw up the papers and drop them off this afternoon."

Still no sound and I really don't know what else to say or do. Taking another breath, I take a step toward the door. "Going once." I take another step. "Twice."

Zack sits up straight before he says, "We need to take a vote first."

He turns his head when Dams speaks up. "Oh, the hell with voting. Just say yes before she changes her fucking mind."

Dams claps his hand on the table and all of them follow, making such a noise I'm afraid they'll break the table.

Zack slams down a hammer. "It's settled then." He stands up and sticks his hand out. "Partners."

I take his hand in mine. "Partners, and I need the forty-five bucks. Now."

He laughs as he pulls out his wallet.

Dams smirks when he says, "Hang on there, Prez. It needs to come out of the club's wallet. Remember?"

"Give it back to me later," Zack throws back at Dams while he hands me a fifty.

My eyes go to the money when I say, "Yeah, that's not gonna work. I need forty-five bucks exactly. I don't have change."

"So keep the five." He throws in a wink.

I shake my head. "Nope, I only need forty-five bucks."

Hearing him curse he turns to Dams, who now has the exact amount in hand.

Spinning back, he hands me the money. "Here you go."

I smile as I take the money and put it in my purse. "Thanks."

"Why only the forty-five bucks? You know we can split the cost," Zack questions.

I shrug. "The money doesn't even make a dent in my bank account. So I don't want to hear about money, I couldn't care less. I owe your sister forty-five bucks and I never have cash on me. I only use plastic, so I figure it was easier this way."

He gives me a hint of a smile before his face turns serious. "Okay. Well, we need to go over some details so I'll come over later tonight."

Shaking my head, I reply, "There are no details to discuss. I'll take the apartment, you guys can deal with the gym. I'm heading to my lawyer right now to have the papers drawn up and I'll sign. They'll drop them off afterwards and that's it."

He takes a step closer to me. "I'll still be over tonight, 'cause we need to talk."

"No talking, and no coming over. Now, I need to leave because I'm not allowed in here. Bye boys!" I give them a wave and walk out the door to the sounds of Zack cursing.

Chapter 5

Zack

Fucking hell. I can't believe that just happened. Fuck, I don't think she even knows what she just did. She hasn't thought this through, I just know it. But fuck if I care. She just tied her ass to the club, *to me*. There is no backing out now and I can't wait to have it in black and white.

"Alright boys, seems like we've got ourselves a gym." The second that statement leaves my mouth, hollers and table slaps fill the room. Things are looking bright again.

When the noise settles down, I look at my VP and say, "Dams, you and Sico do a walkthrough as soon as we have the keys. When you're there, write down where you think what machines might be best, and where the cardio corner will be set up."

"We need a boxing ring in there. I wanna hit shit," Dams replies.

I nod, knowing he's right. The gym, as it is now, is set up in a very weird way. The space could be used in a more efficient way.

Also the idea of hitting shit makes me think of Blue and the stuff that slick prick said about Blue wanting to train fighters again like her dad. "You're right, we need to do this the right way. Get the blueprints or otherwise draw the layout. We need to discuss things and get Blue back in here."

Sico raises his voice. "Why get the hot chick back? I mean, don't get me wrong, she's sexy and all but she didn't want to discuss shit."

I look Sico in the eye, taking a deep breath to calm myself. Right now I want to smack his head to the table and keep it there while I squeeze my hand around his neck and yell his eardrums out not to call my woman hot chick or sexy.

I know she's fucking sexy, but I'm the only one who gets to fucking say so out loud. After another breath I think how best to answer his question. Giving the brothers information that'll make things easier on her, might go a long way.

"Her father was a kickboxing champion, one hell of a trainer and so is she. She knows all about the sport, so this shit is right up her alley. Three weeks ago, she lost her dad and her brother. She might think she doesn't want anything to do with the gym now, but who knows, she might in the long run. I say we force her to help out with the layout because she was born into this shit." I watch as they absorb this information, most of them nod in agreement.

"Do you think she might want to work there too?" I look at Bruce who threw the question out there.

Before the question rolls over in my brain, Dams answers for me. "Nah, I don't think so. She's one of the artists that works in the tattoo shop next door to the gym."

The eruption of laughter and remarks flows through the room as Dams stands and pulls up his shirt to show off the ink she put on him. Brothers discuss when and what they are gonna let her put on their body and especially where her hands will be. The moment I see a brother pull out his phone to make an appointment I see red.

"Hey," I growl, and the voices dim down slightly.

"Everyone shut the fuck up and listen." Surprise fills their faces as the room turns quiet. "Listen real good 'cause I'm only telling ya'll once. She's not club pussy or some random chick to get your hands on and your dick in. She's off limits to all of you. If you wanna get her to ink you, run it by me first. The first one who fucks up is closing his eyes forever, while the worms feast on his meat."

Dams, the fucker, chuckles and shakes his head.

"What? Got something to say, VP?" I bark.

The corner of his mouth turns up into a wicked smile. "You gonna claim her, or just trying to keep our dicks away from her pussy? Because she's…" He chuckles and puts his hands up to air quote as he says, "Club business and all."

I stand up so fast the chair falls back behind me as I put two hands on the table and hover right in front of his face. "She's mine and you know it."

That motherfucker is still laughing, right in my face. "Yeah, I know, brother. But does she?"

"She will." I turn my head and look around the table.

"We're done here. Everybody knows what to do, and especially what not to do. Now get the fuck out." Everybody starts to get up. "Oh, and when the papers get in and we sign that shit? We party. There will be a fucking celebration this Saturday."

The boys have smiles and cheer at the thought of the celebration, clapping each other on the back as they leave the room.

Dams punches me on the shoulder. "You wanna head on over to Butcher and order shit?"

I nod as we both step out of church. "Gotta take a leak first."

Dams walks over to the bar and sits on a stool as I pass him. Hearing him chuckle 'cause he knows what's coming.

Opening the door, I see the backs of two prospects and three brothers standing in front of the urinals. Bruce turns and sees it's me. He gives Pokey a tap with his arm and they both shake it off, zip up and step out of the room. The other fucks don't see me so I clear my throat.

"Out," I bark.

I know it's weird but I don't give a fuck. They don't move fast enough.

"Out. Out, now." I growl the last word and this makes them turn.

The tiny prospect that looks more like a school kid than the twenty-one year old he is, still has his dick hanging out while he turns to look at me.

"Put that shit away before you turn around. Christ, I don't know what's worse, the jungle look or the snake that seems to be missing. Get. The fuck. Out. Now."

He's got that look of disbelief on his face. Yeah, dude suck it up. Better me telling you than the girl you wanna stick it in, or try to stick something in. Bet the guy is still a virgin based on the lack of things or thing, ah shit.

His face turns all red like he's holding his breath. "But Prez."

"Zip it! Both dick and mouth, boy. And get the fuck out."

The moment his ass leaves the room I flip the lock. I don't fucking care what they think. When I need to take a piss or shit, that business is mine and mine alone. I don't need an audience. Yeah, the eyes in front shit doesn't work. Fucking creeps me out. My club, my rules, my fucking toilet.

*** Belle***

Cinnamon rolls or bagels? Why do we have to make choices?

"Can I help you, miss?" The cute waitress smiles at me.

"I'll have three cinnamon rolls and three bagels. Two latte macchiatos and one coffee, black." I decide to make things easy by not making a choice.

I smile at myself and check my watch to see I have forty-five minutes left until my first client shows up. I opened the shop about half an hour ago. Lynn and Lee are getting ready to get to work and I offered to get some coffee.

"Hey, Jazzebelle, that's twice in one day." Feeling a hand pressed on my lower back, I smell a familiar fragrance. It's a spicy musk with a hint of vanilla.

Just three weeks ago I was pressed against his chest for hours. We've only been on one date and had just met the night my dad and brother had their accident. Still, he was the one who was there for me. Taking care of the paperwork, informing people, keeping them away from me.

Our fathers were old business associates. I never got a chance to ask my dad all about it. A lone tear slides down my face as I feel a gentle sweep across my cheek.

"Hey now, are you okay?" His voice goes soft and once again I'm back against his chest.

I take a deep breath. It fills with his scent calming myself as I pull away. "Hi, Frederick."

He places his hands on each side of my face and brushes his lips a hint away from my mouth. "Hey, Petal, how's my beautiful flower?"

I shove myself off his chest, so I'm not leaning against him anymore. "Fine, Rick. I'm fine."

He turns to the waitress who hasn't moved to fill my order. I don't blame her. Frederick is tall, well-built and has black hair that kind of reminds me of the Fonz from the show Happy Days. His hair is all shiny and perfect, it makes me wonder if Rick carries a comb in his pocket. Probably not, since he's always wearing a suit instead of jeans.

His rich voice flows through the air. "Would you hold her order for ten more minutes and send two cappuccinos and two cinnamon rolls to our table?"

The waitress nods and takes off before I can even begin to form a word.

"Hey, I was in the middle of getting my order," I mumble.

"I know, Petal, but you still owe me a second date. We're both here now, so… let's have at it." He winks, takes my hand, and walks us to a table in the back.

It only takes a minute before the waitress comes over and sets a cappuccino and a cinnamon roll in front of each of us.

When she leaves us, Rick's hand brushes over mine. "So, how've you been holding up?"

Taking a deep breath, I nod my head. "Okay, I guess. I love my new job and being back here."

He keeps brushing his thumb over my hand while he looks at me with his deep brown eyes. "Should you be working?"

"Yeah, it's actually kinda therapeutic." I give him a small smile. "It's right across the street from here, the tattoo shop."

His smile is so huge, it shows all his straight white teeth. "So you did it, huh? No more doctor? Trading it all in for a different kind of needle."

"Yes." A warm flash goes through my body.

His smile is so genuine and I totally forgot how easy he was to talk to. I told him about my wish to trade that needle. Even though we only had one date, he was there for me for three days straight, pulling me through the deaths of my father and brother.

"So. Are you dating the biker?" Wow, didn't see that question coming.

Quite the topic changer. My thoughts switch to this morning's confrontation and heat flashes through my cheeks.

"No, I'm not dating anyone." I want to make it clear I'm not interested in dating, my life is crazy as it is right now.

"Good. That means I still have a chance to steal your heart." He lifts my hand to his mouth and kisses my knuckles. "What time are you free tonight?"

My eyes are glued to his lips. "Seven." I hear myself saying.

Looking away from his lips, I pull back my hand to grab hold of my cappuccino with both hands. I'm so not ready for this. Still, he's been so nice to me. Always the perfect gentleman. Safe. Maybe I just need a change, to stop overthinking. The last man I had been with was Zack. He was my first... my only. It's been years and he's clearly not the same guy anymore. Who knows how many women he's been with; it's been three years.

"What's your number?" He's holding his phone.

Before I can change my mind, I grab my phone. "Gimme yours."

He smiles and rattles off the numbers. I send him a quick text with the address. "Pick me up at eight."

Getting up, he grabs my hand and stands up too. "What? No kiss?"

I can't help but smile when I see his cheeks heat at his own question. Sweet and shy, I need this kind man; the step forward to normal. I lean over to give him a kiss on the cheek. At the same time he turns his head so my lips land on his.

His hand grabs the back of my neck while his head slightly turns to deepen the kiss. His tongue slips between my lips and brushes along mine. Giving it a swirl as he pulls back, he slides his tongue between my teeth and upper lip one last time.

His lips leave mine as he gives a low moan in his throat. His face is next to mine, his lips almost touch my ear. His hand at the back of my neck grabs hold of my hair and he gives it a small tug.

"I love the way you taste. When that biker asked me to smell his fingers," his lips trace down my neck and back up to my ear, "I was having a hard time not saying yes to that question. I don't think I can wait very long to take a whiff and taste your other lips, Petal."

His mouth latches onto my neck and I feel him suck my skin into his mouth. His teeth bite down just a little. The moan that escapes my mouth surprises me, just as the wetness that builds up between my thighs. This is so wrong, bad, and naughty.

His hand slides away from my hair. He pulls away from my neck and places his forehead against mine. Both of us are breathing heavy as I hear something placed on the table. I pull back, pull the cash out of my pocket Brandlee gave me, and hand it over to the waitress.

I can't take a chance to look at him again. Guess he's not such a shy, kind man after all. Goose bumps trail over my skin as I feel his eyes trail over my body. Grabbing my order off the table I manage to get three words out of my mouth.

"See you tonight." Then I hightail out of there, at the speed of light.

******

With my last client not showing up, I'm home before six. Believe me when I say he's not a client anymore, nor will he get his fifty dollar deposit back. Or another appointment for that matter. Yeah, I'm good like that. No second chances.

If I make the time for you, you either show up or call to cancel. Action, reaction and that shit. Walking into the kitchen I grab a bottle of water from the fridge. Popping the cap, I down half of it and see Lynn walk in behind me.

"You're home early," Lynn says with a hint of surprise in her voice.

"Yeah my last client was a no-show."

Smiling she says, "Ah. So he's gonna stay a no-show."

She knows me well. Although Lynn is also a tattoo artist, she gives clients a second chance or shoves them toward Brandlee. Too kind for this world I tell you. She doesn't take too many ink appointments, but still.

I know she sounds and looks like her own self but I need to ask, "Feeling better?"

Nodding her head she smiles brightly. "Yeah, and I'm going for a run before dinner. Wanna join me?"

Seeing as I do have time, and running most times lightens my mood, I agree. "Let me go change."

I take a few steps forward and her eyes slide to my neck.

She has a smirk on her face when she tells me, "I thought we agreed no hanky panky with boys and only toys."

"Well, that was your idea," I grumble.

I try to pass her but she points a finger at my throat. "Then why did my brother latch onto your neck, sucking the panky for your hanky?"

"Jesus you nerd, cut the silly words already and what the," I slam my hand across the spot I know she's talking about. "The fuck, he didn't," I squeak and make a run to the bathroom.

I let my hand slide away as I look horrified in the mirror.

"Yeah he did," Lynn says as she leans in to examine it closer.

"No. The. Fuck. He. Didn't," I gasp.

Lynn's eyes go wide. "Oh hell no. Dams?"

I let my hair fall down since I was holding it up for a better look.

"Oh come on Lynn, seriously, that's what you think of me?" I regret the words because right now, I do feel like a slut.

She huffs. "Well don't go all virgin on me now. You're the one that was in the kitchen with my brother and asking me about Dams. Only to turn up with a hickey on your neck and tell me it's not my brother's mouth that has been doing the sucking. So let's hear it. Who. Was. It?"

I actually groan out loud. "It was Fredrick."

Her eyes go wide. "Him? The sweet, understanding, few days before you met and left dude? That Fredrick?"

I nod. Grabbing her wrist, I drag her with me to the couch. She sits down next to me and I tell her all about meeting him at the diner. After I'm done telling her we just stare at each other in silence for a few minutes.

Lynn stands up and begins to pace. "Well shit."

Toeing off my boots, I pull my legs beneath my ass. "Yeah, that's what it is."

She stops in front of me. "You've got two horny alphas out there hunting your pussy. You need to be the mother of all alphas and kick their collective asses," she mumbles something after that.

Scrunching my eyebrows, I ask, "What was that last part?"

She stares straight at me. "I said, we need to get you more toys."

With a snort I reply, "Can I just remind you that I just got a new one? Besides, I'm gonna be the mother of all alphas and mothers don't have time to fuck. Right? So toys it is."

She puts her hand up for a high five and I smack it. Hard. We both rub our hands on our thighs.

"We need to tone that down a bit. That shit hurts."
Laughing out loud, I couldn't agree more.

Her face turns serious. "So. What are you going to
do about the date?"

I shrug my shoulders. "Dunno, I think I'm just going
to go out to dinner. Nothing more. He was there for me
when I needed a shoulder. I kinda feel like I owe him."

"The fuck you owe him. He gave you that!" She
waves her fingers at my neck area. "And that my friend
is a huge fuck you sign for Zack."

Dammit, she's right. "I'm not gonna let him get
close. Again."

She rolls her eyes. "Riiiiiiight."

"Hey! Mother. Alpha. Right here. Now let's go for
that run you promised me." My voice and mind are determined.

******

My run with Lynn gave me a huge energy boost.
Right now, I'm getting ready for my date with Rick. I
never wear makeup. I don't care for that shit. Besides,
I'm the type of woman that tends to rub her eyes without thinking about it. Imagine the way I would look if I
did wear makeup.

The only time I look in the mirror is when I need to check my teeth or pull out a few stray hairs to keep my eyebrows in check. Before two morph into one. No female should ever have that look. So yeah, maybe I do care a little bit about the way I look. Checking my teeth and my two eyebrows in the mirror, I'm good to go.

My hair is pulled back into a tight bun and I'm wearing a tight black dress that stops a little above my knee. My twins are a little on show because of the deep V cut. The dress is just one of the many I still have from my old job. Hospital rules, attend at least two parties a month the investors held. Boring, but that's just the way it is. Or was. Thank God I didn't need to be in that circle anymore. Although I would have given the world for still being there if it meant I would still have my dad and brother.

Hearing the front door, I grab my purse from the bed and hurry with my black Louboutin follies spike heels in my hand. Attempting to put them on while I make my way to the door is a little challenging. With one heel in place, I hop a few times to put on the other one. Off balance, I stumble forward. Two strong arms are around me in a flash as I'm pressed against a hard chest.

"No need to throw yourself at me, Petal." His voice is filled with a hint of laughter.

I shove myself away from his chest and slap him with my purse. "Not throwing, Rick. Just testing your reflexes."

Flashing a bright smile, he chuckles as he grabs the belt on his dark gray Armani suit and adjusts his pants. My eyes flash down to his crotch.

"We'll get to testing my reflexes soon enough, Petal. Soon enough," Rick mutters.

I smack him again with my purse, as his hands now flash to his heart, acting wounded. His hand reaches out to my face and he steps closer.

Leaning in, he gives me a feather light kiss on my lips. "Hi."

Not realizing I closed my eyes when he kissed me, I open them. "Hi."

Jesus, I'm shy all of a sudden. What the hell has gotten into me? I can't seem to get a good read on him. When I got to know him he was the perfect businessman. Today I've seen flashes of a completely different man. The clearing of a throat pulls me from my thoughts, and I look over to see Lynn standing by the front door.

"Hi." She lifts her hand to add a finger wave.

I roll my eyes and give the introductions. "Lynn, Fredrick. Rick, Lynn."

Rick gives her a nod and a smile.

He turns his wrist to look at his watch. "We've gotta go, Petal."

He takes my hand and leads me to the door. Before we get to it, the door opens as Zack walks in with Dams following close behind.

"What the fuck is he doing here?" Zack steps forward, his face filled with anger while his hands turn into fists.

I manage to step forward when I feel Rick's arm going around my waist. "Seems like you're just in time to see that we're going on a date. Now, if you'll excuse us, we were just leaving."

He waves his hand as if Zack is dismissed.

Zack's eyes turn into tiny slits as he steps forward and inches his face close to Rick to growl out his words. "My woman ain't going nowhere with you, suit. But you, on the other hand, can leave. As in. Right. The fuck. Now."

I hear dark laughter coming from Rick. It makes me shiver and the hairs on my arms stand up. That shit ain't funny, it's creepy as hell.

"She isn't your woman, the lady is her own. But as you can see, she's wearing my mark." Rick's voice is firm.

Zack's eyes flash to me as he looks me over. When he sees the hickey on the side of my neck an actual growl leaves his mouth. That's it. I've had it with these cavemen. Fucking alpha bullshit.

"I'm leaving right now. To hell with this shit. You," I press my finger into Rick's chest. "Don't ever think you can pull that mark me shit again, mister. And you," I turn and poke my finger in Zack's chest. "I ain't your woman, not now, not ever."

Before I can pull my finger away from his chest his hand wraps around mine. "You were mine before you left me behind. The moment your tight ass stepped back into my town, you were mine again. We've lost three years, but that's it, Blue. None of that shit will ever happen again. So get used to it, you're my woman. Always have been, always will be."

"No. I'm not. Cut that alpha bullshit out. I am not property you can own." I look between the both of them. "I'm done. With both of you."

I step away and look at Lynn, who is standing at the door staring at the guys. "Lynn." She's is still staring at the two men facing off. "Lynn," I growl.

She manages to shake out of the staring.

"I'm leaving, and you're coming with," I snap out my words.

She nods and steps away to grab her shoes. As I watch her put them on, I hear the guys going at it.

"You need to step out of her life, she's mine. Always has been," Zack barks.

"That's where you're wrong. The moment she wasn't yours? That's when she became mine. I've been there for her more than you've been. I might know her for a shorter period of time than you, but make no mistake, I'll be the one who'll get her in the end." Rick's voice leaves no room for arguments.

Zack shoves Rick against his chest. Dams steps up and grabs his president by hooking his arm around him.

"Keep dreaming, pal. Not happening," Zack growls as he struggles against Dams' hold.

"Do not ever lay a hand on me again." Rick's tone is steady, barely raising his voice.

"Or what, suit? Think before you answer that one, 'cause I don't respond well to threats," Zack snarls.

His struggles against Dams brings him closer to Rick. I feel the need to step in because this isn't going to end well. Like two dogs fighting over a bone, and unfortunately it seems I'm the fucking bone. Almost seems logical to throw myself in between.

I turn to do just that when I see Rick lean in and barely hear him whisper, "Or…I will have someone pushed out of your life."

He steps around Zack and Dams, walks up to me and strokes my cheek.

He leans in and places a soft kiss on my lips. "Sorry we have to cut this night short. Another time, Petal."

I only manage to nod before he's out the door. Okay, that was very creepy. Any other man who fits his business style appearance would have pissed his pants. Or at least ran out the backdoor the moment two bikers stepped in. Lynn's looking at me with the same confused look on her face.

Her eyes meet mine and her face shifts a bit to a question written all over, asking me if we're still going out.

"Oh yeah, we're still leaving alright. I need a drink." Reaching in my purse I grab a piece of gum and throw it in my mouth.

Without a look or a word to Zack, we leave the house.

******

The bar we're sitting in has a large jukebox with pink neon lights. I slide in the coins and pick three songs and walk back to the table. The waitress comes up and collects the empty shot glasses while she places the new round of tequila shots on the table.

"Thanks," I murmur and grab the glass and return it empty before her. "Could you please bring six more?" I give her a smile which she returns.

"Sure, honey, comin' right up." The waitress spins around and walks off.

Lynn groans. "Could you please tone it down a bit? I won't drag your ass into a cab and into the house. Your ass is heavy."

"Ah, just shut your barn to keep the smell inside would ya. That shit's nasty," I reply.

She looks at me, opens her mouth, shuts it again before her eyes twinkle and we both laugh.

When she's finally got her breathing under control her eyes turn serious. "So you've really bought an apartment and a gym. And you're leaving my ass."

I give her a soft smile. "Yeah, but you know I'll be just a few minutes away. Besides, the apartment is right next to the shop. You can sleep over at my house anytime you want. Anytime. And yeah, I sold 49% of the gym to the MC."

Shock fills her face. "You did what?"

"I made them partners but kept the one percent extra since the apartment is attached to the gym. I don't give a shit about the gym." I shrug my shoulders.

Lynn throws back a shot of tequila when I add, "Oh, and I only asked forty-five bucks for it. Made them pay in cash so I could give it back to you for the toy you got me."

She starts to cough and slams her chest. Her eyes water as she struggles to breathe.

"Are you gonna live there, honey?" I ask.

She takes a deep breath, seems to hold it while she keeps slapping her hand on her thigh. Watching for a few seconds that seems more like minutes I start to worry about her. Right when I want to stand up, loud laugher escapes her throat.

"You..." She wipes her eyes and struggles words between laughter. "Sold... A gym... For a... For a ... Rubber dick."

The last few words come out in a high-pitched voice that stands out cause the jukebox decides it's time for a new song. Every head is turned to Lynn and I can't stop myself from laughing along with her.

"So you're gonna run the gym with them?" Her head tilts, awaiting my answer.

I shake mine. "Nope, they can have it. I want nothing to do with it."

"You're not serious." Pointing a finger at me, she continues, "It'll be perfect for you. You need this to get back into your workout vibe."

Again, I shake my head. "I have my workout vibe, Lynn. I don't need a gym for that. I got my treadmill and running outside. That's enough for me."

"No way, Belle, this is too perfect. It's time to do more, it's been too long..." Her voice trails off.

Pain shoots though my chest. "You know why I stopped. I can't do it anymore. Hell, I haven't thrown a punch since that night. The night I lost...

I lost so much that night, not only her. Ugh, and to think the first punch since then was hitting your brother in the gut."

"See?" she insists. "You need this. It wasn't your fault, Belle, you didn't know. There was nothing you could do and now it's time to let it go. Let everything go. You need to look beyond the past and start living again. You owe it to them honey, to yourself. Besides, my brother is an ass. He deserved it. You can use him as a punching bag any time."

I look down, I know she's right. "Maybe they won't add bags to the gym. They need to think about the setup first. I do hope they get good equipment though."

"See? Right there, honey. You need to get involved. Even if it's just business. You need this," Lynn insists.

"Yeah, maybe." I shrug my shoulders. "But what I need right now is more tequila."

"Love it when we're right and we're in agreement." She smiles and raises her hand while she screams out, "Another round."

Chapter 6

I'm sitting at the bar in the compound. Music is still screaming loud while most of my men are already in their room with a piece of ass. Dams is sitting beside me, a prospect behind the bar, and another three of my brothers are sitting around a table playing poker.

I feel a hand sliding over my shoulder as another one is going toward my dick.

Grabbing the hand around the wrist, I lift it away from my body. "I won't be needing your mouth or your hands from now on."

"Oh, come on, Prez. You know my mouth is worth it," she purrs into my ear while her tongue licks my ear-lobe as her lips clamp around it.

I pull my arm up between us to push her away from my body.

"Did I somehow speak in a language you didn't fucking understand?" I growl. "Fuck off, Lau. Go fuck another brother. Plenty to go around."

"What about you, Dams? You want my mouth, hands or my pussy? I know my pussy wants you. How about it, you ready to pound into me?" Lau purrs.

I see Dams shake his head at the unattractive tone of Lau. Doesn't that bitch realize none of us find that dirty mouth attractive? Okay, maybe every once in a while we like it. Just long enough to put a dick in it so she can shut the hell up.

My mind goes back to the one thing my dick does want. Still can't believe I walked in on her getting ready to go out on a date with that suit. The fucker doesn't know who he's dealing with. She's mine and it's time his ass walks out of the fucking picture. Hell, walks out of my fucking town.

My phone vibrates in my pants and I pull it out. "Speak."

"Prez. They just took C.Rash to the hospital. Some fucker pushed him off the road." Walter's words come out in a rush.

"What's that, Walter?"

I hear Walter take a deep breath before he starts over. "We were riding out on 85 when some Chevy comes out of nowhere, drives past us and slides into C.Rash pushing him off the road. He came down hard, Prez. I would have chased the Chevy but I needed to check on C."

"You did the right thing, we'll be right there." I put my phone back into my pocket. Dams stands up, ready to go.

Hearing one side of the story seems to be enough for him. "Where are we going?"

"Someone pushed C.Rash off the road on 85. He's at the hospital right now," I throw out the words while I think shit over.

Dams looks at me and his face goes angry as realization also hits my brain.

"Pushed," both me and Dams state at the same time.

"Jinx," the little fucker says behind the bar, like a little teenage kid who's watching others play a game. "Go on, who's gonna throw the first punch." His fucking eyes sparkle.

"It'll be my fist to your face if you don't shut the hell up, Tyler," Dams snaps. "Man, you're such a baby, no wonder you're not even close to getting patched in yet."

"Motherfucker!" I roar.

Fucking slick as hell, asshole suit. I just fucking knew something was wrong about that guy.

I look Dams in the eye. "Someone pushed C.Rash off the road. He's in the hospital, Walter's there. Pushed. Off. The. Road. That fucker, who tried to claim Blue threatened to push someone out of my life."

Tyler's fist slams into the bar making Dams and my head turn to look at him. He shrugs his shoulders.

Dams shakes his head and grabs his phone. "Knew that guy was trouble the moment I saw his face."

I nod my head in agreement. "Yeah, this could be just a coincidence but, fuck. It's just too obvious."

Seeing Dams scrolling through his phone I glance at mine. "We need to go to the hospital and I want to know where the girls are. I don't trust the fucker, even if he's got nothing to do with this. I need eyes on the girls."

Dams nods as he punches his phone and brings it to his ear. "I'm calling Nerd, run a background check on the fucker."

He steps away and talks into the phone as I dial Blue's number. When she doesn't pick up I try my sister's number. When that goes unanswered too, I feel the need to smash something. Instead I step away from the bar and head to our bikes. Dams falls in step behind me as we leave the clubhouse.

My voice is almost a bark. "We're stopping at Purple Beans first."

Hoping Lynn was smart enough to take Blue there. Dams nods in understanding as we drive off. Purple Beans is a bar the MC owns, next to a welding company and a pig farm we own. Let's not forget the gym we now also seem to have.

Stepping through the door, I take in the scene. The bar is crowded as the jukebox tries to bring its sound above the loud murmur of voices. My eyes search for the one I hope to find between the crowd. It takes a moment to find my sister.

She's on the dance floor swaying her ass to the music. There are two guys dancing with her, one in front of her, and one behind. Both guys have their hands on her body. Anger boils up in me. I know she's a grown ass woman, but she's still my sister and no man gets to put his hands on her body while I'm standing in the same damn space.

Walking across the dance floor I see Blue's body dancing behind my sister. She's got her eyes closed and she's dancing on her own. There are guys watching her, and one tries to sneak a hand around her waist to pull her against him.

My feet are moving fast toward them as I see Blue push the guy away from her. She keeps on dancing as the next guy tries the same move. Before his hand reaches her, I pull her toward me. Her eyes open with a fuck off look that flashes to heat the moment she recognizes me.

My hand goes into her hair and before she can take the next breath, I steal it away from her. Our lips meet in hunger as our tongues fight for dominance. She tastes like tequila and lime. The tip of her tongue slips through my lip ring as she gives it a little pull, activating my dick.

With one hand on her hip, I pull her body closer to me, grinding myself into her body. Letting her feel that my dick is hard and ready to find his way in. It's like I'm getting drunk on her taste. Not the tequila that's obviously on her tongue, but her. I'm hooked; she pulls me in and I'm lost.

My hand slips down her dress and back up her leg, underneath her dress. She hooks her leg behind my ass. I can almost feel the heat coming from her pussy that's now so close only my zipper is keeping us from connecting. My hand reaches between us as I set myself free and slide her panties aside. Before I can bury myself in paradise I feel someone hitting my back.

"Snap out of it, Prez." Dams adds a few more curses.

Pulling my lips away, her leg slides down and I reach to zip myself back up. Fuck. I almost fucked her right here. On a fucking dance floor filled with people.

Dams still continues his rant. "We ain't in the clubhouse, Prez. Besides, I've never seen you put your dick in pussy before. In a bitch's mouth yeah, but a pussy?"

"Shut the hell up, Dams! Fucking now," I growl.

"I just warned you to skip the fucking, Prez." The idiot chuckles as Blue keeps grinding herself onto my dick.

"You gotta stop that, Blue." It pains me to voice those words.

She pushes her bottom lip out. Pouting she says, "Why? We're on the dance floor and I want to dance."

"Blue, my dick wants to dance inside your tight pussy, and that's exactly what's gonna happen if you don't stop offering a way in." I close my eyes and shake my head, before they flash back open.

Her eyes lock on mine as she places her hands on both sides of my head. She pulls my head down for a kiss that has us going right back to where we were. With Dams hitting my fucking back again. I barely manage to drag my lips away.

"Dams, get my sister and meet me out front. We need to leave." I bend my knees slightly and place my shoulder into Blue's belly before I lift her up to my shoulder.

The moment I have her there she starts to hit my back. "My purse! Get my purse, Sally Boy!"

My dick twitches by the sound of my old nickname coming from her mouth. Sure, she called me Sally in front of everybody back then. But Sally Boy was reserved for the bedroom, the pet name for my dick.

My hand slides in between her legs, stroking her pussy through her panties. "No worries, Blue, I got you and your purse."

When I get outside I place her back on those cute little spiked heels she's got on, that are hot and sexy as fuck. I wouldn't mind having her naked, holding her by the ankles as her heels press into my pecs.

"What the fuck, brother? We were having a great time, why come and ruin it?" My sister's mad as hell, shooting fucking daggers out of her eyes but she can suck it up.

She knows how this shit flies, and right now she's gotta follow orders. "We don't have time to get them home, and a brother to watch them. They're comin' with."

Dams nods and grabs for Lynn while he leans in and whispers something in her ear. She nods and gets on the bike with him.

******

98

Everybody steps aside when we're walking through the halls of the hospital as me and Dams pass them by.

Walking up to the desk, the nurse behind it looks scared as she picks up a pen and starts to wiggle it between her fingers. "Ca.. ca... can I help you?" Her voice is almost a whisper.

"Yeah, hun, you can. C.Rash was brought in earlier. He was in a bike accident. Any news on him yet?" I ask.

In the corner of my eye I see Walter walking up to us.

"Are you his next of kin?" the nurse questions.

A little annoyed I fire back. "He's our brother."

"Is that brother, as in same mother and all, or brother in the television series kinda way?" Her eyes go to my patch and she gives me a slight smile. The timid nurse just became slightly cocky.

My voice turns cold. "Take your fucking pick, just give me the information I want."

She craves the television series version to get her panties wet? I'll give her the fucking bad boy vibe. "Now bitch, I ain't asking you nice, now am I?"

She drops the pen, stands up and runs away through the hall. I hear laughter coming from behind me as I see Blue bend over holding her hands on her knees while she struggles to breathe through her laughter.

I look at Dams and Walter, who both shrug their shoulders. Lynn strokes Blue's back with a huge smile. Blue finally pushes her hands away from her knees and stands up straight wiping her hands over her face.

"I'm okay now." She bursts out a laugh or two and keeps her eyes on the floor to prevent more laughter from escaping her.

"You totally scared the piss out of her, you know that right?" Blue's voice is still filled with laughter.

"Yeah well, she shouldn't have pissed me off," I grumble.

Walter shakes his head and says, "Fuck man, they won't give me any news either. Screw this, Prez. Should we storm into his room, pitch a fit, and demand answers?"

I shake my head. "Nah, Walter. We can't do that without them calling the boys in blue."

"I need gum, who's got gum? I'm out of gum... I need it." Blue's voice cuts through our conversation.

All eyes hit Blue. I know she's drunk right now, but come the fuck on. We need to focus. Blue walks up to me as she pulls her hair back into a tight bun that covers the blue that's in her hair.

My voice might carry a hint of anger when I tell her, "Sit down, Blue. We'll get you home soon enough. We gotta take care of something first."

Her shoulders straighten. "Yeah, me too, you degrading fuck. Now gimme a piece of gum."

Fucking bitch, I know she's feisty, but no one talks to me that way. Especially in front two of my brothers, one being my VP for fuck's sake. I can't take that shit from anyone, especially when you're the president of a fucking MC.

I reach into my back pocket to find my gum. Taking a look, I have one piece left. Awesome.

I grab it and throw it in my mouth. "Sorry, seems like I'm all out." I throw the empty wrapper down at her feet.

"Mister smarty pants thinks he's all television series badass right?" She walks up to me as her hands go to my face.

She pulls me down to her lips and bites down hard on my piercing. I give her a growl as I open my mouth. Her tongue touches mine as she strokes and sucks my tongue into her mouth, closing her teeth on my tongue to give me yet another bite. I turn my head to deepen the kiss as she slides back into my mouth. The moment I'm lost in her mouth she pulls away.

"Thank you," she says as she walks behind the desk, pulling a white coat on that she stole from the row of lockers behind it.

Six loud pops come out of her mouth as she smiles back to us. Sneaky little bitch stole my gum.

"Shutting up now… Need to play doctor…." She's got a sing-song voice to her words as her eyes go to the computer.

Her hands move over the keyboard as she types away on it. A few clicks and she walks away from the desk and into the hall.

She looks over her shoulder back to us. "Coming?"

"Fuck me. She's hot. I'll be," Walters voice is barely a mumble, but I still fucking hear him loud enough.

"Finish with 'coming' and I'll be nice enough to allow you to spend a few months here in a private room." I glare at the brother who needs to shut the hell up or I'll make it so he never speaks again.

Walter murmurs out an apology. We all follow her down the hall as she stops in front of room number 214.

She takes out the papers next to the door and looks through them. "Crash seems to be pulling through okay. He's suffered some severe abrasions and lacerations. The injuries he sustained are to his right arm, leg and buttocks."

"Huh?" Walter tilts his head, trying to understand what she just said.

Dams chuckles and says, "Yeah, you kinda lost us there Blue, I mean Doc."

She shakes her head. "Severe road rash."

The moment the words road rash leave her mouth we all burst into a fit of laughter.

"What the fuck, guys?" Blue watches us but isn't laughing at all. "You guys are fucked up. You heard me, right? Road rash is painful and needs a lot of treatment. It's not funny. I've seen some of the worst cases and even to the bone. Fuck this, I might be drunk off my ass but I don't think it's funny at all."

She places the file back and starts to walk away as I grab her by the elbow.

"Hold on, Blue. We're laughing cause his name isn't Crash. It's C. Rash. As in Carpet Rash, a nickname he got when he was still a prospect. At that time he was ordered to take care of three brothers that had passed out. Found them bare ass and drunk with two whores in the hallway of a hotel. He put the girls in a cab, dragged the guys by their hands into the room one at time. Let's just say we had three butts looking the same and with that, owning his new nickname."

The corners of her mouth come up as she bursts out a laugh and covers her mouth with her hand fast.

"Still not funny," she mumbles behind her hand, yet her eyes twinkle and give her away.

I lean in and kiss her nose. "You're adorable, you know that right? Gum stealing, annoying and feisty little cheat. But adorable nonetheless. So he's gonna be okay?"

Blue nods. "He's gonna be okay. World of pain for a few weeks, but okay."

I give her a nod in return and spin around to address my brothers. "Walter, wait till they let you in. Keep me updated. Me and Dams are gonna take the girls home."

Walter lifts his chin and walks over to the chairs across from the door. He picks up a magazine and gets comfortable as we turn to walk out.

Chapter 7

Belle

I open my eyes and instantly regret it. Fuck, my head hurts. I wish I could stay in bed all day but I'm booked up and have to be at the shop by 1:00pm. Opening one eye just a tiny bit so I can glance at the alarm clock I see it says eleven thirty.

Well, shit. That doesn't give me much time for lying down and getting rid of this mother of all hangovers. I can't even think of putting ink on a person right now. I need to keep my eyes closed. There's a noise coming from the hallway. Seems like someone is stumbling out there.

"Everything okay?" Holding my head with both hands, I try to raise my voice.

"I'm dying over here. Come help me out, bitch. Since it's all your fault," a voice mutters.

Lifting my head I see Lynn crawling on her hands and knees.

"Where are you going?" I wonder out loud.

"I need to pee and I need water. Lots and lots of water," she groans.

Thinking fast, I answer, "Water as in shower or drinking it? Hey, go into the shower, you could pee and drink and shower all at the same time. Smart, huh?"

"How is your mind still functioning with all that tequila you had yesterday?" Lynn grumbles.

A groan escapes me. "It's not, it's on autopilot. It keeps flashing, save body, save body, behind my eyes. Very annoying."

Lynn falls on her side laughing while she holds on to her head. "Do not go all funny on me, bitch. I hate you right now. My head hurts too goddamn much. And how the hell did we get home last night?"

"Fuck, I thought you'd know." I think and for the life of me can't remember shit. Wait. "Lynn…"

Soft crooning replies from off the floor near the door.

I have this weird flashback. "Were we at the hospital last night?"

Her head flashes up. "Oh shit. That happened?"

"Erm… pretty sure it did if we both remember it," I state.

"Fuck," she shoots back.

"Yeah, let's just hope it didn't have anything to do with fucking. Right?" Fingers freaking crossed I mentally add.

"Fuck!" Lynn repeats.

Opening my eyes, I look to see if I'm wearing any clothes. "Well at least I still have my bra and panties all in one piece. What the," Throwing off the blanket, I look at my feet. "Why in the hell are my heels still on? That's not right. Why pull off my dress but leave my heels on? What the fuck?"

"Well at least you took off your dress," Lynn groans. "I still had my jacket on and was lying on top of the covers. Woke up cold as hell."

I can hear a very soft buzz. "You hear that? That buzzing noise?"

"What? That's not coming from inside my head? Oh thank God, it's annoying as fuck." Her hands go to her head. "Make it stop, Blue."

"Great, everybody is calling me Blue now, might as well go get me a new freaking license," I grumble to myself as I slowly sit up.

I see my purse on the edge of my bed. Reaching out I grab it as I let myself fall back into my pillow. With my eyes closed I reach inside to grab my phone. Holding it up I see a few text messages from Zack. I scroll through them and curse in my head.

"What? What happened?" Lynn snaps.

Shit, not so much in my head. "Your brother seems to be the one who put me to bed last night."

"Ah, that would explain the heels and me on top of the covers, still in my jacket," Lynn states.

"Yeah." Groaning, I add, "I won't tell you what he's saying about my heels."

"Fuck no. Stop talking right now or I'm gonna barf all over your freaking floor."

"Ummm, that would be your floor, Lynn. And no puking. Oh gosh, the smell alone would have me barfing too." A flash of heat turns my stomach and I barely make it to the bathroom.

I try to hold back my hair as I puke my guts out. I can hear Lynn running down the hall to the other bathroom. Pretty sure she's now doing the same thing.

Taking a shower and getting dressed seems to have drained all the energy I had left. Searching through my bag I find the aspirin bottle. I take one out and place it on the kitchen counter so I can grab a piece of gum from my bag as well. Placing the piece of gum next to the aspirin, I walk to the fridge and grab a bottle of water. My phone indicates I got a new message.

Zack: We need to discuss the gym.
Me: No we don't. You guys can handle it.

Annoyed, I put my phone down on the counter. Lynn walks into the kitchen and grabs herself a bottle of water too. Pulling the cap off the water bottle I reach for the aspirin as my phone starts to buzz. I throw it in my mouth and down half the water, trying to swallow down the pill as I look at my phone.

Zack: We do & we will. Party at the MC Saturday.
Me: No.

I close the water bottle and put it back in the fridge. Reaching for my gum I throw it in my mouth and start to chew vigorously. Mad as hell, because that alpha jerk is now annoying the shit out of me. Crumbling in my mouth indicates it isn't the gum, but the aspirin I threw in my mouth, making me gag and run to the sink spitting and cursing.

Running the tap I rinse out my mouth. Standing up I rub my hands down my face groaning in displeasure.

"What the hell are you doing?" Lynn questions.

"I just swallowed my gum as if it was the aspirin and chewed my aspirin as if it was gum, okay?" I mutter.

"Why in the hell would you do that?" she gasps.

I shake my head. "Oh for fuck's sake. For fun okay? Like my head isn't killing me enough already, I decided I needed a little mindfuck too."

"Well the joke's on you then." I freaking hear the smile in her voice.

"Har har. Shut it, Lynn, just shut it." Walking to my purse I grab another aspirin and hold it in my hand as I grab Lynn's water and swallow the pill down.

Taking out another piece of gum I throw it in my mouth and start walking to the door. "Coming?"

Lynn opens the fridge and grabs two more water bottles. She walks up to me hand hands me one of the bottles.

With her big smile I know exactly what she's thinking. "Feels great huh, drinking water after drinking tequila."

Drinking water always seems to get that drunk on tequila feeling right back, at least for me. One look toward Lynn and I get the reassurance that it isn't just me that gets that feeling.

As if her smile couldn't get any bigger and yet, she succeeds. "Got that right. Cheers, honey, here's to getting through the day."

******

Just one more client, one more client and then I'm done. I should get a medal for pulling this off. The bell above the door rings, and I look up.

There's a huge bouquet walking into the shop accompanied by a set of feet. "Delivery for Miss Crowler."

"That would be me." Walking out of my room, I reach for the flowers as we both put it on the counter. It's huge. It's filled with blue orchids and white wildflowers. The colors are amazing and the smell is pulling me in.

My hands reach out to one of the blue orchids as my fingers feel the velvet flower. My mother loved blue orchids. That's the reason they're one of my favorites. They always remind me of her and of...

"They also wanted me to hand you this." I look back at the guy who is holding his hand out.

There's a black jewelry box with a card. He pushes his hand a bit up and down signaling me to take it from him. I give him a nod of thanks as I take the box.

"Right. My job is done, enjoy your day, Miss." The flower guy nods and heads for the door.

"Thank you," I mumble against his back.

The guy rushes out, and my eyes trail back to the black box that's equally as soft as the blue orchid I just touched. Setting the box on the counter, I open the envelope.

There are only two words on the card. "Miss you."

Knowing Zack would never send me flowers gets me a bit disappointed. Setting the card on the counter while reaching for the jewelry box, I open it and my breath hitches. There's a pendant in the shape of a petal filled with blue shiny sparkles on a silver looking chain.

"Holy shit, are those blue diamonds?" The box is grabbed from my hands as Lynn holds the box close to her head. Her fingers lift the chain so she can get a better look. "Fuck yeah, platinum chain. He. Is. Loaded. It's from creepy gentleman guy, right? Cause, well. Let's face it, my brother would never send flowers."

"Yeah I think so," I answer mindlessly. "He's always called me Petal and knows that blue orchids are special to me."

"You gonna call him?" Lynn chirps.

I shrug my shoulders. "Dunno."

"You should totally keep this. It's awesome. Here." She walks over to me and before I can say anything she puts the choker around my neck.

Reaching out I feel my own necklace first. It feels weird to have something else around my neck. Something that reminds me of blue orchids, of my mother. I was a mother, I should still be. I can't breathe. Waves of panic flow through my body.

"Get it off. Off. I need it off." I start to claw at my neck but the chain won't budge.

I can't breathe, it's too much, my knees start to sway as everything goes black.

I hear voices around me. Lynn's clearly crying and Lee is cursing. I try to open my eyes, and when I blink a few times, I'm looking at the ceiling of my room. Which means I'm lying on my own ink chair.

Footsteps sound as an angry voice booms through the shop. "What the fuck happened? Why is she laying there?"

Bracing myself up on one elbow, I look around at my friends. Turning my head I look into Zack's eyes.

His voice softens. "What happened, Honeybump?"

He steps closer to me, as Lynn answers his question while she's talking to me. "You had a panic attack, Blue, and it was all my fault. I'm so sorry. I'm so fucking sorry."

"Panic attack, huh..." My hands go to my throat. It feels like my skin is on fire.

Hopping off my chair I walk to the mirror. Cursing at myself because I look like I belong in a freaking horror movie where Freddy Krueger slices the shit out of my neck. Zack steps behind me and looks in the mirror at me.

"What happened, why'd ya panic, baby?" His endearment freaks me out, it hits too close to home.

Baby, my baby, our baby. My hand automatically reaches up to grab a hold of my pendant. I need to hold her, he's too close. He doesn't know. My breathing picks up again, black spots come into my vision as two arms grab me from behind.

My back is crushed into Zack's hard chest as his mouth is close to my ear. "Breathe, Blue, in, easy now, breathe out. Feel me, Blue. I'm right here with you. Stay with me, girl."

His voice takes me away from the panic, from the loss I feel. His hand moves from my waist to my hand holding my pendant in a death grip. His eyes meet mine in the mirror. There's so much emotion in his eyes, they pull me right in. I can feel the tears as they flow from my eyes.

There's a second where the feeling of his hard chest leaves me as I'm turned to face him. I bury my head against his chest as the sobs start to get louder and louder.

"Shush, baby, I'm taking you home." His voice is laced with worry.

Another wave of panic hits me. I've got one more client coming and I can't just blow him or her off. I push away from his chest and wipe away the tears in my eyes with the back of my hands.

"I, erm. I'm sorry about that." I wave in front of his now tearstained shirt.

"Not a problem, baby. Let's get you home." He pulls me back into his chest as I take a deep breath and fill my lungs with his scent. Spice, leather all raw and manly.

I groan as I think of the last two hours I still have left here at the shop. "I gotta work, just give me a minute. My client will be here any second. I'll be okay."

"Blue, you're not okay and you're holding on to your client right now. You're a great artist and I trust you completely. But there is no way in hell you're gonna ink me right now when you're like this. No offense, baby."

"Could you fucking stop with the baby shit? It's fucking annoying," I seethe.

He laughs. He fucking laughs at me while his hand cups my face. "There's my Blue. Keep that up and I might let you put some ink on me after all."

I grumble out my words. "So you're my last client of the day, huh? How'd that happen?"

Lynn shrugs her shoulders when I pin her with a mean stare. Right now my eyes should be able to shoot daggers, or at least some kind of laser, so I could burn her hair into a pile of ash. That would teach her.

I give in. "You're probably right, I should go home."

All of my energy is gone and suddenly I'm glad he's my last client so I can go home. I gather my things and walk up to Lynn and give her a hug.

She gives me an extra squeeze as she whispers in my ear, "So sorry, honey, go rest and we'll talk tomorrow if you want to."

I give her a kiss as I say thanks and say goodbye to Lee. Zack gives them a chin lift as we walk out the door.

******

Pulling into the driveway, I click on the remote so the garage door opens, leaving enough space so Zack can park his bike beside mine before I close the garage door. We walk into the living room and I offer him a drink. He sits down on the couch when I walk in holding two beers.

His voice is soft when he asks, "You wanna talk about it?"

I crash down next to him and let my head fall back as I close my eyes. "Nah, no good will come from that. I'd be breathing into a bag within seconds. We do need to talk, I owe you that much. Just. Not right now, okay?"

I'm selfish, I know, but I just can't do it right now. How do you tell a guy he could have been a father? Ah hell, he was. Our baby died. Dead, all because of me. Okay, I never even knew I was pregnant. At least, had been, until the moment I was kicked in my stomach during the one match I wanted to win so badly. The match that would have made me a World Champion for the fourth time in a row.

How my life changed with just that one kick was unimaginable. Lying there bleeding out in the ring. On the verge of losing someone that meant so much to me, even though I didn't know it was there. Waking up in the hospital, going into surgery to have a C-section to try and save the twenty-three week old baby I seemed to have in my belly. The very reason I stopped kickboxing right there and then.

When they couldn't save her, I threw myself deeper into becoming a surgeon. Just like my mom was and what my mother and father wanted me to be. Mom....I was a mom for the few seconds they told me I needed a C-section. I should have known right then. My baby never stood a chance. A piece of me died right along with her that day.

Instinctively my hand goes to the pendant. The need to hold her is strong. It's not much but the pendant holds a part of her, traces of her ashes are locked within.

When I had it made special, I had them make two. I need to give him the other one.

I owe him the truth. Lynn is the only one, next to my father, who knew. She was the one who told me not to say anything. He was in Iraq at the time, and communication was shit. Besides, why throw an emotional ice bucket over him when the two of us were ripped apart as it was? Miles away from each other.

Puppy dog love as my father used to call it. Even though we were both freaking grown-ups. You'll get over it. That's what my dad told me. I knew I never could, we were tied to each other, even more from that moment on. That made it even worse; leaving him out. Not able to share, I know he would have come for me if I told him.

Soft strokes on my cheek bring me back to the present.

"Hey, Honeybump, where did you go?" His voice is as tender as his fingers on my skin.

Taking a deep breath, I debate on telling him now. Either way it's gonna be ugly. I can tell him, and get it over with, or I can drag it out another few days, weeks, or hell even months. I'm sure he's going to be disgusted by me, and leave like everyone else in my life does.

I might as well just get it over with now. "We need to talk. It's only fair I tell you everything. I never should have kept,"

His phone rings. Taking it out of his pocket, he holds up a finger. "Sorry, Blue. I need to take this."

He stands up and walks into the kitchen. He doesn't talk much, only seems to listen intently. My mind is running wild and jumps all over the place. I need to do something before I go insane. I look at Zack, and see he's staring back at me. The look I see is filled with so much lust. Even though he's got the phone glued to his ear.

Keeping our gaze locked on one another, I stalk up to him. My hands go to his belt buckle as his hand goes around my wrist stopping me. He shakes his head, but I just nod. My hands keep working his jeans as he lets go of my wrist, I push down his pants.

Expecting underwear and not seeing any makes me giggle. His cock jumps at me like a little jack in a box. Except the little part, it's quite the opposite and reminds me of a bodybuilder who is all pumped up. Veins are wrapped around his dick and it's not even fully hard yet.

"Tell me you're not laughing at my dick." His hand is holding the speaker on the phone as he whispers the words to me.

Sucking my bottom lip into my mouth as I put my teeth in it, I drop to my knees in front of him.

Zack groans. "Fuck.... No. I. Just. I... Fuck. Gottta go, Dams, check in with ya later."

He puts the phone down on the kitchen counter but his eyes never leave mine. My hands are stroking him and my eyes lock onto where my hands are. I can't help the moan that leaves my throat. His dick is truly a work of art.

He has a Prince Albert, a piercing that goes straight through the tip. But he also has the frenum loop on the underside of his dick and a few more so it looks like a little stairway leading to his balls.

Holy shit, Lynn did tell me a little about all the different kinds of piercings that are out there. It's her job after all but this one I specifically remember. She told me they would feel like speed bumps for the partner.

My fingers slide over them as I let my tongue trail behind them. I feel him shift and lean back against the kitchen counter. He grabs a hold of it with both hands to steady himself. Sliding up, I lick away the pre-cum and get more turned on by his taste. I've never done this to him before.

We only had sex twice all those years ago, and in the same day. The same day my mom was killed and my dad took us away. I never had another guy after that. Never had a dick in my mouth but I sure as hell wouldn't let him know that. I've heard and read enough about it.

Playing with the PA, flicking it with my tongue and putting the tip through the ring as I give it a little tug. By the sounds coming from his mouth he was enjoying everything I gave. Tightening my lips around his cock as I suck and swirl my tongue at the sensitive spot just beneath the mushroom head.

This brings out a string of curses. Pulling away, I needed to look up. A bit shocked because I thought I was doing great, but by the curses leaving his mouth I wasn't sure.

"Don't you dare fucking stop, Blue. Get your mouth back on me." His voice sounds pained.

He pulls his hands away from the counter and guides me back to his cock. Fisting my hair he takes control of my movements. "Harder, Blue. Do that thing with your tongue and lips again. Tight, Honeybump, drive me fucking nuts. That's it. Fuck yeah. Just. Like. That."

His hips come forward with every word that leaves his mouth as he brings my head back with his fist. I feel used, and yet so fucking empowered by the way his voice cracks… it's like he's doing everything he can, just to hold on.

My lips tighten more as I hollow my cheeks, and stay on the head of his cock as my hand pumps up and down. Hard and fast. My tongue working its magic on his sweet spot. He tries to pull me back as a warning; leaving me with a choice. Without thinking I take him down deeper.

I feel his cock harden even more when he starts to pulse in my hand. His piercing hits the back of my throat. Warm fluids enter my mouth with a strange taste that makes me want to swallow and not think about what I'm swallowing down.

It only lasts a few seconds then I feel him soften a bit in my hands and he slips out of my mouth, his hand still wrapped tight in my hair.

He tugs so my face falls back and I have no choice but to look at him. "That, Blue, that was something we need to do again real soon. Nothing else I've had compares to that mouth of yours."

What the fuck did he just say? Oh, no he didn't. Did he just compare me to other women? The jerk must think he's giving me some huge compliment. While all I hear is him bringing up other women into our moment. Fuck that.

"Glad you've had enough women to compare me with. Now fucking leave." I stand up and try to turn.

He grabs both my arms. "That's not what I meant, come on, Blue. I should have, ah fuck. I didn't think, you just blew my mind okay."

"I blew your dick and swallowed your cum, not your brain cells, you idiot," I sneer.

Shrugging off his hands, I leave the kitchen. I hear him stumble and curse as he tries to walk and pull his pants up at the same time. This gives me an advantage to speed walk to my room. I slam the door and lock it. He just needs to fucking leave.

Talk about leaving a bad taste in your mouth. Shit, I need to brush my teeth and pee. Coming out of the bathroom, I hear Zack knocking on my door.

Asking in his version of a sweet voice to open the fuck up. Tired of all this shit I drop myself on the bed.

Not even getting comfortable I grab a pillow and throw it over my head. Taking a deep breath, I let all the crazy shit in the world go as sleep consumes me. I continue hearing faint knocking and curses as well as the ringing of a phone. All of this can't bind me to this fucked up world as I trail off to dreamland.

Chapter 8
Belle

I push my feet harder into the ground to pick up speed. Running always makes me feel liberated. My mind seems clearer now and finally I can think straight.

Well, except for the annoying panting coming from behind me. "Move that ass. You sound like a freaking whale on dry land. Come on already."

With a quick look over my shoulder I can see the anger flash in her eyes and it makes me smile. I know just the right buttons to push to kick her ass. We used to workout together all the time. Even when I was in Japan we used to kick each other's ass online to keep focus. I've missed this, even if I do most of my workouts alone. She sucks as a running partner and I could go laps around her while we're on a run but I love having her with me.

We're almost home. We've got the stone stairs left with a wall running past it at the end. I used to jump over that wall to skip half the stairs so I could beat her. Not that it was a contest or anything. More like a silent competition, to see who can finished first. Not once has she ever made it back before me. And I'm not about to let her this time either.

"I am gonna kick your fat ass," Lynn growls.

"Ha. No way, you've been staring at my ass for the last forty minutes or so. No touching. Not. Even. Close." I push my feet harder as I jump up on to the wall, take a few steps on it and jump back off.

Within a few seconds I'm at the door. I turn just in time to see Lynn come around the wall. She drags her feet panting like she's going to die any minute now.

"Damn girl, you're out of shape!" I throw my words over my shoulder.

"Yeah, well... Not... everybody... is... a... fighter girl..." She struggles with her words between sucking in air.

"I haven't been a fighter in years, Lynn. Hell I haven't even thrown a punch until I hit that asshole brother of yours. I should have punched him yesterday and right in the dick too."

A strangled noise leaves her throat. "Well shit…. What… did… he do… now?"

"Come on, we'll talk." A chuckle escapes me. "Well, I'll talk and you can listen. That way you have time to catch your breath. Then maybe you can attach words together as actual sentences instead of puffing each word out."

"Shut… it… Fatso," Lynn growls.

I chuckle again as I grab the key out of the small pocket in my pants and unlock the door. We go straight into the kitchen where I grab two bottles of water from the fridge. I hand her one as I begin to explain what happened yesterday.

"He's an idiot, Blue. I don't think he meant anything by it. Hell, you had just blown his brain out literally, and let's face it, cavemen don't have too many to begin with. But seriously.... You swallowed? Oh damn girl. That's just." Lynn scrunches up her nose. "Okay, I've done it a few times, but with the last guy I almost choked. I barely swallowed it down and I ended up burping. Oh God, that was humiliating. I never enjoy that shit. Don't get me wrong, I'm all over sucking dick and am fucking great at it if I might say so myself, but the end game... yeah, I'd like a little warning so I can avoid that prize. Hell I'd rather have that nasty, sticky shit in my hair or ear than to swallow it down."

I shake my head. "Jesus, Lynn, that's a little too much information! Did you say ear? Ah, yuck!"

"Oh you shush!" She points a finger in my direction. "You're talking about my brother's cum, and I'm the one who's oversharing? I'm just pretending you're talking about another dude. So, let's hear it...what's the trick, huh? How do you swallow?"

"What?" I try to hold in my laughter. "Without burping?"

Her head tilts to the left, as if she's thinking things through. "Actually, it was kind of in between a burp and a gag."

We both laugh as I make my way to the kitchen. I fix the both of us some oatmeal while letting her words linger in my head.

I may have overreacted just a bit. He probably didn't mean anything by it. It was my insecurities taking over.

"It was a heat of the moment thing. I was so into it that I wanted it. I was so fucking turned on by him. Until he crushed it. But now that I've thought about it," I turn down the gas and let the oatmeal cool down a bit.

"What? Just spit it out," Lynn demands.

"Ha! Funny, Miss Burp Because I Can't Keep Your Cum Down."

She hits me in the shoulder. "I knew I never should have told you."

"Yeah, too little, too late," I inform her. "Because I'm never gonna forget that one. I might have to bring it up at your wedding one day."

Lynn shakes her head. "Fucking hell, bitch, you wouldn't. Gah. Never mind, I know you would because I would."

"Totally. Sorry, not sorry. But yeah... I do feel a bit bad about how I reacted, but you want to know why I did?" My gaze finds hers.

"Spit it out, again...totally pun intended." She smiles at me.

"Ha. Yeah, well...I haven't been with anyone else. Not one guy. Your brother is the only one I've ever had. It felt like he took a knife to my chest. Hearing him talk about all these women and then to compare me to them."

Her smile falters. "Well shit. When you put it like that…I hear ya and would have reacted the same way. He's an ass, honey." She looks over my shoulder to the doorway behind me. Her face grows angry the longer she's looking.

A thought crosses my mind. "I think I need to get laid with a few guys, so I have something to compare."

"No fucking way in hell." The booming voice that comes from behind me sounds more like a lion's growl; ready to attack and conquer.

The hair on the back of my neck stands on end and my heart skips a beat. How much did he hear? Oh my God. The look on Lynn's face. He heard.

I spin on my heels to face him. "Where the fuck did you come from?"

"Couch," he throws at me. "I slept here. We need to talk."

"Yeah… so talk," I snap.

"Later, when we're alone," Zack states. "Now, do you have some oatmeal for me too? Or should I make my own?"

Cursing under my breath, I reach to grab another bowl from the cabinet. Filling all three I set them on the table and we all sit down.

We eat for a few minutes in silence before Zack starts to speak. "I'm gonna put a guy on the both of you. Something's come up and I need to make sure you two are okay at all times."

We both look up at Zack and then at each other. Then back at Zack again.

Before I can ask the question, Lynn's already fired it at him. "This got anything to do with what happened with C.Rash?"

"It might, but it's club business so you both are on need to know basis." His voice clearly indicates no room for arguments.

I snort at his caveman style answer and stand up to put my bowl in the sink. "I'm gonna hit the shower and get ready for work."

"Don't forget the BBQ tonight." Zack's demanding voice fills the air once again.

I shake my head. "I didn't forget, Zack, I'm just not going."

"Your ass needs to be there, Blue. We're celebrating the ownership of the gym. You're a co-owner and that means you're involved in club business."

I can't hold back the automatic eye roll. "Oh, so now I'm involved in club business. Now ain't that convenient."

"Yeah, Blue, so get fucking used to it. We're in bed together. Your ass is mine, business and personal." He steps closer, caging me between his body and the kitchen counter.

His head moves closer to my ear as he whispers slowly, "Just so you know; no man will ever lay a hand on that tight little ass of yours. I like knowing you haven't been with anyone else but me and I meant what I said last night.

Your mouth is the best one I've had on my dick. Since that's the only thing I can compare because I've never put it in another pussy. Just yours, Honeybump. My dick has only seen the inside of your pussy. Mouths are the only thing I could do. Always wrapped it up too. So no fucking mouth touched skin to skin, there was always something in between. No more, Blue, no more. The only mouth, pussy, ass or hands that my dick will know or see is yours. You hear me?"

Sometime during his speech I seem to have lost my voice and my mind. Not to mention that I need a change of underwear because these are now soaked.

"I said, did you hear me?" His voice is slightly raised and it comes out as a growl.

Still no voice as I barely manage a nod.

"Good. Now, I need to handle some shit. Dams will be here soon and he's bringing Pokey with him. You girls both go straight to the shop and Pokey will tag along with you today."

Now we both nod as Lynn steps away from the table and out of the kitchen. Zack grabs my waist as his mouth hits my neck. I feel his teeth and a slight tug as he sucks my neck. My head falls to the side to give him a better angle. He moans and steps closer, pressing me harder against the kitchen counter. His hand slips up from my waist to my breast as he squeezes it gently.

The doorbell rings and both of us ignore it while he keeps sucking my neck. Both of my hands end up in his hair and I pull him closer to me. The doorbell rings again and loud knocking joins the annoying sound.

Zack's mouth leaves my throat as he turns slightly. "Stop fucking hitting me, you twat!"

I look behind Zack as I see Lynn standing there. Water is dripping off her while she is wrapped in a huge purple towel.

"Then get your face off her and open the fucking door! For fuck's sake don't touch each other. The both of you seem to leave to another planet the moment you start touching." She curses some more as she walks away.

"She's right you know." He runs a hand through his hair as he keeps his eyes on the floor. "But fuck how I love that planet we seem to hit the moment we touch. Fuck anyone else. Right now though, right now you need to shower and I need to handle some business. But we're planet hopping soon, sweetheart."

He grabs my chin and slams his lips on mine. There is nothing delicate about that kiss, it's hard, wet and fast. His lips leave mine as does his body while he stalks to the door as the pounding starts up again.

Zack

Getting on my bike and leaving her side is very hard. Another thing that's hard is right between my legs. Damn, I need to be inside her as soon as I can. My cum needs to decorate the insides of her pussy so her body knows it's mine. First I've got to take care of some shit. Dams got more info on the fucker who's trying to steal my woman. I know the fucker is the son of a huge real estate dick here in town.

My anger flairs up as I guide my bike through the compound gates. No way will this fucker ever get his hands on my woman. Dams walks up behind me as I head for church.

He grabs my shoulder and slaps it twice. "His dad is one dirty motherfucker. This is bad, Zack."

"Had a feeling shit was gonna hit the fan. The moment I laid eyes on that motherfucker, I knew he was trouble." Anger clearly laces my words.

The door closes and all my brothers in this chapter are in the same room. Time to get things started. I nod toward Dams so he can inform all of us.

Dams leans his elbows on the table and looks around. "So, Prez and I ran into this dude Frederick Dayans at that auction. He also wanted the gym but Blue ended up with it. Blue seems to know him and he seems interested in her. Long story short, he threatened Prez to push someone out of his life. C.Rash was pushed off the road the other day. We did a background check on him, and while his nose is clean his father's as dirty as they come. This guy goes by the name of Frankie Dayans or Frankie D. who is the big boss of some real-estate scheme that's been going on. He's got a long list of scumbags that handle all the dirty shit. Those scumbags happen to be the Broken Deeds MC."

All hell breaks loose after that. Curses roar and fists slam down on the table. We've had a few run-ins with them in the past when my dad was president. That shit was all cleared up with a truce as long as they stayed out of our town.

"Calm the fuck down, now," I growl.

It takes a minute for everyone to shut the hell up but when they do Dams continues. "They've been able to fly under our radar for quite a while now. They're smart enough that they keep their shit out of our backyard. Frankie D. also owns half the property in town and does business in different cities as well. Nerd also got some intel on Broken Deeds MC. Seems like their president is handling things different. Dog isn't president any more. His son took over. He's an ex-seal and a former MMA. From what Nerd could get on him, it seems like this new president isn't happy with being Frankie D.'s lapdog. There wasn't much info, but Frankie D. must have something solid to tie this MC to him."

Dams sits back down into his chair. The silence in the room is deafening. With all this new info running through my head I know we need to take action, to get ahead of things before they come crushing upon us. "Okay, listen up. We need to squash this fast. The smartest thing to do is have a sit-down with the president of Broken Deeds MC. Even if nothing comes from it, they need to know when to fuck off. I'll handle little Frankie D.'s son. Blue's my ol'lady and I'm gonna make damn sure he knows it."

"Prez…. Does she know she's your ol'lady?" There's a smug fucking smile on Dams' lips.

"Shut it, Dams," I growl. "She knows, or she will know soon enough. Reach out to Broken Deeds MC for a sit-down. In the meantime, everybody keep their eyes and ears open."

******

With the meeting done, the guys are getting everything ready for the BBQ. I made Pokey check in with me every hour so I knew my woman was safe. She'd better get her ass here tonight or I will drag that ass over here myself. Taking another sip of my beer I feel a hand sneaking up my back. It brushes to my front and strokes my dick. Seeing the black nail polish and the uncountable bracelets I know the hand belongs to Lau.

I grab her hand a little rough and slap it away. "I told you to fuck off, bitch. I'm taken."

I might have used her mouth a lot of times but that's just what it was. Used. She knows why she's here, she ain't no ol'lady, she's a quick fuck. To all my men. Nothing more, nothing less. If she doesn't like it, she knows where the door is. We've got a few of these girls. Love to fuck and love our way of living. They get what they need and my boys like to give it to them.

"I thought you were shitting me, Prez. And taken or not, we could still have fun," she purrs and the hairs on the back of my neck stand on end.

I fucking hate clingy bitches. I'm clear as day and she needs to listen and back the fuck off. "Last warning so listen real good. I ain't touching you, you ain't touching me. Ever. Again. Go fuck one of my boys, if you ever walk up to me like you just did and run your mouth, you're out. Are we clear?"

"Sure, Prez, whatever you say." The fucking bitch still has a purr in her voice as she bats her eyes.

Thank fuck she turns and walks away. I never should have used her mouth more than one time.

Before I know it, I get a message from Pokey saying he's heading this way with the girls. Putting my phone back I head up to the bar to grab a beer. Standing next to me is Walter. He's the one handling the pig roasting above the fire.

"Walter." He gives me a chin lift when he hears me addressing him. "The pig done yet?"

He gives a tiny shake with his head. "I'd give it another half hour before you cut the thing off."

"Nice. Any news on C.Rash?" I ask because he's kept me up to date so far.

"Doing better, Prez." Walter chuckles. "Those nurses keep him all happy and smooth. He gets released tomorrow. I'll pick him up and take him home once the Doc says it's okay."

I nod and turn just in time to see my sister walking toward me. My breath hitches as I see Blue next to her. God-fucking-dammit! I look around and for fuck's sake all my men are staring at her as if she was the pig roasting on the fire and they haven't been eating all fucking week. Fuck me for my thoughts and she would be fucking offended by my comparison yet again but this cannot be fucking happening.

She's wearing a short denim skirt with patches of leather on it. Biker boots with pieces of red and yellow leather flames on them. Her hair is loose and falls on the red tank she's wearing. On her tits the words "Eyes up, F*cker" are written in black sequins.

Every one of my boys seem to ignore the statement because, well her tits are almost spilling out. My steps pick up speed and I'm in front of her within the next second. Dams senses my anger and is standing right beside me, holding on to his beer.

"What the hell are you wearing, Blue?" My words might resemble a growl.

She looks down at her clothes. Her eyes meet mine in an innocent stare. "What? You don't like it? Should I take it off?"

Before I can answer her there's a hand curling around my waist, sliding down to cup my dick. "Come dance with me, hun." The annoying voice purrs and I see anger flash in Blue's eyes.

Blue takes a step forward. "Would you mind getting your hands off his dick? We were talking here before you opened your mouth."

Lau steps in front of me and gets in Blue's face. She looks at her and smirks. "I can put my hands on his dick anytime I want. As for opening my mouth, yeah... that too. Since I've had him in my mouth lots of times."

Blue narrows her eyes at Lau. I can't help the wave of pride that hits me to see that she's jealous. She fucking cares about me or that comment wouldn't have hurt her.

"Well, congratulations. Since you like to suck and all. Why don't you buy a lollipop and go celebrate," Blue states as Dams showers Lau with the sip of beer he just took, and coughs loud.

Blue reaches over and slaps him on the back a few times. "You okay there, honey?"

His coughing turns into laughter as he wipes his hands over his mouth. Lau is pissed as fuck as she reaches her hand back to smack Blue in the face.

My fingers go around her wrist as I turn it around to her back. "You're done here. Leave and never step foot on my property ever again. Yeah?"

She fumes as Pokey steps up and grabs her elbow to guide her out. My eyes go to Blue, my arm reaches around her waist as I pull her against my body. Wrapping my hand around her hair I pull her head back and swipe my tongue over her lip.

She keeps her lips shut as she grabs a hold of my piercing with her lips to give it a little tug. I growl at her. She gives a little laugh. Taking advantage of her lips opening, I force my tongue in her mouth and wrestle with hers.

I pull her closer to my dick, her legs wrap around my waist and I cup her ass with one hand. The rest of the world just falls away as I turn and push her against the wall. My hand finds the edge of her skirt as I slide down underneath it. Fuck she's not wearing any panties. Holding her pinned to the wall and my body, I reach in front of me to pull down the zipper.

Setting my dick lose, she moans in my neck and whispers for me to hurry. She doesn't need to tell me because within seconds my dick is coated with her cream. Running the head up and down her lips I can't hold back.

With one hard thrust, I'm balls deep where I belong. She screams in agreement. Her nails go into my back as she bites down on my shoulder. Pulling out and slamming right back in, I have the need for more. I need to fuck her hard and I need a good hold on her body, and I can't do that if I'm holding her up at the same time.

Without thinking things through I look to my right and open the door to church. As I lay her down on the table, it's the perfect height for pounding right into her. I want to pull her top down to see her tits slam back and forth from thrusting into her. Instead, one of my hands goes around her neck to keep her down.

She moans loud as she asks me to tighten the hold I have on her. My other hand is on her hip, fingers pressing into her skin so deep, I'm sure she'll have my handprint as a bruise there days to come. She grabs the edge of the table with both hands to keep in place as I keep slamming back and forth.

Feeling her tightening her walls she screams my name as her body begins to shake and her back arches. My dick is getting squeezed tight and I get harder by the sight I have before me. Feeling my balls starting to overload, I launch my seed, into the pussy that's all mine, in full force.

I growl out her name while I keep her pinned to the table. Just a few seconds more to enjoy this magic moment before we're brought out of our haze by a loud applause.

Blue's confused look is just as good as mine as I look around the room.

Chapter 9

Zack

"Oh fuck," I mumble as reality sets in on what just went down.

Dams smacks me on the back and congratulates me as he looks down at Blue. I follow his eyes and thank fuck I didn't pull her top down, so her tits are still covered. With my dick still inside her and her tight little skirt around her hips, that part is pretty well covered too. I pull out and make sure she doesn't flash anyone. My eye falls on her leg as I see my seed sliding down. Well fuck, isn't that just the best thing I've seen in years.

"Why is he congratulating you, Zack?" She looks around the room and sees most of my men standing there.

The douchey prospect, Tyler, is standing in the doorway since he's not allowed in church yet.

Tyler shakes his head. "He can't take a piss with others in the room, but he doesn't have a problem with fucking in front of the whole chapter? I just don't get it, makes no sense at all."

Heads turn to the comment that's just been made by Tyler. Fucking hell I gotta get a handle on this, right now.

Pokey's voice is filled with appreciation when he says, "I must say, Prez, old school claiming is something that needed to be brought back. Heard about that shit but that was way before our time. Thank fuck you reinstated it."

138

"Zack. What the fuck is he talking about?" Blue demands.

"Out. Out. Everybody out." My voice bounces off the walls.

"See… you just gotta wait for it." That fucking prospect and his shitty remarks, he's gonna fucking die.

In two steps I'm in front of Tyler and my fist connects with his nose. There's a crunching noise and blood pours as I pull my fist out of his face.

"Clear this fucking room. Now." My own ears ring as I bellow those words.

My sister walks up and I shake my head. "I need a word with her, Lynn. Alone."

I slam the door shut when the last person leaves the room. Leaving only me and the woman I love. Shit. Well, no denying now. I fucking love this woman and I'd do anything to keep her with me. Time to put my mouth where my head is so we're on the same planet, page, or wherever the fuck we are. Together, once and for fucking always.

Belle

What the hell just happened? The best sex, that's what happened. I can't even enjoy the afterglow. My pussy still throbs between my legs from the visit it got from Zack's dick.

Oh shit, even the thought of his dick, or better yet, those piercings. Oh man, that was amazing. Even the reminder makes me want to clench my thighs. I could just have an orgasm solely based on a memory. Oh Fuck. Why the hell does any type of sexual interaction with us have to end weird. This is fucked up in more ways than one.

Zack pins me with his gaze. "Blue, before you go all crazy, just hear me out okay?"

I grit my teeth because I know I can't make that promise. "Just tell me, I ain't making any promises."

"Blue, remember us and our own planet." I nod, because I know exactly what he's talking about.

When we touch everything else fades and we end up wrapped up in each other. Sometimes literally. Oh, shit. That could end bad in one point in time, I gotta say something to make sure that doesn't happen.

"We need to stop touching each other in public. I mean, what if we were at a mall or something. Oh hell, no more touching. Just behind closed doors with no one else around, okay? Oh fuck, we need to not touch anymore, 'cause I bet at some point we'd get arrested for indecent exposure. I definitely don't want a record, not with that listed on it at least. Oh, shit. With all the cell phones out there we'd end up all over YouTube. Or they'd tag our asses on Facebook or some shit. Seriously. No. More. Touching. In. Public. Say it."

"Fine," Zack grumbles. "No more touching in public. Now, for what just happened. Us fucking, that is. Well. Damn. I have no fucking words. We just need to do that again. Soon."

"Well that's the second thing we both agree on then, moving on to number three. Hey, do all the things discussed here go over that easy?" I look toward the table. "Can I swing the hammer now? Not your hammer, a hammer. Fuck. Quit looking at me like that. Shit, I'm rambling. You were talking. Go on, get it out with, why was Dams congratulating you?"

Taking a deep breath, he puts a hand on the back of his neck before he looks at me. A soft smile on his lips as he starts to talk. "By fucking you in this room, on this table. According to the old rules, I officially claimed you as my ol'lady."

My head rears back. "How does that work? Like boyfriend, girlfriend?"

He shrugs his shoulders. "More like married for life, biker style."

"What the hell, dude?" I gasp. "We're not fucking married. I didn't even say yes for Christ's sake!"

"We did the fucking and by that the married part happened." A smug smile spreads on his face. "I'm pretty sure you said yes more than once before you screamed my name. Remember? When you came all over my pierced cock, while I was slamming it deep inside you."

He's right, fuck. I was a few seconds away from going full out crazy. I take a few steps toward him and I can feel his cum as it oozes down my leg and the smell of him surrounds me. Oh fuck, how could I fucking forget? He didn't use a condom and I'm not on birth control.

"You didn't use a condom, you dick. How in the hell did we let that happen?" I am so angry at him, at myself, married, ol'lady, this fucking situation.

I can't breathe. My hand reaches for my pendant.

Zack closes the distance between us as he places his hands on my face. "Breathe, Blue, in... out.... breathe with me. Stay with me. Calm down. We'll handle it, together. You and me. Hell, we just got married, we might as well have a kid together."

My heart stops. My breathing stops. My world stops. Life itself stops. My blood runs cold as I push away my panic attack.

My eyes lock onto his. "We had a kid together. She died. I.... Killed because of me, it's all my fault, I killed her."

His eyes widen as he takes in the words that stumbled from my mouth. I can see the wheels turning in his head. "You mean the first time we... turned into a... I had a daughter? You said she? How old was she? How…Why did you fucking kill her? What in the hell are you talking about? How can you fucking kill a kid? Did you have an abortion? No. Because then you couldn't know it was a she. What the fuck happened, Blue? Fucking tell me. Right fucking now."

His arms go from my face to my shoulders as he shakes me roughly. He's scaring me with his grip and hard words.

I close my eyes and bring back the memories that haunt me. "My last World Championship match..."

"Yeah, the last one where you got your ass handed to you and lost your title and you let that stop your career. What about it?" Zack asks impatiently.

"Bitch kicked me in the fucking stomach. Was bleeding bad and ended up passing out. Before I knew what was happening I woke up in the hospital. They were telling me I'm being rushed in for an emergency C-section. She didn't make it. I didn't know and I fucking should have, okay? She died. I fucking got her killed while I should have protected her. I never should have been in that fucking ring. I should have known I was pregnant instead of listening to the doc why I didn't get my period. Should have thought about the sex we had instead of blaming the stress of my mom, the fights, the training, losing you, the moving, every fucking thing was another fucking excuse. I didn't think, I never think, shit doesn't just happen. It happens to me, this is all on me. Don't you see? This doesn't end well. Everything around me... Hell...everything in me even, dies. Dies, Zack. Dies. She died. Our baby died before she got a chance to live."

His hands fall from my shoulders as he takes a step away from me. His gaze falls to the ground. I did this. He's as disgusted by me as I am at myself. I step around him and walk out the door, out of the compound as I hear footsteps behind me. Lynn's arm goes around my shoulder as we walk to her car.

She guides me into the passenger seat. I click on my seat belt as Lynn walks around and gets in the car. Without a word we drive home.

******

It's been three days. Three fucking days and not one word from Zack. He hates me, I'm pretty sure he hates Lynn too. She told me he called her that same night. Asking if she knew. Lynn admitted she advised me not to tell him, because he was deployed in Iraq. He hung up on her. This whole mess is on me, I need to take responsibility.

Lynn and her brother shouldn't argue over me. I got the keys to my apartment above the gym, and had it renovated and furnished within two days. They even managed to put in a whole new bathroom in that timeframe. Yeah, okay, so I paid a small fortune but it was worth it. I packed all my things in the duffel bag.

Looking down, it was kinda sad how all my personal belongings seem to fit in that one duffel bag. Throwing it around my shoulder, I walk up to Lynn, who is standing in the middle of the living room, a sad smile on her face.

"So you're really leaving?" Lynn's voice is filled with sadness.

My shoulders sag. "You know where to find me. Hell, we work right next door, Lynn. Don't you get all dramatic on me."

She pulls me in for a hug and I close my arms around her.

Feeling her shake I know she's crying. "Don't get my shirt wet, I don't wanna freaking change."

"Oh shut it, bitch," Lynn mumbles. "I'm gonna cry and get mascara all over your shirt so you can fucking remember me."

We laugh and cry at the same time.

Hearing the house phone, Lynn pulls away and answers it. "Talk, stupid!"

I smile big. I know I'm going to miss living with her crazy ass. She always seems to pick up the phone with a different insult, every damn time. Zack forwards his calls to her phone when he's out of reach, so it can be awkward when she answers the phone that way.

Lynn's eyes go big and then narrow. "Don't you get your panties in a twist because you feel stupid.... Oh, do not blame me, you're the one who's...

What the fuck did you just call me? Oh hell no. You can just rip off your dick, stick it up your ass, pull it back out and shove that shit up your nose."

She slams the phone down as she mutters something about someone calling her a cunt, but I swear I also hear cocksucker, and bitch somewhere in the middle of her rant.

"Who the hell did you just piss off, or pissed you off?" I have to bite my lip to keep the laughter inside.

"Some crazy ass asking for Zack. Fuck, he had such a sexy voice though. What a total..." The phone starts ringing again. Lynn picks up.

"Masturbating here, so talk fast." Oh no she didn't.

Lynn gives me a bright smile but it falters and morphs into anger the second the person on the other end speaks.

"Yeah well with your dick cut off, there's not much else for me to do. What? No. Yeah, you wish. No, I ain't no fucking ho, or club pussy. No, no I ain't no guy's girlfriend, or ol'lady either. I ain't giving anyone a message for you, you impotent little fucker. No, you fucking listen to me. Hear this." She slams down the phone.

This time, my laughter slips free. "Normally people speak actual words after one says hear this."

The phone starts to ring again.

"Yeah, no way I'm picking it up again. You do it. He wants to leave a message and I'm no one's damn secretary," Lynn states.

I can't help but chuckle as I reach for the phone.

"Hello, can I help you?" My voice is smooth as silk as I can manage.

A rough voice on the other side of the line answers me. "What happened to Hotlips? The one that answered the phone two times before this call?"

"Yeah, she's done. Said she's not a fucking secretary, so now you've got me. Make it fast. Because I'm not a secretary either, and I'm kinda in the middle of leaving."

"Right. Just get a message to Zack, can you do that?"

"Sure, what's the message?" Like hell I will, but Lynn can pass that message or write a freaking note for all I care.

"Tell him we're okay for a sit-down, yeah? You got that? Oh, and what's Hotlips' name, the one I just talked to two times? Can you give me her number? I'm not done talking to her yet."

Thinking about how Lynn's technically to blame for Zack getting my number. And with me leaving and all, she's bound to be bored. I might give her a little something to do. Before I can think things through I rattle off Lynn's cell number as her eyes go wide. "And that would be her number. And who shall I say is okay with a sit-down?"

"That would Broken Deeds MC. Say hi to Hotlips for me. Tell her I'll be in touch."

Oh fuck. The line goes dead and I'm pretty sure I might have just signed my own death certificate, or Lynn's. I turn to look into her eyes. Yeah, most definitely my own.

"Who the fuck did you just give my number to, Blue? Not the asshole that kept calling for Zack, right? The one who called me a ho, cunt and pussy in one fucking sentence! Tell me you didn't just do that, Blue," Lynn seethes.

I scrub a hand down my face. "Yeah.... about that... I might have given your number to one of the guys of Broken Deeds MC."

"Oh fuck," Lynn mumbles.

"Yeah, that's what went through my mind too. Hey, at least he called ya Hotlips."

"He what?" she squeaks.

"Yeah... I think you turned him on. Anyway... I gotta go, and you've got to call Zack and tell him Broken Deeds MC is okay with a sit-down."

Lynn tilts her head. "Did you get his number?"

"Huh? Shit. Didn't think to ask that. He just asked for yours. Fuck. Well, all of this is so not my problem."

Lynn is about to say something as her phone starts to buzz with a message. Grabbing it off the table she looks at the screen. Swiping her finger over the screen she looks at the message for a few seconds before she furiously starts typing back.

"He just fucking texted me saying I'm his personal secretary. And from now on I'll be taking his notes. Well guess again, fucker, I ain't nobody's fucking…"

It only takes a few seconds before her phone starts to buzz again and the same thing happens all over again. Watching for a few minutes, and a lot of short texts later, I remind myself I need to leave.

I give my best friend a hug and walk out of the house. Slinging the duffle bag over my shoulder as I straddle my bike.

I can hear two bikes coming around the corner. Just as I'm about to start my bike, they pull up next to me. I recognize Zack and before he can get off his bike, I start mine. Backing up I hear his voice crack my name. One last glance over my shoulder, I see Dams holding him back.

It took three days for him to come here. Who knows, maybe he came to see his sister instead of me. I need to start seeing this the way it is. Another loss in my life. Everyone is better off. Hell, I'm better off not having anyone close. If he feels the same way inside as I feel, knowing what we'd lost… It took me years to give it a place in my heart. Yet still it feels like my heart was ripped out yesterday.

Trying to concentrate on driving instead of the worries that flow to my mind, I'm glad it only takes me a few minutes to reach the gym. Driving around back, I find the personal parking space that came with the gym. I park my bike and get my keys out to walk into my very own property.

Don't get me wrong, I own lots of property. All of it I'd inherited from my father. He invested in a lot of things, all of which I still need to read up on.

Shit, I don't even know what and how much I own. The lawyers called and asked if I could drop by to pick up a few files to get me up to speed on these things. They've also gotten a request for a sale of one of the properties I seemed to own. But this, the one I'm walking into? This is mine. I've researched it. I bought it. I'm going to live in it. Mine.

There are two ways to reach my apartment above the gym. Outside through the fire escape stairway. Or the one I'm taking now, straight through the gym. I haven't been inside of the gym yet. I've been in my apartment twice through the fire escape. Once to check it out along with the contractor I hired to fix everything up the way I wanted. The other time was when the contractor was done. I needed to check if everything was according to the plans we discussed. Turns out they did a great job. They even helped out getting all the furniture I ordered in place. Now I want to have a look at the gym before I go home.

Home, I need to say it a few times to believe it myself. Have to build a life for me, a new home. I throw down my duffle bag and walk through the gym. The space is huge with big white pillars keeping my apartment up. One wall is filled with mirrors, nothing is broken or cracked. Not all the gym equipment was removed. They took or sold some of the good stuff and left the old machines behind. Everything needed to be cleared out.

I'm surprised to find the floor brand new. It looked great, like they just had it done. Hearing an engine roar, I walk up to the front windows. My breathing picks up. I don't want to talk to him or anyone else for that matter.

Chapter 10

Belle

It took a few minutes before the door opened. Holding onto my pendant with one hand I see only Dams stepping inside. My hand slips from the pendant and I let out the breath I didn't even realize I was holding.

"Hey," Dams' voice fills the empty gym space.

I manage to give him a small smile as a return greeting.

It's then that I notice the black dossier in his hands. "What are you doing here?"

"Came to see you and check out the gym. I need to draw a map to see how we're going to set this place up."

My interest spikes. "That's great. What do you have there? Equipment lists… magazines?"

"Yeah." One of his eyebrows shoot up. "Wanna have a look? Go through it with me? I could use some advice here. My experience is more from using the gym, rather than setting it up and running it."

I kinda see through the scheme of things. But I gotta admire him for trying to trick me into helping. Being the VP, and from what I've heard and seen, he's Zack's best friend. Lynn told me they served together and had each other's back ever since. Pretty sure Zack told him about us, who knows even about our loss.

I decide right then I need to step forward instead of letting everything hold me back. "Sure, lemme see what you got."

Dams walks to the counter and places the dossier on it. Grabs a piece of paper and picks up a pencil while he takes some magazines out from different kind of machines. He looks around and starts to draw a map of the place. He does so twice. When he's finished he hands me one of the maps and a pencil.

He takes his and starts to walk through the gym. "I'm gonna make a setup and so are you. When we're both done, we're gonna compare and discuss, kay?"

"Well aren't we Mr. BrilliantMind all of a sudden," I tell him with a smile.

"Hey, I happen to like Mr. JewelDick much better." His smile is huge. "No need to compliment my other head. I choose to enjoy myself rather than impress others."

I snort at his reply before I shoot back. "Ha. Smartass, you can impress people with both heads."

He winks and my laugh bounces off the mirrored wall making Dams laugh right along with me. I start to relax as I conduct my walk through and map out where I think everything should go. I've learned enough from my father over the years to know what's best and what works best. Besides, I kinda want to show off in front of Dams. He wanted my help and I sure as hell would give it to him.

Okay, this wasn't my only reason. I wanted to get back into a gym too. It's been years since I had a full-blown workout like I used to have.

The last few years, since I quit competing, I've only kept up cardio and a little barbell action at home. I've got a brand new treadmill waiting for me in my living room that happens to be right above this gym.

Silly to have it in my living room when there's gonna be a complete gym beneath it. But that's what it's been like for the last few years. I couldn't get back into the ring, back into a gym to get back to training. But being here in this gym right now. Yeah, that itch flared up. I need to get my ass back into shape. Setting the piece of paper down on the counter, I grab one of the magazines with different brands and models of a bench press.

I look up at him while he is still sketching on his map. "Hey, ever hear about this bench press machine that was designed with a safety peddle? You press on it with your foot if you find yourself trapped underneath. The bench goes down and when you stand up it automatically rises up again. Good piece of equipment to have when you don't have anyone to spot for you."

Dams takes in the info and nods slowly. "That sounds great and all, but price tag on it must be huge. Unfortunately, we can't afford to spend that kind of money right now."

"Nah, you can't let that stop us." I make sure to steel my voice a bit so he knows how serious I am right now. "We're not going to pay attention to the price tag since I'll be the one who's going to deal with that part. You guys are going to handle running the gym. I won't be a part of that.

But I do demand you guys get a few ladies in here to make the woman more comfortable."

Mr. JewelDick wiggles his eyebrows. "I'll get right on that, ma'am."

"Dude. Don't ever call me ma'am and stop wiggling your fucking eyebrows at me. We need a good woman behind the desk here. One who can keep an eye on things. And by things I do not mean dicks. I mean this business, and to make sure the customers know their way around. So I'll be sitting in on those interviews to get a good person. Clear?"

His smile only brightens more and his eyes twinkle. I slap my hand over my eyes. What in the hell have I gotten myself into?

"Okay, Miss Business." Dams chuckles. "Let me see yours and I'll show you mine."

I pull my hand away with lightning speed and my mouth drops open. The last time he said that, he was about to show me his dick. Seeing my reaction, he puts both of his hands up and in front of him.

"Yeah, that's not gonna happen." Dams firmly shakes his head. "Who's got their head in the gutter now, huh? You're the Prez's ol'lady. No fucking way am I ever gonna disrespect that."

"Yeah, I knew that," I snap.

He chuckles as he steps closer and places his sketch next to mine. I'm surprised at his details. In some lines he's almost got the same setup as mine.

Except for the cardio corner. "Why did you put the cardio in front of the windows?"

"Well, you might want to check out the view when you're doing cardio. Also, when we've got hot chicks on those things, we'd have a nice window shopping thing going on." Again with the eyebrow wiggle.

"Yeah, and that right there will be the reason why cardio needs, and is going, to be in the back." I shoot him a glare as he thinks things over.

"So cardio right next to the ring?" he questions.

I like the fact that he placed the boxing ring in the back. I have the same set up, except mine leaves way more space around it.

"When you switch up cardio, we clear a space right here. This allows us to use this," I point behind us to the open space, "to be used as a row of heavy bags as well as a row speed bags. We can offer classes on training with both."

He nods and reaches for a new piece of paper. He starts drawing a map adding in the changes we just made. We iron out a few more details here and there and I think to myself that the place is going to look great. We're almost done when we hear a knock. Looking through the glass front door, I can see Fredrick standing there. Our eyes meet and he gives a smile and a wave.

I start to walk to the door when I feel Dams' hand going around my wrist. "You sure you wanna talk to this guy?"

I nod. "Yeah, he's a friend."

"Do all friends have a dad who's a mob real estate evil gangster fucker? Just think about it, Blue, he's probably already following in daddy's footsteps. Now what I just said is club business. You're not allowed to know club business. But since we're standing in club business and we're in it together and you being my Prez's ol'lady and all, I feel the need to give you a heads-up about that slick friend of yours."

I'm kinda baffled by what he's telling me. Somehow it all makes sense. I knew he wasn't just the sweet gentleman he appeared to be. Still, I never felt like I couldn't trust him. He'd never hurt me, I was sure of that, at least not intentionally.

"Thanks, Dams, I really appreciate it. Oh and this also." I pointed to the sketches. The corner of his mouth comes up in a small smile.

"Give me a minute to talk with Mr. GangsterSon and we'll talk some more and order some shit too. That okay with you?"

He gives me a tight nod. "That's more than okay with me."

I give him a smile and he lets his fingers slip from my wrist as I walk to the glass door. After I try the third key on the set of keys I have of the gym, I finally find the correct one. Giving Frederick an apologetic smile to say I was sorry for keeping him waiting like that, I open the door.

"Still getting to know your new property, huh?" Frederick states.

I tuck away the keys. "First time I've been in here, so yeah, you might say that."

He gives me a kiss on my cheek as he whispers in my ear that he missed me. I kinda missed talking to him too. He was a good listener when I needed him in Japan.

He looks toward Dams. "They helping you get the old stuff out or did they buy the old machines?"

Not wanting to explain too much I deflect the question. "Everything will be removed. I'm gonna order new equipment. Actually I was looking through brochures when you showed up."

"Need any help?" Frederick asks gently.

"Actually Dams is already helping me, but I appreciate the offer." He is still standing very close to me, so I take a step back.

I'm weird like that. Everybody's got their own personal space and I get agitated if people stand too close. I need my bubble. Taking in my move, his smile brightens in understanding. The look on his face told me he remembered I told him about this.

He stood by my side at the day of the funeral of my father and brother. Holding on to me and keeping people at a distance without me flipping out.

"Thanks," I whisper softly.

He gives a small nod, understanding I wasn't thanking him for his offer to help. "You could do me a favor."

"What?" I question.

He tilts his head. "That date?"

Now that makes me smile. He still wants to go out? Even after the whole Zack thing at Lynn's house. Even with Dams standing just a few feet away. Dams, who I am pretty sure can hear everything we discussed.

I take a glance at Dams. Shit. He is tapping his phone to his leg. I hoped he had it out so he could check the time and not to call in the cavalry.

"So how about it, Petal? We could also discuss some business," Frederick presses.

"Business?" I pull my head back in confusion.

"Yeah, you seem to own some property that my dad's interested in. We also wanted this gym. My father was kinda pissed I let it slip through my fingers."

I have to laugh about that.

He didn't let it slip through his fingers, he stopped the bid and let me have it. "You mean the one you let me have? Well, buddy, I was going to get it even if you did try to put up a fight."

He steps into my personal space. His face leans closer, brushing his nose against mine, our lips almost touching.

"That so?" Frederick throws out those two words in a menacing tone.

I was kind of going for "uh-huh" but it might have sounded more like a strangled gasp.

Mainly cause I can't think with his lips almost touching mine. His hand slips around me, between my shoulder blades.

Before I know what's happening, he slams his lips down on mine, as he pulls me forward with his hand on my back. His other hand cups my face. His tongue slips between my lips and touch mine as I taste him. Coffee, cinnamon and caramel.

Oh shit, he had my favorite coffee right before he came here. That's the only reason my brain is frozen. Why in the hell does he have to taste like coffee, and why in the hell is he still kissing me? He shouldn't. I don't want to…I should...

"Would you mind getting your fucking face off my woman?" Zack's voice booms through the gym.

Frederick's tongue swirls a few more times before he releases a moan, places one more soft kiss on my lips, and pulls back.

"Funny," he says as he turns around to face Zack. "She doesn't taste or sound like your woman."

Zack actually growls as Dams walks up, flanking Zack. Getting very annoyed and not ready for a bad re-run of what took place at Lynn's house, I decide to step up.

"Alright, boys, drop your pants and whip 'em out." All eyes flash to me as I wave my hands at dick level. "Come on, I ain't got all day."

Confused looks pass amongst all of them as I explain myself. "Since we're at an alpha pissing contest, let's see who's got the biggest dick of all ya'll. Let's get 'em out and get this shit over with, so I can move the fuck on."

"I'm not in this contest, right?" Dams asks as he barely manages to keep his laughter in.

"Well, since you're standing here, and being Mr. Jewel-Dick and all. Yeah, you can join. Whatcha say boys? Am I right?"

Dams is trying very hard to keep from laughing by biting down on his fist. I step forward.

"Alright then, let me be the winner with my giant lady boner I seem to have from being in the very presence of all this alpha male shit. You." I point to Frederick. "I'll see you at seven. Dinner. Just dinner to discuss business. Now go 'cause I need to have a word with these two and I can't concentrate if I have to keep ya'll from going at it."

Frederick smiles at me and steps closer.

He tries to lean in for a kiss and just as Zack is about step in, my finger goes to Frederick's lips. "No more kissing! For now at least." Yeah, I totally threw that last part in as a punch in the gut for Zack. Just because he pisses me off. I need to work on me and get my life back together.

161

"Alright, Petal, see you at seven." Frederick walks around Zack, watching the glass door close softly behind him.

I turn my attention to Zack. "Who the hell do you think you are coming in here like that, huh?"

"Your ol'man. That's who, and who the hell do you think you are kissing another man with those lips that belong to me, huh?" Zack growls back.

What the hell? He fucks me over and still acts like I belong to him? Fucked me over two times actually, once on the table and the other relationship wise. I spill my guts and he walks out of my life for three whole days. Suddenly acting like nothing happened and I don't even exist to him, and for him all this time we're one fucking happy couple.

"Who I'm kissing, or fucking, or doing whatever the fuck I like, ain't your business. We're not even together for fuck's sake!" I seethe.

Zack shakes his head. "You're my ol'lady, no denying that. So yeah, it is my fucking business. You're mine, no other man is going to touch you. Ever. Again."

Now I'm the one shaking my head. "I am not anyone's property, Sally. You fucked me over, literally. So why don't you just go jerk off on that church table of yours, or go fuck a ho on that fucking table, or whatever you guys do to get a divorce or un-ol'lady it. You've got enough reasons to hate me, hate us. Those three days walking away, ignoring me,

162

says it all. There is no us. For what it's worth, I don't even care anymore. The only family I have in this fucked up world is me. So fuck off, I don't need this shit. I have enough problems dealing with myself. You,"

I point at Dams, I'm done with Zack and this crap he seems to pull. Coming here at God's speed to drive a guy away from me. While he stays the fuck away for those days when I really needed him or when he had every chance to talk to me. Maybe, just maybe we'd be together. Not a fuck-ing chance now.

"Get your ass to the counter, we're gonna order some shit." I pin him with a glare. "Oh and thanks for tattle tailing on me, you're a real sport."

Dams nods and walks toward the counter.

Zack's eyes go to Dams and back to me again. "Already taking the lead and ordering my VP around? Yet you still deny you're my ol'lady, Blue? You were born to be by my side and you always will be."

He takes four steps and wraps his hand in my hair. He pulls my head back and slams his lips on mine, our teeth clash. His other hand goes to my ass, gripping it hard, pull-ing me into his body. I can't hold back the moan that escapes me as I feel his hard dick pressing into my belly.

My fists fill with fabric as my hands find his shirt. I need to get his clothes off.

I hear faint tearing as my lips leave his for only a second. "I need you inside me. Need to feel you, Sally. Now."

"Fuck yeah," Zack growls. "My dick wants in, Blue. I need to see my cum slide out of that tight pussy. All mine. All fucking mine."

One of my hands reaches between our bodies to pull down his zipper. Both of us are smashed out of our moment when we're hit on the head with a magazine.

"Fucking stop, you freaking fuck bunnies. Let go of each other. Fuck man, look. A fucking glass wall here. Busy street. About to fuck in front of a fucking window. Let's not forget; with me standing right the fuck here. My ears are hurting from all that dirty talk. Fucking bunnies I tell ya. Cut that shit out."

Holy fuck. We really need to stop touching while in the presence of other people. Only behind closed doors. Fuck. I need a taser to pry him off me. Would I remember to use it in time? Oh shit.

We need rules and rule number one? No touching. Rule number two. Keep rule number one intact at all times. "No touching. Remember, gotta remember okay? Oh shit, that was close."

When I look at Zack there's a smile on his face telling me he's not sorry at all. Well, maybe a bit sorry Dams pried us apart.

Dams is still shaking his head in disbelief. "Yeah, tell me about it, I fucking warned you two a few times by yelling.

No fucking response whatsoever. Like you guys were locked away in each other soundproof walls and all. Thank fuck you respond to physical assault. That shit would have burned my corneas right the fuck off."

Chapter 11

Belle

I walk over to the counter to pick up the rest of the magazines, the sketches and all the other stuff, and place it in the file folders. Looking at both guys, I walk past them and lock the glass door. Because my fucking body betrays me every time he touches me, I might as well give him a chance to talk.

Talk, with huge distance between us. No touching. Remember not to touch. Rule number one must stay intact at all times.

Zack might as well join me and Dams with the ordering. I've been standing for a very long time and right now I need to sit down and have some coffee. Oh fuck, coffee. Frederick's kiss. Nope, can't think about that. He's a good guy, deep down I know that. Bad father and bad vibe and all, sure. But he's not the guy for me. The all-consuming Zack may appear to be, but that's also very scary. I need to take one thing at a time.

Me first; I need to get back to my old self. Frederick; I need to keep as a friend. Maybe business partner, but I'd hear what that was about at seven. Now Zack, that's a whole different matter.

Walking toward the upper stairs that lead to my apartment, I look back at them. "Coming?"

They both look at me as they start to walk forward taking the steps two at a time. Unlocking my door I step in and let the guys walk in after me. I close the door and smell that all new smell my apartment has going on. Stepping out of my shoes, I walk barefoot into the living room. I love the feel of the soft carpet between my toes.

Placing the dossier on the couch, I walk into the open kitchen and grab a few beers out of the fridge. Opening a few drawers I can't seem to find an opener so I take two bottles, turn one upside down beneath the lid of the other one and pop the lid of the one I'm holding up. I hand the open beer to Dams who takes it from me with a huge smile. Lifts it a bit as a thank you and drains half of it. I repeat the opening of another bottle as I hand that one to Zack. He mimics Dams' thanks as I slam the last bottle on the corner of the kitchen counter.

"Blue. That shit is brand new, nobody does that," Zack snaps.

I look down to see scratches on the kitchen counter. Shit, I didn't think. I need to focus. With all that shit going on around me, I seem to have burned down more than a few brain cells. This is how my brother always opened his beer.

My shoulders shrug. "My house, my rules. Sit, so we can discuss and order equipment."

Pulling my laptop out of the duffel bag, I plant my ass next to Dams on the couch. Zack is shooting daggers at Dams and he tries to get up. Zack walks up so he can take his place next to me on the couch.

"No way. Sit your ass down over there. Rule number one, no touching," I scold.

The corner of his mouth goes up as he smirks at me. Yeah, down boy. Pulling my eyes to the screen I let my fingers dance and it takes a few seconds for the page to load.

As the pictures and the info slowly come up I turn toward Dams. "See, this is what I talked about earlier. It'll be perfect for the gym."

Dams nods. "Yeah, I see what you mean, but did you see the price tag on that thing? How many did you have in mind to order, only one?"

"Nah, I think three is best, what do you think?" I reach for the sketch Dams made earlier where he molded both of our sketches into one. "Yeah, we had three marked right here. There's enough space to place four, what do you think?"

I reach over to Zack and hold out the sketch. He looks it over, eyebrows frown. "Your idea to put cardio near the ring, Blue?"

"That obvious, huh?" I shake my head. Men. "You'd put the woman on display in the window too?"

Zack shrugs. "Well yeah, that'll draw in customers. And yeah, I'd go for three too, there's enough space to place four but I think it's good to place three. That way when you're working the bench there'll be enough space to work around."

We both nod as Dams stands up and hands Zack the laptop.

Reaching over I grab the sketch back and turn to Dams. "Hey, you know the space here? If we cut one punch bag from this row. We could use this corner differently. Like place a large mat there and add mirrors here and here. This could be a corner where woman have their own space. You know… so they have their own dumbbells and space, when they step into beast mode."

"Beast mode? Seriously Blue? But, I do get where you're coming from. You think they'd be more comfortable having a space on the side? Yeah, you don't have to answer, I know what you're getting at. This way they don't have to walk amongst us or grab our weights. Those are way too heavy for them anyway. This is smart thinking, I like this angle. Maybe we could have the mat pink or some shit." Dams holds my gaze as if he's not sure about his last sentence.

I give him an eye roll. "Yeah, not gonna happen, Dams, don't push it. We're not gonna add pink to our gym. Girls corner or not, no freaking pink."

Dams releases a breath between his teeth. "Thank fuck, I only mentioned it since, hell... since you suggested girly shit and... Never mind. Thank fuck no pink, no comment. Like the idea."

"This is a great bench. How did you know this was out there, Blue?" Zack asks.

A tiny smile tugs my lips at the memory. "Heard my dad talk to the engineer who designed it. He wanted to implement it in his gym. Actually, my dad was one of the investors in the project to get the design out there."

Reaching for my laptop, Zack hands it over and I place an order to get three of them. I also send a more personal message with it so he knows it's me and I'm willing to pay more to get them here fast.

When I press send, I turn toward Dams. "I wanna open next week. The stuff will be here in three days, we're gonna order it now and I'll make a few calls tomorrow morning. You need to place an ad for help. We want at least two girls. We need someone who can check in new members and show them around. Not full-time, two part-time jobs. Give me a heads-up when the interviews start. I wasn't kidding, I need to be there and it will be my final vote who gets the job."

"I hear ya, boss." Dams' voice is filled with appreciation.

It's a nice feeling to be on top of things again, even if I wasn't planning on getting mixed into handling the gym.

"Great, now grab a magazine and show me what we need to order so I can go online and do so."

By the time we're done, I've got about an hour left before Frederick gets here.

"That's the last one. You guys need to get out of here, so I can grab a shower and get ready for my business meeting." There, I'm playing nice.

I didn't say date, I said business meeting. That's what it is. I need to set things straight with Frederick, no more kissing. With the way Zack makes me feel and the way I need to think about myself first, it's only fair to be straight with Frederick. I don't want a relationship with him. Even more, I don't want to be the fucking bone that these two dogs are fighting over.

"I wanna talk with you, Blue." Zack's voice is low and demanding.

I should have expected it. We should talk but I'm afraid the hour I have left to get ready isn't enough. Besides, us talking might lead to getting close. Getting close might lead to touching and might lead to dirty talking and having sex. Pressing my thighs together at the thought of his magnificent cock with those piercings and the extra special friction that comes with each thrust.

"Open your goddamn eyes and stop moaning or I'm breaking rule number one with Dams sitting right next to you," Zack growls.

Oh fuck. "I'm sorry, okay? Shit. I don't think we should talk right now. Or, wait. How much does Dams know?"

"I have no secrets from my VP," Zack states.

"So he knows about..." My voice trails off.

A slight nod. "He knows our kid died, yes."

"I'm gonna leave you two to talk." Dams stands up.

Before he can move, I grab his sleeve. "Please, stay. We need to talk. And not touch. Since you already know, I would like for you to help out and just sit here okay. Or when the need comes, smack our heads with a magazine or something."

He sits back down as he crosses his arms in front of his chest and leans back. I turn to look at Zack who is studying me intensely.

"I have something for you." Standing up I reach inside my duffle bag.

Grabbing a hold of a small metal safety deposit box I sit back down on the couch. Opening it I take out a black jewelry box. Reaching over, Zack takes it from my hand and opens it. Inside is the same pendant, as the one I´m wearing, on a leather string. On one side there are two dates, the day she was born and died. The other side has her name. Hearing him swallow I know he´s reading the name. He takes out the necklace and puts it on.

"There's a little piece of her in the pendant. I had both of the pendants made special." My voice cracks at the end and I need to swallow at the tightness in my throat.

"Thank you." His voice cracks with emotion.

With his body flowing with emotion I´m sure he´s not ready for what I´m holding in my hand. Putting the safety deposit box on the table I place a hand on Dams' knee for support.

He shifts toward me and places his hand at my lower back. Dams sees the envelope in my hand. We both look at Zack who is still holding his pendant in his hand while he looks at it. Dams pats my hand and takes the envelope out of my hand. He walks over to Zack and places his hand on his shoulder as the other brings the envelope into his line of sight.

His head turns to Dams as he gives a slight nod and takes the envelope. The moment he opens the envelope and pulls out the picture, my heart breaks all over again. His face twists into a scream except there is no sound. His hand goes to his face and he frantically twists his fist into his eyes one after the other. While his other hand holds on to the picture.

The picture where I´m lying in a hospital bed. Holding our little girl as I say goodbye. My dad took the picture. There are a few more, but this is the only one where I´m holding her. I want to walk over and hold him, comfort him, but I'm afraid. Not afraid about breaking rule number one. I´m afraid of rejection.

I'm the one to blame, I should have known I was pregnant. I shouldn't have been in the ring. I'm so caught up in my own thoughts I didn't even see him move until I feel his arms around me. His head nuzzles into my neck as he breathes me in. Hugging me closer as I feel his body shake.

Shocked by his reaction, my eyes meet Dams as he signals me with his hands. He points at the door and to his chest, letting me know he is leaving. Giving him a nod, I let my arms go around Zack's huge body. We hold each other for what might seem hours but in fact are only a few minutes before he takes a deep breath and kisses my neck.

He pulls back as he cups my face. "Thank you, Blue."

I'm shocked into silence. He is thanking me? "Why Sally? I only cause you pain, I'm so sorry. I…"

"Shush, Blue, just shut up right there. I don't blame you, and you shouldn't be blaming yourself either. Fucking turn of events that none of us had a handle on. As fucked up as all of this is, we need to move forward. Together. We're strong enough to give this a place in our hearts, to keep her memory alive. So yeah, Blue. Thank you. Even if she didn't get a chance in this world, the thought of you and me and this little girl? A family. We will become a family, Blue. Give her a little sister or brother. Hell, I want at least five kids.

It's you, Honeybump, you're everything to me. I need you with me. You're with me, aren't you? We're in this together, right?"

"Five kids, Zack? What the hell, dude? Are you gonna push them out of your dick? Sallybelle was a C-section, I can't even begin to think about popping things out of my VG. Number five will fall right out if I don't keep my legs closed. Oh. My. God."

"How about popping things in? Can we just focus on that for now?" And just like that, he has me smiling.

Damn, I was feeling so raw inside. Looking into his eyes, so is he. His eyes are filled to the brim with emotion. He pushes me onto my back on the couch and molds his body down next to me. Holding me close, his hand strokes gently over my belly as he suddenly shifts up onto his elbow. He looks me in the eye with a question on his face. As I gave him the slightest nod, he pushes up my shirt.

With my belly exposed his finger trails along the scar of the C-section. "This is beautiful."

His fingers now trace the lines of the ink that is tangled with the scar. Thin green lines going over and seem to go under the scar. Tiny leaves and at the end there is one bright blue orchid. The name Sallybelle and the date beneath it.

Understanding reaches his face. "That´s why you had the panic attack in the shop. Blue orchids."

I give him a nod as he reaches forward. He places kisses along the scar. My hand goes into his hair as I stroke it back, repeating a few times. He reaches up and gives me a very soft kiss on my lips.

Pulling his head back, he stares into my eyes. "I never want to lose you, you belong to me. You're my very heart, you need to know that. Don't you ever fucking leave me." His voice is raw.

The only thing I can do is nod.

My throat is locked down with the biggest emotional lump of the century. "So you want to start a family?"

"As in right now?" His smile goes wicked.

My mind goes back to the moment when he came inside me. "I could be pregnant right now since you didn't put a condom on and blew your load inside me."

"So that's a yes, Blue," he growls, clearly remembering the moment now too.

He shifts so his body is hanging over me. He rotates his hips, making his dick press against me. The friction gives me a wave of pleasure through my body as I start to rock back into him.

His nose traces my jaw. "So you're not on any birth control are ya?"

"No. My periods are practically nonexistent. Between the heavy training and stress it usually only lasts two or three... oh."

He rotates his hips harder this time and my mind just goes blank. "A simple yes or no would have been enough."

"No birth control," I whisper. "Never needed it. Better?"

"This is better." He grinds himself against me as his lips find mine.

His hand goes into my hair and he pulls it to the side. Gaining more access to my mouth he takes full advantage. His tongue swirls around and slips past the front of my teeth.

"I need you," I breathe those words into his mouth as he pulls back.

"I need you more, Blue. More than the clothes I have on my back or the breath that I wasted these words on."

He peels off his clothes. Lifting my ass off the couch, he takes my clothes off just as quickly. For a moment I think he´s going to fuck me hard like he did at the clubhouse. But he proves me very wrong when his hands slide up and down my body. His eyes follow each stroke of his hands while he leans over to place a soft kiss on my skin. His tongue finds my nipple as he gently takes it in his mouth.

The tug of him sucking on me sends a jolt of pleasure through my body and finds a place to gather low in my belly. My nipples are still very sensitive with the piercings. He gives it one more swirl with his tongue as he switches to my other nipple giving that piercing the same attention. Needing more, my legs go around his waist and I tighten them, caging him in.

"Careful there, Honeybump. I'm barely holding on as it is. I need this to last so I can enjoy every inch of your body before I explode inside you. I ain't fucking you this time. Maybe later tonight, but now? Now we need the slow and feel shit."

"Such a romantic," I grumble. "Stick your dick in already, I need to feel you. Now."

I grind my pelvis against his dick as his tip brushes past my clit. Repeating the action this time I manage to twist my hips a bit so he's right in front of my opening. As wet as I am now, I know I can make my move. Before he manages to process what I'm about to do I take his lip ring into my mouth and suck hard. Pushing my feet against his ass while I bring my hips forward, his dick slides in me.

Smooth; like a sled sliding off a mountain top. The feeling that goes with it is the same euphoric pleasure. I moan loud as he curses in my mouth. He slowly pulls out and slides back in. His eyes are closed as he tries to keep focus. My hand grabs a hold of his bicep, digging my nails in. My lips let go of his as I bring my head next to his.

My lips close to his ears. "I can't live without you, Sally. I'm yours, I want it all. Fucking give me all, Sally boy."

His name sounds more like a moan causing his focus to snap. His hand goes around my neck as his thrusts become harder. His knees dig deeper into the couch as he quickly grabs my hips. He turns me slightly and places his knee over my leg. My leg is now beneath him as I'm lying slightly turned to my side.

He slams back into me as I scream at the mix of pleasure and pain. This position gives him deeper access and I can feel every inch and every movement that the piercings give inside me. His hands put my knee down as he pushes my ass toward me, opening me more. His eyes lock to where we're connected, watching himself slide in and out of me.

"What a fucking sight. Nothing can be more perfect than this. Fuck, you were made for my dick. Fucking perfect. Come for me, squeeze them walls for me. Hug my cock like you never want it to leave that tight pussy of yours. Oh yeah, just like that, come on Blue, I can't hold on with you like, oh fuck, oh fuck yeah. Aaaah." He screams my name as I scream out his.

Delicious waves of pleasure wash over me as I feel the hot streams of his cum coating my inner walls. The doorbell rings as I'm still caught up in my orgasm. This causes me to release half moan and half a growl. I feel Zack chuckle above me, making his dick move deep inside my walls.

"Is it too fucking much to ask to have an afterglow after we have sex? Why the fuck do we always have to blow and roll?" The words leave my mouth in an unhappy growl of frustration.

Zack is laughing loud, as he pulls out but keeps his eyes between my legs. His fingers go between my legs as I feel him play with our juices.

"Fucking beautiful, this mix, mine and yours. Feel this." He slides his fingers wet with our juices over my clit as the doorbell rings again.

I glance over to the clock and see it´s six forty-five.

Zack's raw voice flows through the air. "Someone´s early... are you going to yell that you´re coming?"

His fingers speed up and before I can give a snarky reply he has me seeing stars as my orgasm flows through my body.

Chapter 12

Belle

"Five minutes and I'll be down."

Not waiting for a reply from Frederick through the intercom, I dash into the bathroom to clean myself up. I put on a red thong and black bra I got from my duffle bag. Before I put on my long black dress, I brush my hair. Because I don't want any loose hair on my black dress.

Because this is a business meeting, I tie my hair up in a tight bun. Hiding the bright colors so it seems all white. Not bothering with make-up because I never wear any, I'm done within the five minutes.

Walking out of the bathroom Zack looks at me with a huge smile. "Normally when my sister says I'm ready in five, it's more like five hours than the five minutes."

I shrug my shoulders. "Yeah, well… I'm not that big on caring how I look."

Putting on my black Louboutin follies spike heels, I see Zack walking toward me. "Strange, since you always look so perfect."

"Keep talking, pretty boy, you might get lucky," I mutter.

He chuckles into my neck as he slides his lip ring across my skin. Opening his mouth and sucking a piece of skin in his mouth giving it a tug. Knowing what he's about to do I give him a slight shove in the chest. Not that it does any good since he didn't move an inch.

"No need for that, Sally." My voice sounds firm.

"Hmmm," Zack croons. "There's a need, Honeybump."

He rotates his hips, making his need clear.

I reach down and stroke him through his jeans. "Will you stay here and wait for me? I'll be two hours, tops. Maybe sooner."

Stepping out of his grip I make my way to the door. Seems like we can touch and go if we just had sex so I'd best leave now while I still have the chance to do so.

I look down at his massive erection that is trying to find its way out of his jeans. "With the need and all."

He smiles and walks toward me.

"No, no." I hold my hand up. "Stay there, I got lucky with the touching and still managed to walk away. I need to go. Will you stay here?"

"Yeah Blue, I'll stay. But that fucker ain't touching you," Zack growls.

"I am not a fucking cheat, Zack. We're together now, right? So, no other men for me and no other women for you."

"The moment that I saw your ass was back in town, I was yours. That's forever, Blue. Let's be clear about that right fucking now."

I give him a huge smile and a nod while opening the door and grabbing my purse. "Be back soon."

******

182

Sitting in the limo with Frederick right next to me, I feel like a bitch leaving Zack alone. Just a few hours ago things were different. Hell, a little over an hour ago we weren't even together, together. Now that we talked and sealed the deal again with having sex? Yeah, no more denying anything.

"Where are your thoughts, Petal?"

How do you explain when the answer is; not with you. I better rephrase so I don't hurt his feelings, but he needs to know before we get out of this limo.

I need to remind him this is business and not a date. "Thinking about how I should tell you that Zack and I are together now."

His face turns sad and he looks away from me. "So he claimed you, did he?"

A little anger rises inside of me. "It's not like that. It's just that… Never mind. We're together, the why and how doesn't matter."

His head turns so fast, I'm sure he's got whiplash.

The look he gives me scares me a bit. "That's where you're wrong, it does matter. You have a choice here. Don't be with that biker just because he says you're his. I could make him disappear from your life very easily."

Holy shit, did he just? Oh fuck no, he's got to be kidding. Right? Remembering what Dams told me and the way his eyes are ice cold makes the hairs on the back of my neck stand on end.

"We were together before I lived in Japan. As a matter of fact, we never broke it off. My father just took us away when my mother was killed," I explain.

He shakes his head as if my words mean nothing. "You should give us a chance. Back in Japan, we were starting something good. I'd like to think we're a good match. You don't belong on the back of a bike. You belong right here, next to me in a limo. All you need to do is say yes."

What the actual fuck? All I have to do is say yes? That sounds like a freaking marriage proposal.

"If you like, then it is. We could hop on a plane to Vegas right now," Frederick states.

What the... "Fuck. I said that out loud didn't I?" My face turns bright red.

I need to stop letting the shit I say in my head come out through my lips at the same time.

He smiles at me and brushes his knuckles down my face. "You would make me one hell of a lucky man."

"Lucky and Vegas huh? That never ends well. It's just that I wasn't looking for anything. A few weeks ago I lost my whole family. I simply came back to my hometown, to the one and only friend I had left. I need to build things up for me. Zack was a part of my old life. Our feelings for one another never went away. He makes me feel safe. He annoys the shit out of me and the whole planet hop thing, but he's there for me."

Frederick takes my hand as the limo pulls in front of the restaurant. "You're safe with me too, Petal. Even if you don't want me, I'm still here for you. Not wanting to be my wife doesn't rule you out from being my friend. Right?"

A sigh of relief escapes me. "Your friendship would mean a lot to me, Rick. Even though you deserve so much more."

He kisses my knuckles and gives me a sad smile. "Let's enjoy a friendly dinner."

Frederick places the order for his favorite wine, while I notice a prospect at the end of the bar. We have a table in the corner of the restaurant. Frederick's back is to the bar since he wanted a view of the doors. I'd rather have a wall at my back so I have a perfect view of all the angles in front of me. Okay, I admit… Frederick wanted this spot but with a few fast steps my ass was on this chair first.

Giving a little wave while Frederick is now checking out the menu, the prospect shakes his head and types something on his phone. Probably telling Zack that I know he's keeping an eye on me. I'm sure Zack trusts me and the prospect being there had more to do with the fact that he doesn't trust Frederick.

The waitress comes over with the wine and gives Frederick the first taste, waiting for his nod of approval before she fills both of our glasses.

When she leaves, Frederick turns his attention to me. "Any problems with the gym?"

"Nope, I just ordered everything online and hope to have it up and running within the week." My smile is bright.

His eyebrows shoot up. "That fast, huh?"

"Yes, kind of surprised myself there. But the rush when I got there tonight and with Dams helping me out? Yeah, I want to get involved more. I know I told the guys to run it but I'm going to get my hands dirty too."

His eyes first get a bit wide and then narrow. Shit, I didn't think. He makes me too comfortable and cue the flowing tongue. Shit, I need to think before I speak.

I try to change the subject and hope he doesn't ask about the guys running it. "So, what did you want to talk to me about? Property you wanted?"

His eyes soften a bit and I'm sure he's going to ask about it later. "Yes, as I told you my dad wasn't very happy with the fact I didn't get the gym. I was kind of hoping you'd sell it to me, or make us partners."

Okay, time to burst yet another one of his bubbles with us being partners. "I kinda already have a partner. Like I said, the guys are helping me out with the gym and this is something that's also in black and white."

"You sold them half?" he growls.

My mind goes back to the fact that I kinda traded forty-nine percent of the gym for a pink vibrator that Lynn pierced for me.

Trying hard to keep the smile from my face while answering, I say, "Nah, I kept the upper hand. Sold forty-nine percent of the gym. The apartment above it is fully mine. It's a good deal since they will run the gym. Win, win for both of us."

Not liking the fact that I'm business partners with the MC, he nods to the fact that it is a good deal. "Smart move with keeping the upper hand."

"Thanks." I smile as I take a huge sip of the wine.

Loving the taste, I take a few more. Frederick smiles as he fills my glass that seems to be empty now. His eyes go to the door and his face turns angry. Turning my head, I expect to see Zack standing there.

"Well, well, well. Who do we have here?" There is a huge man standing at our table.

He's not too muscular but huge as in well-built and solid. And you can't say that he's fat but he's not exactly skinny either. He has no hair and even his eyebrows are missing. His neck and forehead are full of wrinkles but those give way to a smooth bald head.

I can't see the color of his eyes because they are set deep in his head. Small wide nose and thin lips. He looks scary, yet funny at the same time.

The suit he's wearing is high class. The way this man is making Frederick uncomfortable, I'm pretty sure this is his father.

Holding my hand out I don't bother with getting up. "Blue."

Oh fuck, did I just introduce myself with a nickname everybody seems to keep calling me?

"Blue?" the guy throws out in disgust.

Woops, yeah guess I did. His face turns in slight disgust, at least I guess since that face of his is kind of disgusting as it is so that would be a safe guess.

He looks toward Frederick. "Did you seal the deal yet?"

"No he did not." I take the liberty to answer. His rudeness makes my inner bitch wanna play too.

"And why didn't he?" The guy sneers at me.

"Because I'm not selling," I quip.

He never even looks at me but keeps his head, eyes and anger pinned on his son. "You should marry her so we'd own all. Get it done."

"Excuse me mister rude," I growl. "We don't live in a country where we walk all over women. You can't make decisions to marry off your son or a woman you don't know."

"You need to keep your diarrhea mouth shut angel face." His voice is void of emotion.

"Wow! Kicking someone and throwing in a compliment right after, still isn't considered very nice, asshole. No wonder you can't handle business deals like normal people do." Fuck. Me and my big mouth.

The moment that slips out of my mouth Rick stands up, but it's too late.

His father is right in my personal space, spit flying in my face as he speaks his words. "Your mother experienced the way I handle my business first. Your father and brother didn't enjoy it much either now did they, angel face? How about you make that choice right now. Marry my son or follow in your family's footsteps."

The air is gone. I can't breathe. My hand turns into a fist, holding on to the tablecloth. He didn't just say straight to my face that he killed my mother as well as my father and brother, did he? I find the air, my breathing picks up. Black spots are flying into my eyesight. I needed my strength, I can't blackout in front of this evil man. Gathering all my strength, my fist makes my nails dig deep into my own flesh. I lift myself off the chair but instead of standing in front of that evil man, I'm now facing Frederick's back.

"What in the hell are you implying?" Frederick snaps.

"What little boy? Are things suddenly different when she's involved?" He grabs Rick's head and whispers something in his ear. Not low enough though, because I could pick up what he told him.

"Your hands are as dirty as mine. Maybe not with her family's blood. But hey I'll wash their blood off my hands. And you, you can mix our blood with hers. Fuck her good so she can pop me a few grandkids."

I could puke right here, right now. If I had a gun on me I could have pulled the trigger and would have loved to see the impact of the bullet right between his fucking eyes. The feeling I always got when I stepped in the ring is as close as to what I'm feeling right now. Adrenaline pumping through my veins, the need to kick ass. Before I can step forward, to start throwing punches, Rick pushes his father off him.

"You're insane!" Rick roars as his arm pulls back and slams forward so his fist connects with his father's eye.

Withdrawing and hitting him again, this time he hits him in the nose. You can hear the crunch as he goes down, like a wiener sliding out of the bread. No longer a hotdog, just the wiener lying on the ground, not moving.

The prospect comes up next to me and grabs my arm. "I need you to leave with me. Right now."

Rick hears him and looks my way. Fury blazing in his eyes. "Leave, Petal, go with him. You can't, you don't need. You…. Just go."

His head turns away from me. In that slightest moment I see regret, shame and defeat all rolled into one.

In that look, I know he cares for me. And in more ways than just friendship.

My jaw keeps clenching. I know what both men are saying but my body just doesn't seem to move. The prospect takes my arm and leads me out of the restaurant. He puts me in the front seat of a huge truck and buckles up the seat belt. My hands are tight fists as I look out of the window.

Suddenly I'm aware I'm in a truck and not on the back of a bike. "You don't ride a bike?"

He looks at me like I just told him the truck is on fire. "You're not allowed on the back of another man's bike. That's why we're in a cage."

His phone rings and he takes it out and puts it to his ear. Without a word he hands it over to me.

"Hello?" I ask confused.

"You okay, Honeybump?" Zack's voice is soft.

"Dunno," I whisper.

"Just breathe, you're just a few minutes out. Then you'll be in my arms. Can you hold on for me? Then I'll hold onto you. We clear?"

I swallow against the tightness in my throat. "I miss you."

"Did you get any food in?" Zack asks.

I snort. Such a guy thing to ask about food. I know what he's doing, trying to focus on other things. Come to think of it, no I didn't even get any food in. I did manage to throw down two, or was it three, glasses of wine though.

"Did you?" he presses.

"Did I what?"

"Food, Blue. Did you eat?"

Hearing the roar of bikes I turn in my seat and see them coming up behind the truck. "Your friends are behind us."

I hear the smile in his voice as he tells me. "They're my brothers. Family, Blue. They are also your family now. Get used to it." Feeling the truck turn, I look out the front window. "There you are."

He's standing in the parking lot walking up to the truck. Pulling open the door before the prospect even pulls the truck to a stop. Taking just a second to unbuckle the seat belt, he pulls me into his strong arms and lifts me out of the cab.

My arms circle his neck as I tuck my head to his chest. He's not wearing a shirt and his skin feels cold. He must have been standing outside waiting for a long time. He's here for me. He cares enough to stand in the cold, waiting to hold me. Even when he wasn't with me during that business dinner, he made sure I was looked after. I feel safe in his arms.

"I've got you, and I'm never letting you go. You hear me?"

I love this man. He's it for me. I never did stop loving him. My first love and I now realize, my last. I can never love anyone as I love him. My arms tighten as I breathe him in.

"You might wanna loosen up a bit there, Blue. I do need some oxygen to enter my brain."

I chuckle and loosen my grip, not much but enough to let him breathe. I'm not letting go either, he's mine.

Chapter 13
Belle

I glance around my living room, somehow it seems smaller. Although it might be due to the fact there are at least twelve bikers scattered around it. Sitting on the couch, I feel Zack's hand sliding up and down the small of my back.

He needs to stop touching me. Rule number one. Although we're not jumping each other's bones right now, that might change any second.

As my body leans into his touch, his hand disappears as he shifts beside me. "Rule number one, Honeybump, we need to talk right now. Then, once we lose all my brothers, it's time to say fuck the rules."

I can't help but smile because I was thinking the same thing. Well not about the talking, but the rule number one and the fuck was indeed on my mind.

The prospect from the restaurant walks up to where I'm sitting. "Can I have my phone back now?"

Looking down, I see I still have his phone in a death grip without even knowing I'm holding onto it. Dumping it in the hand he's holding out to me, he stares at it in disgust. Pokey stands next to him and their eyes go to the phone and back to each other.

Tyler murmurs silently to Pokey. "She must have gotten her period or something."

It's a statement, not a question.

Pokey looks at the blood and has his own brilliant solution that he feels the need to share with the rest of us. "You know, maybe she just got a little rough masturbating. Once I jerked off until I bled. Maybe she just,"

"Shut your filthy mouth, you idiot. Of course she didn't. What's wrong with you, man? That's just. Jerk off till you bleed? What fucking idiot does that?" Zack bellows as yet again Pokey tries to explain.

"Well Pete said I couldn't jerk off ten times in twenty minutes and I had to prove him wrong." Pokey shrugs.

"Prove him wrong? By jerking off till you bleed?" Zack shakes his head.

Pokey rubs a finger against his chin. "Nah, that happened when I was at fourteen and still within those twenty minutes until,"

"Shut your mouth!" Zack cuts him off. "Fucker, that's just. Just. Fuck I don't even have the words, you sick fuck!"

I tilt my head. "Did the blood come with the cum or did you just bleed, from you know, your hand and the rubbing? Shit, why do I even ask? Never mind, even the medically educated part of my brain doesn't want to hear the answer to that. That might just actually be the weirdest thing I've ever heard. Quite the accomplishment, yet very disturbing."

"Thank you." Pokey smiles as if I just gave him the biggest compliment.

Fuck, that guy is strange. Tyler walks into the kitchen area and starts to clean his phone with tissues. Zack reaches over and takes my hand as he turns both palms up. I look down and see why the phone is covered in blood. My blood. Blood that is still oozing out of the four half-moons in both of my palms.

Clenching my fists without keeping in mind my nails are too long was not a good idea, because I apparently sliced open my palms while doing so. Zack asks if I have any first aid stuff and one of his men turns to walk into the bathroom as I answer.

Grabbing the first aid kit where I told him he could find it, he hands the kit to Zack so he can tend to my hands. First cleaning them and then bandaging my hands. It reminds me of getting taped up before a fight. This leads me straight to the memory of my last fight. My dad taping me, getting kneed in the stomach, losing our...

The tear that falls from my eye is caught by Zack's thumb. "Talk to me, Blue, what happened tonight?"

My mind goes back to what Frederick's father said. This can't be happening. They never did find the reason why she was killed or who killed her. They haven't even come close to solving my mother's case. The circumstances of my dad and brother's accident were also suspicious.

"Blue."

My head snaps to Zack, startled by the rough tone when he calls out my name. "What?"

"You kind of got lost in your thoughts there." His voice softens. "Called your name three times before you snapped out of it. Talk to me, what happened?"

"I think Mr. RealEstateGangsterDude just confessed to me that he's killed every family member I had." My voice is barely a whisper.

The room turns eerily silent for a few seconds before all hell breaks loose. Dams walks up next to Zack as he yells for everyone to shut the hell up. When some of the cursing has quieted down, Dams crouches down next to me and places his hands on my knees. He looks me in the eye and with a very soft voice he asks me to repeat exactly what the bastard said.

I look toward Zack who is sitting with his hands holding on to his knees. Like if he doesn't, he's going to explode. Facing Dams, I quietly explain how Frederick's father interrupted dinner. The reason why and what he said to me and then to Frederick. As soon as the last words leaves my mouth, Zack stands up and his hand goes into the back of his pants.

Pulling his hand back to his front I hear the click of a gun as his hand comes to rest at his side. "Tyler, you stay here with Blue. The rest of you, come with me."

Oh fuck. I didn't even see or feel that he had a gun on him. Did he always have it on him? How the hell did he get it? Shit, he's going to off him. Can he do that? That's just fucked up. What in the fucking hell? This isn't some kind of shitty movie my ass is in. Fuck.

"Sit back down you trigger-happy, shoot first ask questions later, ass. This is how we're gonna deal with that fuckhead." My voice echos from the walls.

All biker eyes turn to me as Dams smiles. "First, I want to know why. That fucker can't just throw that shit out there. He's fucking dead, that's for sure, but not before I know why. Besides, I'm the one who gets to punch the ever fucking life out of that piece of real estate shithead."

Zack's smile joins Dams' as different voices from all over my apartment yell their agreement.

The hard voice of Zack makes them quiet down and listen. "Get Nerd on the phone and dig deep into both her mother's murder and the accident concerning her father and brother. Every one of you, put your ear to the ground and your eyes everywhere. We need to know what happened at least two weeks before all of their deaths. We also need to see all of property owned, bought or sold right before and after. We need to check for a connection. Honeybump..."

He turns to me as he sits back down.

His face softens as sympathy and sadness enters his face. "Can you… will you, please…. Can you tell us what happened when your dad and brother died? We need to know what you know so we can go from there. You up for that, Blue?"

I take a deep breath and hold it for a few seconds. Reaching over I take Zack's hand in mine as I give him a squeeze. I can't look at him but I need his support.

Feeling at ease with Dams, I decide to look him in the eyes as I start to explain. "We were all on the drive back from a match. One of my dad's fighters had a championship fight. He didn't win though. My dad was kind of upset since he took an elbow to the eye that he should have seen coming. Hell, I even turned as a reflex it was that obvious. But he. Shit, never mind. Yeah, anyway...I should have been in that car with them too except... Except my dad just introduced Frederick to me a few hours before. He was in the seat next to me during the match and we kind of hit it off straight away. His father should have been in the seat next to him, but it stayed empty. He never showed. Frederick asked me to join him for a late dinner after the match and I said yes. My brother got in the driver's seat and my dad in the passenger seat. We followed behind them in Rick's car but my brother was driving faster than Rick was. Knowing my brother he was probably talking through the details of the fight with my dad.

My dad was more than pissed off at the guy losing like that. Hell, my dad was in a shitty mood before the fight. Losing only made it worse. There were at least two cars between us when a huge Chevy came from behind us. The thing was speeding and I wasn't paying that much attention to it. At least, not until I heard Rick cursing about the car. It happened real fast and somehow real slow. The car made a swirl past the two cars and tipped the side of my brother's car. Pushing side to side he stayed next to it. The tunnel came up so fast and the Chevy pushed my brother's car closer to the wall. The Chevy turned the wheel to just barely avoid crashing but my brother had no choice. They hit the wall. Full front collision."

I listen to myself retell the story, realizing something. For weeks I've been reliving that night and now my mind has been replaying it very differently in my head. Knowing what Frederick's father said, things seem to fall into place.

My dad expected Frederick's father and even asked him why he couldn't make it to the fight. They had some kind of meeting and my dad was pretty nervous. More than upset with his guy losing, it was something more that was bugging him. He didn't even give me a hug before he got in the car.

"The hell with a drunk driver who didn't know what he did or the other option they had... road rage. Road rage my fucking ass. Those cops don't know shit. He did that! That's why the fucker was a no show at the fight. He was there, he just…. Fuck," I seethe.

My hand leaves Zack's as I lean forward letting my hand slip to his back. I stand up in a flash and walk toward the door. I have a score to settle. Right fucking now.

"Blue," a very dominating voice booms through my apartment. "Do not take another step, woman."

Turning very slowly, I see the anger in his face, along with understanding. But I needed to say it, just to be clear. "You're not taking this away from me."

He walks up to me very slowly, I feel like I still need to do this on my own. I can't drag him into my shit, I need to take care of this. Me. Not him, me. I've got nothing left to lose. He's got his sister, his friends.

"This isn't your fight, it's mine." My voice is determined.

Zack tilts his head. "I'm in your corner, Blue, you know that as well as anybody here in this room. What you also know, even more than any other person here in this building, is that you need to prepare. Study your opponent before you enter that fight. Am I right?"

Fuck. I know he's right but there is just no time. This needs to be dealt with. Now.

And I'm the one to settle the score. "Consider it the surprise part of the solution. He's not allowed to breathe through another night. He's living on borrowed time the moment he messed with my family."

"Look at me, Blue." He sticks his hand into the back of my hair and he roughly pulls it so my head falls back.

All I can do is stare in his eyes. His lips come down as I feel his other hand sliding over mine, gently taking his gun out of it. My now free hand grips his hair as I pull him closer to me.

Biting down on his lip ring, I hear a low rumble in his throat as his tongue fights with mine. Zack breaks the kiss and pulls away, shouting in an angry voice toward Dams.

Dams, who is yet again hitting us with a magazine, while trying not to smirk.

"I had a handle on it, dick!" Zack growls.

Dams rolls his eyes. "Yeah I could see that. You know, with your tongue so deep down her throat it practically came out of her pussy. Hell, your hand was starting to spread those other lips open to give your tongue access out. Thank fuck you had a few brain cells active enough to put that gun into the back of your pants. Or even still had your pants...."

"Out. Out, everybody out!" Zack bellows.

"Yeah, here we go again," Tyler mutters. "He could at least give us another show, but nooooo."

Dams pats Tyler on the shoulder. "Get the fuck out, kid, before Prez activates some more brain cells and kicks your ass. Oh hell, if you don't shut it and leave, I will be glad to kick your ass. Learn when to shut it, kid."

Zack and Dams talk for a little while longer at the door before Dams walks out. Zack and I are now alone in my brand new apartment. Walking up to me, Zack takes my hand and walks to the bathroom. He twists the knobs in the shower and turns to undress me while waiting for the water to heat up.

When he finishes with me, he starts to undress himself. I can't take my eyes off his magnificent body covered in ink. His rippled abs, and the V that leads to the pierced master-piece, his dick. That stairway to his balls, reminding me how it felt deep inside me.

"Stop looking at me, Blue, you ain't getting any." His voice comes out raw.

Popping my lower lip out in a pout, I take a step toward him as he sidesteps into the shower.

"We're not going to fuck. Not right now at least," Zack states.

Getting a bit pissed off and not at the very least under-standing why the hell we can't have sex, I take the bottle of body wash and start to clean my body. We could totally have sex right now. That would get my mind off of things.

All I need to do is touch him, except he's being a dick and pissing me off. Trying very hard, I succeed in ignoring the very hot and hard body behind me.

He growls low in my ear. "We need to shower and eat. Believe me, I'd rather lick you clean right now and make no mistake, honey, we are going to fuck. Tonight is almost over, but just so you know, guys are much hornier in the morning. So I don't mind putting it on hold until tomorrow morning. I am going to fuck you. Just not right this second, are we clear?"

All I can do is swallow and give a slight nod as I hurry to wash away the soap and step out of the shower that is way too hot right now.

******

I wake up to something brushing up my legs. Still very sleepy, I shift and try to doze back off. That something is still there and now I can't seem to close my legs. Something wet and hot slides through my pussy as I hear a loud moan. Holy shit. I have never felt anything like that. Trying once more to close my legs, I am now convinced there's a head stuck between them.

I can't pretend to be asleep now with the movement of my legs but I also don't want to open my eyes. I just want it to…

"Holy shit," I breathe out as it flows into a loud moan when two fingers are pushed inside me.

A tongue slides through my pussy, teeth grab hold of one of my lips and give a tug.

"I might need to do this a few times a day, Honeybump. Your taste. Damn, no other man can ever have this. This," He pushes his fingers deeper in me, pulls out and slides back in as his tongue plays with my clit.

"This is all mine. You hear me? Mine. Open your pretty eyes, Blue, watch me. Watch how my face fits perfectly between your legs. Watch how my lips latch onto yours. Watch as my tongue digs deep inside your pussy. Watch how I lick you clean and demand more of your taste, Blue. I need more, give me more, Blue. Wait, I'll just bring out more taste from deep inside you." He pushes himself up and places his hands on each side of my head.

My legs now fall on his hips as he balances himself on one hand and uses the other to guide his dick and place it at my entrance. He slides inside me with one hard push. My head falls back and I feel his piercings rubbing on the inside. He stretches me with every pump he makes. My nails press into his biceps as I feel the hot sparks of my orgasm building low in my belly.

"Don't you dare fucking come, Blue. My dick is only bringing your taste up for me. I'm going to fire you up with my tongue to drag out that orgasm. After that, you can have my dick. Then you can come all over my dick as much as you want."

He pumps a few times more with so much force I feel his balls smacking against my body. Suddenly he stops and slides down my body until his face is back between my legs, lapping from my ass to my clit and pushing his tongue inside me.

"Love this sweet pussy, love tasting it. This pussy is fucking made for me."

His mouth goes over my clit, sucking it hard as he slams three fingers inside me, sliding in and out while he curls them slightly and pushes down. He speeds up and shifts his mouth to suck even more. I'm lost. My mind goes blank as fire starts to spread through my body.

Moaning loud, without any shame, I call out his name. Struggling to breathe, my pussy becomes too sensitive and I want to pull his mouth off. I can't handle anymore touching. Reaching over, my hands go into his hair as he stops sucking but flicks his tongue over my clit and digs his fingers deeper.

Zack's hand goes to my nipple and he tugs slightly at my piercing. Heat slides through my body. I need more. I pull his mouth harder onto my clit. Another flick with his tongue and it's either another orgasm or just the special edition running overtime.

Trying to catch my breath with my eyes closed, my hands fall beside me as my body goes limp. Hearing a faint chuckle, I open my eyes.

Zack is hovering above me with a huge smile on his face. His face is wet like a dog who just had a huge bowl of water. I smile back at him and look at his mouth. His tongue goes around his lips and I follow the movement. His face drops closer to mine as I press my head into the bed.

"What are you doing?" His face inches closer to mine but he doesn't answer my question.

There isn't anywhere else for me to go when he kisses me full on the mouth. His tongue that was very deep in my own pussy just moments ago now swirls around in my mouth.

He pulls back smiling. "Taste that, that's you. Fucking love that taste."

Not that it's something you can put in a cup so I'll drink it with my sandwich, but it is quite a turn on having his lips on me, right after, well, right after he had his lips on me.

Makes me wonder. "Shall I kiss you the next time your cum fills my mouth?"

He actually growls at me. His eyes turn hot as his face inches closer to mine. "When my cum slides down your throat and I'm finished pumping it into that sweet little mouth of yours? After you swallow everything I give you, you bet I will put my tongue down that throat next."

Without using his hands, his dick finds his way to my opening all on his own. Pushing his hips forward he slams into me so hard, there might just be a blueprint of his balls on my ass. My head falls back when he pulls out and slams back in again.

His face leaves mine as he sits up. Putting one of my legs onto his shoulder and one leg of mine between his legs. Going deeper inside me, I try to shift, afraid of the pain that might come when he slams into me. His hand curls around my calf and his other goes to my hip. I'm unable to move but he pushes himself deeper. Rotating his hips, I feel his piercings stroke inside me, sending out a massive flow of feelings I can't begin to describe. Overflowing with everything my body explodes into waves of pleasure.

"That's it, grab hold, fucking hug my dick, Blue. Take it, take. Oh, fuck. Blue." He roars as I feel hot pulses inside me.

His cum coats me, branding me on the inside. Letting go of my leg, he lets himself drop on top of me. His phone starts to buzz and ring as we are both trying to catch our breath.

"No, no, no, don't get that," I groan. "Ah, just once, once would be nice."

"Oh shush, sweetheart, we've got forever. That's a long fucking time to enjoy catching our breath once after mind-blowing sex."

"Mind-blowing huh? Well…. If you keep pumping that cum of yours so deep inside me, we're bound to have a tiny person screaming for attention in nine months. Talk about no sex then, huh."

A smug smile paints Zack's lips. "Honey, we've got enough brothers to watch our kid for twenty minutes."

My left eyebrow raises. "Just twenty minutes?"

"Yeah, you know if Pokey can jerk off at least fourteen times in twenty minutes then how many times do you think we can get off?" The phone doesn't stop buzzing and ringing. Zack lifts himself off me as he answers his phone. "Talk fast."

Or die slow. He should add that too, that would sound real cool. Except for the fact that he's naked and that firm ass of his is looking right at me. Oh damn, his muscled back is filled with ink. The club's patch with the running horse and flames instead of manes. Not one section of ink is in color, believe me, I've checked.

His arm flexes and the words that are inked on there catch my eye. 'We shall overcome' At this moment, those words hold so much more meaning than just ink on skin. We shall overcome, Zack and me, the fucked up mess I'm in. I'll make fucking sure we overcome.

Zack throws the phone on the bed and reaches for his jeans. "Gotta go, darlin'. Church. Dams called a meeting."

Sliding off the bed, I reach for my duffle bag to get clothes out, so I can get dressed too.

"You're staying here, Blue. I need to keep you safe and you're not allowed in church anyway."

"You've gotta be fucking kidding me," I snap. "This is about me. I should be there."

He shakes his head and walks up to me. Getting angry, I take a few steps back so there's enough space to pull my arm back and punch him in the gut if needed.

His gaze softens. "Blue, you're an ol'lady now. This club hasn't had an ol'lady in its circle for years. With all of us being the new generation of Areion Fury MC, it only holds stallions. You're the first mare in our midst."

Anger rises within me. "Are you comparing me with a horse, Zack? Is it my ass or is it my mouth that's too big?"

"Fucking hell, Blue," Zack grumbles. "There is no bigger picture for you, is there? Always so damn literal, taking the words exactly as they come to you?"

"Duh, I know what you meant by it, I'm not stupid. I just like to take both options and give hell for the insult that it holds first. Just to be clear, I ain't taking shit."

He takes out the space between us by pulling me into his body. His lips cover mine in a wet and slow kiss that makes the part between my legs tingle and wet.

He pulls back and looks me in the eyes. "The choice will be mine to tell you club info. If it'll be all, some or none, that will be my choice. You're the Prez's ol'lady. So you're top rank in the line of females. You're in charge of them, they will look to you first. For you to handle it, if one might step out of line."

"You just said I'm the first woman there, so what's there to rule, huh? And don't start with the big picture 'cause I know there are more females in there. Calling them females is nice because I could have said ho's." I can't see the upside in all of this.

He takes a deep breath and places his hands on each side of my face. "Yes, you're in charge of the ho's but also every new ol'lady. And hey, even Lynn has to listen to you since she's part of our club."

Hell yes, there's an upside. "Ha. Oh, that's just too good to be true. I'm gonna have so much fun."

"I knew you'd like that part." Zack chuckles.

I kiss his nose and pull away, getting underwear, yoga pants, a shirt and my running shoes out of my duffle bag. Somehow it's easier to step away from him right after we have sex. Walking into the bathroom, I wash up fast and put my clothes on.

Zack is standing in the doorway just as I'm putting on my shoes. "You're going for a run? Because that would mean I need to switch Tyler watching you with one of the other brothers. Not many do cardio and since me,

Dams, and Pokey will be in church the choice is limited."

Smiling I walk up to him. "I'm hitting the treadmill that's in my living room. Tyler can sit on the couch and watch."

"Tyler's not watching you," Zack growls. "Well he'll watch you, but he won't be fucking looking."

"Yeah, big boy, I get it," I mumble softly and add under my breath, "Seems like I'm not the only one jumping on words instead of looking at the big freaking picture. Hello pot, this is kettle. Freaking caveman."

By the look on his face he heard my muttered comment, so before he can say something, I give him a kiss.

Pulling back, I look in his eyes. I need to let him know what I think about what he said earlier. "That part about you deciding what I'm told about club business? I trust you, completely. There's not a doubt in my mind you'll handle everything the way I would handle things. So don't tell me, tell me something, tell me everything. I vow to forever trust your judgement."

"Nice to soften things up, Honeybump. But you and I both know I'll end up telling you all about the skeletons, mud, blood spatter, paperwork, beer, toothpaste, and every other fucking detail. We both know your ass doesn't function well on just a few details or none at all."

My face turns into a beaming smile. Fuck, this guy knows me too well. "Great, now we've got that settled. Get your ass to church. The sooner you do so, the sooner I get to know."

Zack chuckles as he leaves the room.

Chapter 14

I walk into church to find every brother already seated. The look on Dams' face does not look promising. It makes me wonder if it's bad news or no news at all. Bad shit would suck, but no news at all might complicate the fuck out of things. Sitting down, the chair makes a noise like it might just break in half any minute now. Glancing around the room, the faces of each of my brothers are pinned to me.

My eyes go to Dams and I nod, giving him the lead to lay it all out. "Nerd did a background check and it doesn't look pretty. Seems like Blue's father and Frankie D. were once friends. Tight as fuck friends, also business partners until things went south. They both owned several properties around town. Seems like they partnered up on the health center on Third. Blue's dad wanted to make it a nonprofit thing but Frankie D. wanted to make a profit. Blue's mom worked there. Seems like there was a huge fight between the three of them two days before she was killed. No one knew what it was about. People remembered the yelling. Frankie D. and Blue's father threw some punches. Funny thing though,"

Dams throws a folder on the table. "That's a copy of the deed. The health center was signed over to Blue's mom the same date as the fight. Rumor is that Frankie D. had feelings for Blue's mom. Don't know for how long though, since they have known each other since high school and it seems like Frankie D. may have been trying to patch things up with her that day. Still waiting for the police and the autopsy report from Nerd for more details. Told her to bring it over as soon as she got it."

"She's coming here?" Pokey stands quickly and leans over the table. "Chick sounds hot as fuck when you have her on the phone. No one has ever seen her either."

Dams shakes his head. "Yeah well keep your dick in your pants, Pokey, and your tongue behind your teeth. She just might have a face covered in zits, pigtails and glasses. Oh and a fat ass from sitting on it all day."

"Are you done, Dams? Cause, we've got more important things to discuss than your fetish fantasies about Nerd," I snap.

The whole room fills with laughter as Dams growls in frustration. "Shut the fuck up. I don't have a fucking fetish for anything. Okay, maybe the pigtails, or the whole librarian glasses, oh fuck, never mind. My dick is getting hard."

I growl right back at the fucker. "Yeah, that would be; shut the hell up, Dams. Get to the rest of the intel already."

"Right Prez." Dams seems to snap out of it. "Well according to the police report, the accident involving Blue's brother and father happened just like she explained. Report lists accident as a road rage gone bad. Something about their car cutting a Chevy off first and the Chevy trying to scare them. So they're leaning toward accident, a conflict gone wrong. They never found the Chevy so that doesn't help the case. They haven't closed the case yet, but it's been a few weeks now. Seems to me that they've shoved it off the table and stuffed it in a closet so far it might as well be a closed case to them."

There's a knock at the door. I yell so whoever it is can just come in. The door opens and a tiny person stands in the doorway. Her head is down and she's holding a file. She looks like she's barely eighteen and just walked out of class.

She's wearing socks that go way over her knees, black with yellow dots I might add. Yellow skirt that falls right above the knee, and a black tight t-shirt that says; You're Fucked, Lucky Me. Honey colored hair with a bit of a red glow to it. And in honest to God pigtails.

She's wearing pink mirrored sunglasses. Her head sweeps slowly from left to right as she finally steps into the room. This must be Nerd. And oh, would you look at that?

For being so tiny she does have a big ass, and somehow she pulls it off as sexy. Not that my dick notices though, since it doesn't come alive for another woman anymore.

"Who's the ass that calls himself Dams?" Nerd snaps.

All fingers point to Dams as he stands up slowly.

Pokey chuckles as he mumbles loud enough for all of us to hear. "At least you got the pigtails right, and that fine looking ass."

Her head turns to Pokey and gives him a death glare. Walking across the room, she closes the distance between her and Dams. Nerd smashes the folder against his chest and she holds onto it with one hand. Dams' hand goes to the folder keeping it in place as she tries to put her face close to Dams.

I mean, she's tiny as fuck and even with those black gothic like boots with heels that seem to resemble the Eiffel tower, she's not even close to his chin.

"If you ever fucking threaten me again, I'll wipe your measly existence out of the freaking system. You got me? Asshole," she seethes.

Nerd pushes against his chest and turns to leave the room. The door slams shut with a loud noise and everyone looks from the door to Dams as we burst into a booming wave of laughter.

Pokey recovers first and pushes Dams' buttons by saying, "You're fucked and she's lucky. Fucking love her shirt. Fuck, I love that chick. Can we get her back? I need her number. Can I have her number?"

Dams is furious, his tone is solid and threatening. "Shut your shit spewing jaw, you idiot. You're not getting her number. Forget about her, she's none of your fucking business."

Sounds like Pokey pushed the right buttons, so he adds a bit more pressure. "Getting all hot and horny for Madame Pigtails are we, Dams? Laying claim already? Yeah…. You're fucked alright," Pokey taunts as Dams is getting visibly frustrated.

Funny how Dams has been the only contact so far between Nerd and the club. We used the number we got from my dad. In the beginning it was her father that worked with mine. She just picked up the phone one day and took over six months ago. Dams didn't seem to mind and I didn't give a shit either. I mean, she always got us the info we wanted so why complain?

"What's in the file, Dams?" I need this shit over with, too much at stake for taunting bullshit. Besides that I want to get back to Blue as soon as I can. Dams opens the file and looks through it.

He passes me the file as he begins to give us the short version. "Report says it was a gunshot to the chest, and it hit at an odd angle. The strange thing is, the report says there was a witness that saw two men arguing before hearing a gunshot. There was some kind of a struggle, she heard a gunshot. Then she saw the woman fall to the ground. Both men ran to her aid before one of them ended up running off. Police report says they found Blue's father applying pressure to the wound upon their arrival. Too little, too late she was already DOA. Since the witness couldn't tell who pulled the trigger and Blue's father was found on scene and fully cooperated, he wasn't a suspect. Not to mention he is very tight with the chief. His statement indicates he didn't know who the male was. Started yelling without any reason, he wanted the guy gone, turned into a fight, blah, blah, blah."

"That's the whole report?" I question. "How could you have read that shit so fast?"

Dams looks over at me and gives a tight smile. "Nah, Nerd placed a yellow Post-it inside the file. She even wrote the blah, blah, blah. See."

When I open the file to look, I see it. I'll be damned, there is definitely more to the death of Blue's mother. That is something I can tell from miles away.

My gaze hits Dams. "Get Nerd to find out who the witness was. We need to have a little talk with him or her."

Hearing Dams groan and Pokey's chuckle, I just knew Pokey wouldn't keep his mouth shut. "Better wait a few minutes there, Dams. She might just hightail it back here and chew your balls off."

"She's gonna have my balls in her mouth soon enough. But there won't be any chewing, just lots of sucking. Fucking pigtails," Dams mutters.

Dams pulls out his phone and turns from the table. Knowing that all we can do is wait for more intel, I wave my hand dismissing everyone from church. I need to get back to my woman. Besides that, we have a gym to set up.

******

It's been two weeks and Nerd can't seem to find out who the witness is. She says she's close though. The gym should have opened a week ago. At least, that was Blue's intention. Apparently that was wishful thinking. We got the final shipment of gear yesterday and we just finished getting everything into place. Blue hired two women who will each take a shift behind the counter.

A simple job really, sign in new members, help out the women and let them feel more at home and shit. But yeah, smart thinking on Blue's part. We need members to feel comfortable. Hell, Blue did a great job with making a part of the gym women only.

With the opening tomorrow and everything in place, we're having a BBQ at the clubhouse tonight. Taking a sip of my beer, my eyes stay focused on the door. Any minute now Blue's gonna walk through it. I fucking love that woman, and I need to tell her soon. She needs to know. I'm sure she knows I care about her. A lot. Hell, she might already fucking know I love her. But I've never actually said the words to her. She needs to hear it. I need to say it.

The door swings open and Lynn walks in with Blue behind her. Tyler walks in after them, giving me a nod. With that, he walks behind the bar to get himself a beer. Blue's wearing some kind of black dress that's longer on one side and very short on the other.

The fucking thing looks shredded like she sat on the back of a bike and the fucking dress was caught slightly by the wheel ripping it in half. Blue's wearing red heels with little skulls on them. Her hair is pulled up and she's looking sexy as fuck.

I need to adjust my dick because it wants out. My other head wants to take a look for himself. Or better yet, slam deep to feel the tight and hot as hell place he wants to hibernate in for the rest of his life. I don't have to move because she walks right up to me wrapping herself tight against my body.

My hands go willingly to her ass and push her against my rock hard dick. "You feel what you do to me?

Just by walking into the fucking room. Now put that tongue to good use. And don't be a smartass by using it to talk, 'cause you know that's not what I'm implying."

She smiles brightly and leans in. Her tongue sweeps over my lower lip as it finds my piercing. She puts the tip of her tongue through it and gives it a tug.

I growl and shift my hips to press even deeper into her body. "Every fucking time you do that I feel the jolt in my dick. You know that, Honeybump? Two fucking places at once."

A playful smile on her lips. "So I don't even have to touch your dick anymore, I'll just do this."

Oh fuck, she drives me nuts. My hand goes around her neck, giving it a small squeeze. My thumb presses beneath her chin as I drag her off my lips. I turn her head with a tight grip and bite down on her neck. I need to be inside her in the next few seconds or I'll combust.

My lips go to her ear, my tongue slides over it and I bite down on her earlobe, giving a little tug. "My dick is going to find out if you feel as good as you did this morning. Will you open those legs so he can find his way home?"

Blue groans. "Does he have hands to help him with barriers along the way? Or can he work through a few obstacles all by himself? Unstoppable and all that."

My hand slips beneath her dress, slides beneath her thong and I slide two fingers deep within her.

She gasps and I swallow it with a wet and open mouth kiss. "What obstacles, honey? With us, there are no fucking obstacles."

The smack on my head with something hard and the noise that goes with it makes me slip my fingers out of Blue's tight little pussy.

"What the fuck!" I growl as my other hand rubs the sore spot at the back of my head.

"Yeah, sorry or actually, so not sorry about that. Didn't have a magazine this time." Dams holds up his drink. "Did have a bottle of beer in my hand though."

Blue chuckles and she says thanks. She actually fucking thanked Dams for smacking me on the head with a beer bottle. Pulling the two fingers that were deep inside her a few seconds ago close to my face, I hold them to my nose and with my eyes closed I inhale her sweet scent.

Opening my eyes, I then bring my fingers into my mouth and suck them clean. When my eyes find Blue's, I see her visibly swallow. Yeah, take that, honey. You're gonna be begging me tonight. I smile as I turn away to take a piss. It's gonna be hard as fuck to aim with my dick pointing up.

When I come back I see Lynn talking with Dams and Blue. Walking up slowly I try to pick up on their conversation.

Lynn speaks very quietly. At least, she's trying because I can easily pick up her words with the loud music around us. "That's why I pierced the toy to make it look like your dick. So she knows what it looks like."

Seeing the twinkle in Blue's eyes sends of a bolt of jealousy through me. Why the fuck does she needs a toy? And, a pierced one, no less. But most of all, why the hell is it pierced like Dams? I need to know more so I bite down on the inside of my cheek and I taste blood.

I keep quiet so I can hear Blue's reply. "Yeah well, I never got to use it or even got it out of the box. Besides, I have Zack now so I won't be needing it anyway."

That settles my rage a bit but the next words out of Lynn's mouth set my temper on fire. Now it's threatening to burst free at full force.

"That's a shame since the rubber dick cost you half of a gym." Lynn chuckles.

In two steps, I'm in front of Lynn. "What the fuck did you just say?"

Behind me I hear Blue furiously pop her gum. Four very loud rapid pops that express her agitation. Turning around, I slam my lips to hers. My tongue forces its way between her lips. That's when she loses it. My lips leave hers and I walk over to the trashcan across the room and spit out her fucking gum.

"Nice move, dick," Blue snaps.

My gaze locks on hers. "Yeah well, stop with that nasty old habit, it's annoying as fuck."

"None of your freaking business. If I want to pop, I'm gonna pop." Her mouth twists into a dirty smile and her mouth opens slightly.

Before she can form any words to roll off those pretty plump lips, I shut her up. "The only words I want to hear out of your mouth are the ones that explain why the fuck you'd trade a gym for an all pink pierced rubber dick?"

With every word of my voice getting louder I think everyone within the clubhouse just heard the word dick bounce off the walls.

"How do you know it's pink?" That's the only fucking thing she has to say?

By the way my face scrunches up she knows she's just said that out loud.

"I said that out loud didn't I?" Blue mutters.

I'm seconds away from losing it and grabbing her shoulders to shake some sense into her. Why the fuck would someone sell a piece of huge property… Fuck, that's what that money was for. She didn't need the money but wanted to give the cash to Lynn. The dick was probably her idea too. I turn so fast Lynn gives a little scream as she drops the bottle of beer she's holding.

"You! The plastic dick was your idea wasn't it?" I growl.

I feel Blue's arms around me as I turn again to look straight into her eyes.

She reaches over to put two hands in my hair as she turns her head to Dams. "Give us a minute, Dams. But if my ass, tits or pussy threaten to show, start smacking."

He gives her a nod. "I'm gonna go look for a magazine."

Blue pulls my face to her, sliding her lips softly against mine.

Her tongue gives my lip ring a little tug. "Lynn made me the toy. I asked her if it was possible to pierce a toy, because you didn't want me to see Dams' piercing the night I gave him his ink. I owed her the money for the toy, and since I asked her to get it for me, I paid up. I always pay up. You know this. I wanted you guys to have the gym and I would have given it to you for free. But I needed the money to give back to Lynn. Two birds, one stone, that simple. So I didn't see it as trading. Well, not until your sister here was nice enough to point it out to me. She almost choked and died from tequila though."

She pushes her hips against my dick. Her lips go to my lip ring as she gives another tug. "You still mad at me?"

"That depends." My voice is husky.

Her head pulls back slightly as she looks into my eyes. "On what?"

An idea slides through my mind. "Do you still have it?"

She nods in slow motion, trying to figure out where I'm going with this.

My mouth goes to her ear as I whisper to her and grab her ass with both hands. "Then we'll play with it when we get home. I can't wait to fill you up, front and back. Would you rather have the toy up your ass or me, Honeybump?"

She gasps and shoves herself away from me. Yeah, I can't help but bark out a fucking laugh. Payback is a bitch and she just came for a long freaking visit.

******

Walking into the empty gym, my hand rubs at the back of my neck. Fuck, my head hurts. I need the aspirin I took a few minutes ago to kick in real fucking fast. I look back into the direction I just came from. At the stairs to Blue's apartment.

What a night. First shocking the hell out of her at the clubhouse and then again the moment we got home by pretending to look for the toy. Bet she knows exactly where the damn thing is. No way is she going to hand it over now though. I reach into my pocket for my phone when I hear the door of the gym opening. I look up to see Dams walk in.

My eyes focus on my phone as I shoot a quick text to my sister. Yeah, I'm a dick and I'm not afraid to shove it in her face. Or better yet, shove the rubber dick in her face. A toy, I'll just ask my sister to make another one. I'm not letting this go. I'm gonna have a little fun with this, even if I'm not gonna use it. Fuck. Just the thought makes me hard as a fucking rock. She's gonna squirm like her ass depends on it. Sure as fuck will be too.

"You ready for this?" I look my VP in the eyes and by the pumped up expression on his face, it looks like he's ready enough for the both of us.

I can't deny the fact that I'm a bit nervous. It's healthy, keeps me sharp. At that thought my hand goes to my .44 at my back.

Hearing the rumble of bikes, we both look out the large front window. Five bikes pull into the spaces at the front of the gym. Two men swing their legs off their bikes and walk up to the door. The other three stay seated on their bikes. Dams holds the door open as they walk in.

The president of Broken Deeds MC is wearing practically the same clothes as me. Jeans and a black wife beater. His cut is rough, shows years of wear and tear, while his face is still young. Or maybe that's because he's a bit of a smooth baby face, model kind of guy. I bet chicks fall all over this guy with their legs open and holding on to their tits so they won't shake as much as he fucks them.

He's also covered in ink, hands too. Can't tell what the art is from this distance though. Looks like it's all lines and swirls or some shit.

The guy next to him, presumably his VP, is one scary dude. Not scary in size since he doesn't even reach my shoulder, but scary, as in, his face is covered in ink. I bet people cross the street when they see him coming. He reminds me of those New Zealand fuckers, all inked up. Maybe that's where he's from. His features seem to add up. I should mention there's a shop next door where he can add some piercings. That might just add more to his whole scary as fuck appearance.

Dams walks up and comes to a stop next to me. The two guys look around, both with looks of approval all over their faces.

The president takes a step forward with his hand out. "Name is Deeds, this place yours?"

"Zack." I shake his hand once with a firm grip and drop it. "Yeah, club property. Opening is just two hours from now."

The president walks though the gym. Doesn't introduce his VP, so I sure ain't gonna introduce mine. Walking straight for the corner Blue designed for the fighters, his hand goes to one of the punching bags.

He slaps it with a flat hand like you would smack a chick's ass. "This is a great setup you guys have. Haven't seen anything like it in a very long time.

Hell, I'm not sure if I've ever seen anything like it…it's like fucking heaven to me."

I nod. "Appreciate it. We've had someone with a fighter's heart set this up."

All the info he needs. Turning this into business since that's why the guy is here.

I'm just gonna throw it out there. "Listen, I wanted to meet because word around is that you're Frankie D.'s guard dog. The one that handles the shit he doesn't want to get his hands dirty with."

"Not his guard dog," Deeds growls, clearly offended by the words. "We do some business for that asshole since my old man had a contract with him. If it was up to me, we'd put him in the ground already. It's been hard to work around him since we have the contract, but we need the hard cash that comes with it. Been different lately since the son took over, though. Now we only get what, how many we need to mess up?"

He looks at his VP as he takes a deep breath and scratches his neck. "Doesn't matter. The difference is that Frankie D. likes to put his business problems in the ground and his son rather keeps them above. Now what's…"

His phone vibrates in his pocket. Taking it out and looking at it he types back furiously and shoves it back in his pants. Only to have it vibrate again after a second and take it back out.

The sequence repeats four more times before his VP slaps him on the back. "Quit texting the cunt."

Deeds shoots his VP a glare as his phone vibrates again. His VP reaches for it and in one swift moment Deeds' fist moves forward and connect with the VP's nose.

The VP steps back with two hands pressed to his nose. "Fucking cunt loving, asshole of a motherfucker."

"Shut it, I didn't even hit you that hard. Just a little tap on the nose, you big pussy." Reading his text, Deeds murmurs, "Speak of the real estate devil."

He puts his phone in his pocket and looks me in the face with a whole different glint in his eyes. "Get to the fucking point, why did you bring up Frankie D.?"

The tone of his voice and the look in his eyes puts me on my toes. I have this strange feeling that he's only giving me one shot.

Instead of fishing for information to see where his loyalty stands with this guy, I choose to give him a piece of the truth and hope he takes our side. "Frankie D. crossed paths with my ol'lady. He might be connected with murdering her whole family. We want to hear if you heard or know anything about it."

"Does she live at this address?" Deeds asks.

My skin crawls at the question. Giving a slight nod with my head, my hands clench into fists as one of them inches towards my back. He pulls out his phone.

"Really? Again? Cunt before business?" his VP growls his frustration.

"You want me to make your face even more pretty, Goffa? No? Then learn when to shut it." Deeds puts his thumb on the button and hits an icon and turns the screen to me.

There's a message, all I read is the address of the gym we're standing in, and that he needs to get the bitch that owns it.

My eyes look up from the screen. "Why are you showing me this?"

He puts his phone back in his pocket while he shrugs his shoulders. "Told you, I owe him no loyalty whatsoever. I don't like the fucker and how he handles his business. The contract was made with my father, not with the club. The money is good and since the son took over some parts of the business, there's less dirty shit. But what I just showed you? That's from the big boss himself. That can only lead to one thing."

I feel a hand on my shoulder and I try to keep a steady breath and not lose my shit right here. Apparently honesty was the way to go, and he's giving me honesty in return. I need to respect him and I'm trying my hardest here. Dams pushes me back a bit with his hand still on my shoulder.

I steel myself and my voice. "Look, Deeds, we appreciate your honesty and all. But since we have no foundation of trust between our MC's, we either build that shit up starting now or you need to walk out that door and leave us to deal with our problems. Meaning we add you to the shit pile. So, what's it gonna be?"

Deeds holds up his two hands defensively. "Look man, like I said. If it was up to me, he would be pig shit by now. Hell I've even wished he'd die of a heart attack so his son could take over. But like everything you wish for, some things just don't happen that way. You mentioned your ol'lady. Well, I have more respect for a fellow president's ol'lady than for the fucker who just placed an order to take her to him."

We all seem to let this shit sink in because none of us talks for a few minutes.

Deeds puts his head up and looks around the gym. "What if we made a deal?"

My interest spikes. "What did you have in mind?"

"Work, cash, partners in some shit, I scratch your back you scratch mine. Work together in the future. I'd rather have an MC as a friend than that douche nozzle." Deeds glances around the gym again. "Besides that, I fucking love this gym. I wanna train here."

I nod, appreciating the offer. "Guess we have to get into more details before we can agree to all of that shit but I do like the sound of teaming up. So, that being said, you wanna train here? You hear that, Dams? Sounds like we've got our first member. We'd love to have you here."

"Good, I'll be here about every night. Or morning, depends when I can fit that shit in. I get full access right, or does this thing close during the night?" Deeds questions.

I shrug my shoulder. "Nah, I'll make sure you get full access so you can get in whenever you want."

"Been waiting to switch things up, this might be it. Can't wait to workout here. Fuck, I feel all pumped up just standing here." Deeds looks around again, nods his head.

He takes out his phone and starts texting. "I'll let Frankie D. know we're handling it. We need to discuss what and how we're gonna put him in the ground."

"Say what?" I bark.

"Yeah, we need to get rid of him." Deeds doesn't even lift his gaze from his phone. "That would be the best option. Step ahead of him, 'cause he never backs away from something he wants to get done. Now I don't know why he wants her brought to him, but if he's asking us to bring her. Nah man, that shit never leads to anything good."

Fuck, it's been a while since we had to swipe somebody under the rug. Shit, I know he's right, there might not be another option.

Reaching out my hand I step forward. "We'll get the details settled."

He takes my hand while texting with the other.

Looks me in the eye and gives my hand a firm pump and releases it. "Talk to you later. Goffa, let's go."

Watching the five members of Broken Deeds MC ride off, I feel Dams' eyes on me.

"You trust 'em?" Dams asks.

I take a moment to answer. I sure as fuck don't trust them but that doesn't mean I have to take a chance. He could have left out the info from the message he got. By the way he was talking about the contract and Frankie D. it made me want to trust his word. Trust this MC with our lives or Blue's? Yeah, whole different thing right there.

"Trust isn't given, it's earned," I state. "Guess we have no choice but to wait and see how things will unfold."

Dams nods and locks the door. Just another few hours until the grand opening. Or just opening since we already celebrated yesterday. That reminds me of the message I got earlier. Must have been Lynn getting back at me. Unlike that ass Deeds texting during a conversation, I waited until now.

Pulling out my phone I start to walk in the direction of Blue's apartment. "You'll be here the moment we're going to open the doors to the gym later on?"

Dams thinks about it before he answers. "Yeah, I'll be here. Need to handle a few things before then."

Meeting his gaze, I ask, "Like what?"

He waves a hand in front of himself. "Check in with Nerd, see if she found anything yet."

"You want coffee?" Dams nods as we both walk up the stairs to Blue's apartment.

Chapter 15

It's been a helluva few days. Since we opened the gym, there's been a steady flow of people coming and going. The few classes scheduled were full within a day. I still need to hire a new trainer for the 'Get your ass into that bikini' work-out class. I printed out information on a few of the trainers that had applied.

Standing in Lynn's kitchen, I have them spread out over the kitchen counter. While my eyes are focused on the information about the trainers, Lynn's eyes are on her phone, her fingers typing furiously on the screen.

She mumbles to herself or to her phone. "Oh hell, no."

Her phone vibrates just seconds after she hits send.

My interest is spiked. "What are you doing, and who are you texting?"

"He's asking for a picture of my tits," Lynn gasps.

Can't help but smile. Now I know exactly who she's talking about because Lynn doesn't have another guy she texts or sees without telling me about it. "Still in touch with Mr. TakeAMessage huh? Show me your tits. Classy. What did you reply to that?"

"Yeah. And I told him I only show tits if the guy is in front of me so he can suck it." Lynn snickers.

I burst out laughing. Watching as she sticks her middle finger into her mouth, wraps her tongue around it, which now shows her tongue piercing. She snaps a picture up close so only her lips and part of her hand is showing off the bird.

She's also got a snake bite piercing, that's one left and right on the bottom lip, near the corners of her mouth. She turns the phone to me to show the picture. I laugh because it's perfect.

Not showing her face at all but somehow it's very sexy. Even if she's flipping him off. She laughs as she presses send.

It takes a few seconds as the phone in her hand starts ringing. "Oh shit, it's him."

My hand slides over my mouth to contain the laughter. "Well, what did ya expect sending a picture like that? Answer the phone, you big cow."

"You answer it!" Lynn snaps.

"Fuck no, it's your phone. Your picture, your words, your mess. Suck it up and answer it, you chicken. It's not like the pig can bite you through the freaking phone," I grumble.

Lynn's eyebrows scrunch up. "What's up with all the farm animals?"

My stomach rumbles. "I'm freaking hungry 'cause I've put myself on a meal plan and I've put together a workout schedule."

Lynn puts her phone in her pocket and with three more rings it stops. A few seconds later her phone vibrates and we both look at her jeans pocket. Knowing that's probably the indication she has a voicemail, she takes out her phone. She swipes the screen, punches it a few times with her finger and puts it to her ear. Her eyes go wide.

A moment later she pulls the phone away from her ear and tucks it back into her jeans pocket. "So you're back full force getting into shape, huh? Good for you. Have you punched the hell out of something yet?"

I shake my head slowly. "Oh no the fuck you don't. Speak up, bitch. My ears want to know what yours just heard. Spill."

Her face flames up, and I know it's bad. This only makes me want to know even more what the guy said.

I push a little harder. "You owe me, bitch. Remember my pink rubber friend? Come, the fuck, on. Tell me, or at least let me hear the freaking message."

She thinks about it and decides to let me listen to the message. Looking it up on her phone she hands it to me and I listen.

One very low, husky voice breathes the words into my ear. "Very soon I will be sucking that finger into my mouth and my cock will be treated to the feel of those sexy as fuck piercings. You make me want to coat my fucking phone with my cum while I fuck my hand just looking at the sexy picture you just sent. Pick up the next time I call you, or I'll hunt those Hotlips down. You hear me, love? I. Will. Hunt. You. Down."

Holy hell! What in the fuck did I get her into? Well, she kind of started it. I just gave him some digits, not my fault he used them to text her. So her and her Hotlips are indeed to blame.

Fuck yeah, I'm so not taking the blame for this one. "What in the hell have you gotten yourself into?"

"I don't know!" Lynn screams in frustration. "Shit. I'm so fucked. I'm just gonna ignore him from now on."

I snort. "Yeah, that's a solid plan, mastermind. You are indeed fucked, or will be soon. By him. You know this right?"

"Fuck," Lynn growls.

I nod my head in agreement. "Yeah."

My hand goes to the papers scattered on the kitchen counter.

Mindlessly looking over them, I hear Lynn whisper. "I'm kinda hoping he fucks me. He sounds like a screw your brains out kind of guy. Just once I would like a good lay. Shit, this is such a clusterfuck."

"Yes, it is. But that's your clusterfuck, or fuck. So, there you go. My advice?" My gaze meets hers. "Meet the guy, screw your brains out. Hey, maybe he's good and hot so you'll swallow his cum without burping."

"Or gagging." Lynn chuckles. "Yeah, worth a shot right there."

We both laugh as Lynn turns to the fridge, pulls out a homemade container of ice cream and two spoons. "Made this earlier. Greek yogurt and chocolate whey, and some other healthy ingredient shit."

"You did? Ooooooh, that's why I love you!" I croon.

"Cut the crap, I know you just love my ice cream. Zack already kind of told me you were back at it again so I made it for you. Now show me the hotties you want to pay so we can look at them while they are getting our asses into shape." She leans over to take a peek at the papers on the counter.

I give a snort but throw my arm around her neck to pull her close and plant a kiss on her cheek. "Thanks."

******

It took us about three hours to nail it down to two trainers. One chick and one dude. Because they both look really good on paper, I invited them both to an interview the next day and ended up hiring them both. This way, we have more classes and members could choose to either have a female trainer or a male trainer. Needless to say the guy had his class full within a few hours and the female has a few places left.

My own workouts have been going really well. I've been lifting and adding more cardio each day. I have yet to start punching but I'm working up the nerve. Having people in the gym at all times made me nervous too. Now as I'm lying in the dark I feel the need to workout. Lifting my legs out of my bed and sliding carefully out from under Zack's muscled arms I sneak out of the bed.

Walking to the closet, I grab my workout clothes and a pair of sneakers. I dress in my living room and grab my phone and earbuds. Because I know the gym is closed, I can leave the door to my apartment open and I don't have to take keys or anything else.

Hopping down the stairs, I put in my earbuds and thumb through my phone to find a good playlist. Clicking the one with the most Steve Earle tunes, I tuck my phone into a pocket I've add to my pants. Most pants don't have a good pocket to carry my iPhone, I've added internal pockets to all of my workout pants.

I walk toward the row of treadmills and out of the corner of my eye I see movement. Turning my head, I see a guy working out in the ring. He's punching into the air in front of him with dumbbells clenched in his fists. Like he's beating the shit out of someone with dumbbells in his hands.

He's wearing a training mask and it covers his nose and mouth. I know it's used to strengthen the lungs but fuck, it just oozes sex. His skin is covered with ink. At least the parts that are showing. His body and movement show that he's a skilled fighter. He's wearing a black tank and shorts. His feet and hands are taped and he's looking right at me. Fuck.

I smile and nod. From where I'm standing, his eyes indicate he's smiling too. Can't confirm due to the mask and all, but fuck even those eye crinkles are sexy. He gives me a wink and a nod and looks away, back to punching the air in front of him.

I know Zack handed out a few so called VIP cards to men who don't have the time to workout during normal times so they are allowed to come here whenever they want. So if Zack trusts him, I'm assuming it's all good. Stepping onto the treadmill I take out my phone and shoot a short text to Lynn.

Me: Went down to the gym. There's a hottie working out here!

I put my phone back into my pocket while I program the treadmill. My phone vibrates so I take it out and there's a message from Lynn. Figures she's still awake since the addict either reads or watches documentaries at the weirdest times.

Lynn: Pictures or it didn't happen.

Me: I'm not taking his picture!

Lynn: Yes you r. Why the fuck tease me? SHOW ME THE HOTTIE

Lynn: NOW

Me: I can't just snap a picture, he'll know. Hell, I own the gym, that's a felony or a lawsuit, right there.

Lynn: Everybody has ninja moves. Go exploit yours. Act like you're taking a selfie or looking through your phone and snap, there you go!

Fuck that shit. I can't do that. My head turns to look at the guy. He's focused on his workout and doesn't even have his head my way. Cringing inside, I hold my phone up and snap a picture, pressing send the same time as I'm hitting the start button on the treadmill. It only takes a few seconds for Lynn to reply.

Lynn: Holy freaking hotness. You just found my dream man! Can you give him my addy and send him my way? Tell him I'm in bed waiting for his cock!

Me: Christ Lynn. You got your picture, remember what your Mr. ImGonnaPutMyDickInYourMouth said? Go and masturbate to the picture. I need to smash my workout. Night Night.

Lynn: Night oh, fuck yeah, right there, night!

Me: Nasty bitch

Thirty minutes later and I'm dripping with sweat. I dare to take a glance in the direction the hottie was working out. Glad to see he's gone. Walking to the storage room I find myself some tape and start to tape my hands. It's time, I need to get over myself and get some light punches in. Walking up to the last punching bag near the corner, I plant my feet and pull my hands up. Taking a deep breath, I let my hands slowly hit the bag. Just to take in the movement and the feel of the bag.

Something peels away inside of me. My hands start to move naturally. How could I not have missed this all these years? Punching away I let myself get lost in the feeling. Before I know it I feel strong hands wrap around my waist and I'm pulled against a hard chest. Reflex brings up my elbow, only to find it blocked by a solid grip.

"Calm down, Honeybump, it's me." I'm panting like crazy but it's not from Zack scaring the shit out of me just now. Zack is holding my hands in his. "Look at what you're doing, honey. Too much, too fast."

He drops one of my hands and pulls the other with him as he walks us in the direction of my apartment. Sitting down on the couch, I watch as Zack grabs the first aid kit and sits down beside me, stripping away the tape and cleaning my bruised knuckles.

"Felt good, didn't it?" His voice is as soft as his touch.

Taking a deep breath I know he's right. It's like something heavy was lifted off me. "Yeah, felt amazing. *I feel amazing.* Never knew I'd miss…"

As the dick wipes alcohol across my knuckles I inhale sharply.

He chuckles and continues to dress my hands, placing a kiss on each hand as he finishes. "Try to stick to short active time on the bag and not go all in for long periods of time. And wear your damn gloves. You know this."

I nod absently. "Yeah, I know but I was just gonna work on freshening up my technique by hitting slowly. I guess it just kinda turned into a frenzy there, huh?"

He smiles and kisses my nose. Grabs my hand while he tugs me up off the couch. "We're going back to bed. No more sneaking out while I'm sleeping, yeah?"

"Hmmm hmm," I answer as the words flow over in a yawn.

"You need to stay awake a little while longer, Blue. My dick needs to feel that pussy. Seeing you workout like that? Muscles all slick with sweat and little moans coming out of your mouth. You're lucky I didn't fuck you right there in the gym. Naked. Against the mirrors." He actually growls out that last part.

Holy fuck. And fuck, that would have been a pain to clean those mirrors after that, or forget and leave a print of my ass for all to see in the morning. I'm brought out of those thoughts when my ass hits the bed. Strong hands rip off my pants and panties in one swift move.

The next second the tip of his dick is pressing against my entrance. I didn't even see him take off his clothes. He grips his dick in one hand as he strokes his piercing up and down the lips of my pussy. He smacks his dick hard a few times right on my clit, sending fire jolts through my body. Building hunger deep within my VG and I feel myself getting wetter by the second.

Still sliding his dick up and down my slit he sees my juices coating his dick. "Fucking beautiful, open up that tap of honey. All for me, right? Christ, look at that."

Feeling the same need, his hips pull back and he enters me in one hard thrust. Gripping my hips with both hands he pulls me harder to him. Not moving in or out but only rotating his hips he seems to relish in the feeling of being buried deep inside of me.

He leans over. "Lift your shirt honey, I need to see your tits."

While he's holding my hips in place I manage to pull off my tank and sports bra. His eyes lock onto my left breast and his mouth goes slowly to my nipple.

His tongue flicks over my piercing and a loud moan leaves my mouth. He starts to move his hips, pulling back and slamming full force back in me.

One of my hands finds his biceps to hold on as the other holds his head in place. My nails digging into both. The slight burn of his huge dick filling me up, stretching me is wrapped up with the intense feeling of pleasure. I pull his hair back and he releases my nipple with a popping sound.

Bringing his face to mine, I let my tongue slide over his bottom lip. His mouth is open as he grunts from slamming into me. I move my head forward so I can get even closer to his face. Still pumped up with adrenaline from my workout I feel the need for more. Of what, I have no idea but I need something.

My mouth presses hard against his and I bite down hard on his bottom lip. Tasting blood I hear him growl out a curse. Before I know what's happening he pulls out and I'm flipped onto my belly. His hand comes down to my ass hard and I scream at the top of my lungs.

Fuck, that hurt. Not even managing to get a breath in after my scream the next smack lands on my ass. I look back to find his face admiring his work. Seeing his hand pull back for another smack I make a run for it.

He laughs. "You're quick, I'll give you that. But honey? You've just made me hungry for more. Get that tight ass of yours over here or I will pin it down to the bed using my dick."

My little scream of terror makes his smile grow. I need to get him the fuck away from me. No way in hell is that giant cannon of a dick going up my ass. He climbs off the bed slowly, walking to me in slow-motion. I whip my head toward the bathroom, if I'm fast enough I can lock myself in.

I take four steps in that direction before my back hits his chest. "No escaping now, honey."

I try to give him a headbutt, which he dodges easily. His hand slides down my body and finds my clit as his fingers make small circles. My legs relax first and I lay my head back on his shoulder.

"That's it, darlin', hmmm." His mouth is near my ear as he whispers into it.

He licks and tugs with his teeth on my earlobe then his mouth goes to my neck as he sucks and bites down. His other hand moves over my breast kneading. The fingers on my clit slide deep within me while his palm now rubs my clit.

My hips move back and forth as I rock myself in his hand. I feel his dick pressing between my ass cheeks. His hips start to rock into me, seeking the friction my ass is giving his dick. I can't help but feel excitement building. Pushing back I hear his low growl of approval.

His fingers curl inside me and rub the perfect spot. Jolts of pleasure shoot through my body as I come harder than ever before.

My upper body falls slightly forward and Zack's hand pushes my upper body further down. Sliding his hand back to my hip, his grip tightens slightly.

I feel his fingers pull out and wipe my juices back and forth over my ass. His dick finds the right friction to slide between my ass cheeks. I turn my head slightly and my eyes find the mirrored door of my closet.

Seeing him moving his hips back and forth while the tip of his cock pops up above my back with every push forward. It only takes two more thrusts of his hips to see spurts of cum flying through the air and I feel the heat of it landing on my back.

His body relaxes against mine. His fingers move on my back, going up and down. "You should see this. Fucking beautiful."

"That would be kinda hard to do, buddy." I chuckle.

"I could snap you a picture."

I gasp. "Hell no. You can't take or have pictures of me that way, you idiot."

"Well then," Zack croons. "We need to do this a lot in the future, because I like what I see."

"Now that is doable," I croak.

He chuckles as we move to the bathroom to hit the shower.

******

I'm hearing voices. Opening my eyes slowly, I move my arms to push myself off the bed. My face smacks back into my pillow and my eyes close. My arms feel like jello and I moan at the soreness in my muscles reminding me of the awesome workout I had last night.

Well, not so awesome now since I will be having a hard time working today. The thought of putting ink on a person, holding my arms steady and concentrating? Oh I am so fucked.

Another moan slips out and hear the voices in my head again. Well not so much in my head, but they seem to come from my kitchen. They sound far away enough. After last night I think I'm allowed to skip an ab workout. Making the fast decision that I won't be doing my morning ab routine, I stand up in one swift move instead of taking it slow.

I remember it's better to move fast and get my body moving, instead of trying to avoid the soreness. My dad always used to say to his fighters 'Embrace that shit. Move through it and get back at it.' I learned so much from him. He might have kept me out of the down and dirty, but he was always there for me. There was no need for me to be involved and I never felt like he shut me out or anything like that.

I'm sure my brother knew every dirty little secret and then some. He was practically my father's right hand. I mean, when you have a son it's only natural that he knows everything.

Especially if he's taking over family business, walking in his footsteps and so on. They just pushed me out of the fighters' business instead of in deeper. Always told me 'Become a great doctor like your mom' or something else you'll be great at.

Looking into the mirror I see myself smiling. It's kind of a shock to me. This is the first time I remember something about them and am not feeling hurt, pain or sadness. I smile at their memories. Yet another step in the right direction. It feels good. Moving forward, working on my inner self.

Finishing up my business in the bathroom, I walk back into the bedroom to put on some clothes. I'm pretty sure it's Zack and Dams' voices that have been floating from the kitchen. Strolling into the living room my suspicions are confirmed as I see Zack leaning against the counter in the kitchen with a mug in his hand.

Dams is standing in front of him so all I can see is his back when I hear him speak up. "You gotta admit that this stirs shit up. Fuck man, think about it. Would you want to know? Shit like that would change how you feel about a person. Fucking hell maybe the way she would feel about herself. Like I said, think about it. If it was my ol'lady I'd think twice before telling her…"

"Think twice about what, Dams?" I see his shoulders stiffen at the sound of my voice.

He turns on his heels and looks at me. With, pity? What the fuck is that all about? My family is dead. The man I love is standing a few feet away from me. What the hell could he possibly say that would make him pity me?

My eyes go to Zack. "What about you, Zack, are you thinking twice about it?"

The fucker smiles at me. His eyes show no pity at all. Laughter with a hint of pride are the only things that show in his eyes until they drop to my chest and flash hot with lust. Figures. The top I'm wearing is a low V cut that is kind of snug, hugging my tits. But it's pink and comfortable. So is my new pushup bra and by the looks of Zack's pants it's really pushing things up.

"Well?" That might have come out a little snappy, but I really want an answer from him.

He turns slightly to set the cup down. Pushing himself off the counter, he walks past Dams and stops to stand in front of me.

His eyes looking straight into mine. "The presidents ol'lady can handle anything. My woman can handle anything. My soon to be wife by the law of this state, can handle anything. Isn't that right, Honeybump?"

That son of a bitch nasty alpha piece of shit motherfucker. Does he actually expect me to answer that question with a yes so he fucking tricks me into marrying his nail that shit down ass? Fuck.

What the hell should I do? Do I love him? Yes. Is he there for me? Always. Does he make me feel safe and cherished? Hell yeah. Do I need him? More than my next breath and in more ways than one.

He's still watching me. The fucker's face twists from a smile into a shit eating grin, as if he knows my train of thought. His hand reaches out toward my face. I take a step back, because we both know what happens when we touch. I'd be screaming yes within seconds and Dams wouldn't be so glad to see another show.

Closing my eyes, I whisper my answer. "Yes, Zack."

I open my eyes the moment I feel his lips meet mine. His kiss is swift and smooth as he steps away fast, turns and stands in the exact spot and pose he was just moments ago when he was talking to Dams.

"You do know you just agreed to marry me, right?" His smile is blinding.

I should walk up to him and smack the smile off his face. "Yeah, well it doesn't really count unless you put a ring on a woman's finger, buddy."

Stick that in your pipe and smoke... wait, what the hell is he doing? He reaches into his pocket, pulls something out and throws it into the air toward me. My eyes follow the small object and I reach out and catch it with both of my hands. Zack's aim is always spot on. Mine, not so much. I am good at catching things though, and right now I'm holding a silver looking ring in my hands.

Turning it around in my fingers I read the platinum mark and Zack's name is inside of it. It's delicate and yet rough. Engraved lines twist around the surface to resemble fire. I slide it around my finger, a perfect fit.

"Well that was fucking romantic. Remind me never to ask you for anything woman related. You guys deserve each other," Dams mutters as he pours himself another cup of coffee.

Ignoring him, I ask, "Can you make me one of those? Only a tiny bit of milk in there for me."

Taking my cup of coffee with me to the couch, I sit down. Zack takes his place in the chair that's to the right of me, as Dams moves to sit beside me on the couch.

Zack gives a slight nod toward Dams, indicating he can start to lay it all on me. "So. Long story short, because I don't want to bore the hell out of you with the how we got the info and why it took so long and shit like that."

I nod and make a gesture with my hand telling him to spill the details already.

Dams doesn't take another breath before he states, "We think either your dad or Frankie D. shot your mom."

I clench my teeth and close my eyes, only for a second before I open them back up. Looking at him I throw out one word that might have sounded like a high-pitched squeak. Because I know there's more to it than just the one sentence he just threw on me. "And?"

"We found out there was a witness who saw the whole thing. She told us that there was an argument between two guys. The yelling outside made her walk to the window to see what was going on. She heard something about a daughter and the two guys started to fight as your mom came out of the house. She begged them to stop fighting. Asking them to both be there for her or something, the witness wasn't quite sure. Your mom never really got to finish her plea. The guys fought and a gun went off hitting your mother in the chest. The witness said they both ran to your mother and she left the window for a few seconds to call 911. When she looked back out, there was only your dad holding on to your mother. The description of the other guy sounds a hell of a lot like Frankie D. With the gun and him missing from the scene when the cops showed up and your father not telling the cops Frankie D. did it or even mentioning he was present he wasn't a suspect… Yeah, that doesn't add up. Maybe he felt guilty or was a part of it or something? That's the part we're having a hard time with. It's like an open gap we don't know how to close or with what. We haven't been able to make much sense of it all. Sorry darlin'." Dams shakes his head. "Wish it wasn't this fucked up. It doesn't make any fucking sense."

I turn to look at Zack who is watching me intently. Tilting my head, I think it all over. My dad and Frankie D. My dad mentioned back in Japan that Frankie D. was an old business partner. Business deal gone wrong?

They mentioned a daughter, so did they fight about me or did Frankie D. have a daughter too?

I raise my eyebrows and looked back at Dams. "Well isn't that just fucking peachy, huh?"

He bursts out laughing and wipes his hand over his face as if he can wipe away his laughter. "That's all you've got to say? That it's fucking peachy?"

"Yeah, well you gotta admit. It kinda is. I dunno what there is to say about it. Much less do." I shrug. "We need to think things over or get more info or something. Shall I go talk to the witness? Who is she anyway?"

This time Zack answers. "The old woman that lived two houses away from yours."

Right, I remember that old lady. She was old back then. She is like what? A hundred by now? Did she even have her glasses or hearing aid in or something? Oh shit, the hatred. I need to cut off the nasty bitch inside me, that isn't who I am. The old woman was nosy but kind. That I remember.

Maybe I do need to visit her. "I should go visit."

Dams and Zack look at each other. Dams raises his eyebrows as Zack lifts his shoulders. "I see no harm in that."

"Good, it's settled." I stand up from the couch.

Zack stands up with me. "We'll go with you, she lives in a retirement home now. We need to swing by Lynn's first, I need to pick something up."

******

Zack wasn't too happy that I didn't want to put my ass on the back of his bike. So he's driving half beside me and Dams behind us. When we stop for the red light, I know he wants to say something. Ignoring him I keep my eyes on the lights.

When it turns green, Zack's eyes are still on me. I could tell because I launch my bike forward, leaving him and Dams behind. Speeding up feels great. Just what I need to get a few seconds without thinking.

I park my bike in Lynn's driveway. Hearing Dams and Zack coming up, I move my ass into the house with lightning speed. I can only imagine how pissed Zack is, with me leaving his ass behind.

Practically running inside the house I bump into Lynn, and we both stumble to the ground. "What the hell, Blue? Ouch, my ass. Could you…"

"Nowhere to fucking hide, Blue," Zack bellows. "Get that tight ass over here. Now."

The couch is blocking us from Zack's view. I cut Lynn off with a hand over her mouth. Her eyes going wide when she hears her brother's booming voice. Then they fill with laughter, and I try my best to smother the sounds. One moment my body was bent over Lynn's, the next I'm being lifted up by my hips and pulled into Zack's solid chest.

His mouth is close to my ear. "Don't ever pull a fucking stunt like that again. Ever. You hear me? Or I will spank that ass again. And this time, honey, this time I won't let you run off while I'm coloring your ass a nice shade of red. Maybe I'll just tie your arms and legs to the bed, does that sound good, sweetheart?"

His nose slides up and down my neck while his hand sneaks from my hip to my belly, his fingers sliding beneath my tight shirt. Moving them back and forth and dipping them into my pants. His mouth finds my neck as he sucks my skin and nips with his teeth. My head falls back and the next feeling is a smack on the head.

Turning, I see it's Dams holding a rolled up newspaper in his hand. "Move the fuck away from each other."

Stepping away from Zack, I hear him growl at Dams. "You know I'll hit back someday soon. Won't be using a fucking magazine, newspaper or beer bottle. You'll have my knuckles in the face for every smack."

Dams shakes his head. "Keep that wedgie under control, peckerhead, I'm only trying to save your sorry ass. Stop fucking touching each other in public. Or maybe I'll just let you guys fuck your brains out in public the next time."

Zack mutters a few curses and there might have been an apology and saying Dams was right. By the look on Dams' face he heard it too. Lynn comes in from the kitchen. I didn't even see her leave, that's how wrapped up I was with Zack and Dams.

She walks up to Zack and hands him a package. A package that looks similar to the one she…. Oh fuck no. Zack looks at me with a smug smile on his face and gives me a wink. Fuck. I just know he paid Lynn to get a new rubber dick and pierce it.

Oh, maybe this time she pierced it like Zack's dick. Hearing Zack chuckle I just know the fucker knows what I'm thinking.

I glare at Lynn and she just shrugs. "What? He paid me a hundred bucks extra."

"I would have given you five if you hadn't," I snap.

She chokes. "As in hundred?"

I point my finger at her. "Yeah. As in five fucking hundred, you double crossing, money loving, little back-stabbing bitch."

"I have no fucking idea what ya'll are talking about, but I have a lot more to do. So could we move the fuck on and go already?" Dams moves toward the door and I turn with him.

Lynn steps closer to Zack. "Where are ya'll going anyway?"

I look back at Zack, hoping he sees my question. It would be nice to talk to someone later about all of this. She's my one and only friend and with her being his sister and close to the club she has a loyalty that runs deep. His eyes flash away for a second.

I'm sure it's to get his VP's approval. Then he gives me a slight nod. I feel myself release a puff of air that I was holding on to.

Walking back to the couch, I grab Lynn's wrist as I tug her down next to me. "We are on our way to see that old lady that lived two houses down the road from my parents' house."

"You're talking about the one with the crazy hair and the glasses. Always behind those curtains acting like nobody sees her standing there?" Lynn asks.

I chuckle as I remember her crazy hair. Always in wavy curls. If she didn't have curls she had her head filled with rag rollers.

A timid smile stays on my face. "Yeah, that would be her. She witnessed my mom's murder? Uh, when she was killed. They already talked to her. Said it was Frankie D. and my dad who got in an argument, yelling something about a daughter, my mom walks out and says something about them needing to be there for her and then they struggle as the gun went off hitting her in the chest. Then they both ran to her while the old lady stepped away to call 911. When she got back to the window, Frankie D. was gone. With my dad not telling the police about Frankie D. being there it's all weird and fucked up."

Discussing how they all knew each other and with Frankie D. signing his part of the property over to my mom and so on, Lynn just looks at me without saying anything. Her eyes travel to Zack and then to Dams and back at me. Her lips purse and wiggle from left to right. I know she's playing with her tongue piercing. She does it a lot when she's thinking, mad or annoyed. This time I know she's thinking.

She gets up and starts to pace back and forth in the living room. She stops and points at me. Wants to say something but her hand falls away and she's walking again.

She turns back and lifts her finger. "You know... It's weird how they let your dad and ya'll take off to Japan without this case being closed and all. Also, why the fuck hasn't he been questioned or brought in based on this witness statement?"

"Oh, I can answer that," Dams says while he steps closer to the couch. "Frankie D. went to her house and threatened the witness. She was questioned at the time, since she was the one who called 911. The only thing that went into the police report was her seeing two men argue, struggle and hearing the gunshot. With the gun and the shooter gone, they labeled it as a drive by hit or some shit like that. She only talked to us because she's only got a few more weeks left in this world. Cancer is eating her up inside. She'd said, if I'm lucky I might have three weeks. Didn't want treatment to prolong it, so she'd have three more months. Something about not wanting to spend the last few days she had left puking over a toilet."

Lynn looks at me and we both hang our heads. After a moment Lynn starts to pace again.

She stops mid stroll as she begins to jump up and down, clapping her hands. "What if, and bear with me here... what if? Oh my God, you didn't have sex with Frederick did you?"

"What?" I gasp at the same time as Zack growls the words out.

Still in shock I add, "No. And where the fuck did that question come from?"

"Okay, what if your mother cheated on your dad with Frankie D.? That would explain the daughter and the 'being there for her' arguments they had. Also explains the fighting between them if she dropped the 'who's Blue's daddy bomb'." We all stare at Lynn.

None of us has anything to say about that. Lynn puts her arms in front of her chest and lifts her tits up. Huge smile of satisfaction on her face.

I shake my head. "Lynn."

"Yeah."

"Look behind you," I grumble.

She turns and stares at her bookcase. "What?"

"You read way too fucking much of those romance novels. Frankie D.'s my father? No fucking way," I seethe.

"Hey, never judge my porn, you cunt. It's what keeps me sane, my escape to another world. There are freaking life lessons in there. Do. Not. Judge. The. Porn. Ever. Besides, you gotta admit, I might just be on to something here." For Lynn using the word cunt, I know she's serious.

Pissed off, but serious. I look at Zack and his eyes are on Dams. My head turns back and forth between them.

"No!" I yell.

Maybe if I yell hard enough that stupid idea might just blow out of their minds.

"I hate to say this," Dams' voice fills the room. "But it does explain a lot. Sure as hell should be something we look into."

Zack nods at what Dams just said. The fucker. I don't need that shit, I had a dad. Now maybe my dad killed the one I thought was my dad and has been a dad to me all my life? Fuck that. Holy fuck, what if there is a slightest of chance?

"Oh my God, that's why you asked if I fucked him. Holy shit. Oh that would be wrong in so many ways!" My body vibrates in disgust.

"Yeah but you didn't know it back then so…" Lynn tries.

"Don't fucking finish that sentence," I snap. "It didn't happen. Fuck. All we did was freaking kiss. Oh yuck, with tongue. That's just. Oh. Fuck. Well, he might not even be my brother."

"Yeah, but what if..." Lynn tries again. "Even if he is a half-brother, that's a teeny, tiny piece of lost family found right there."

Fuck. I know Lynn is right and all of this could be swiped off the table or thrown on it with one simple test. Grabbing my phone I look up his number.

"What are you doing, Honeybump?" Zack's voice softens.

"Calling Frederick to tell him to get his ass over here. Then I'm making a few other calls to see if I can get us in, to get a blood test, DNA whatever. Then we can move past this and kill other ideas. Or just put Frankie D. in the ground so we don't have to figure this thing out anymore." I push connect on my phone and put it to my ear.

Chapter 16
Belle

"You can't be serious about this?" Frederick shakes his head. His face looks like I just told him a joke, but the punchline is missing.

So I carry on explaining myself. "I damn well am. Listen, this wasn't my brilliant idea but Lynn does have a good point. Think about it. It makes sense this way. I can't just kill him and not know the reason why."

"You want to kill my father? Or, let me get this right… with what you just said, 'Our father'. Believe me, with the childhood I had, the way he does business. I've thought about how it would be easier to have him out of the way, but still…" Frederick shakes his head, thinking shit over.

"The guy is living on borrowed time, Rick, he killed my family," I press. "You were right there with me, when he insinuated that. Or do you think his hands are clean?"

"Then why would my father wanted me to marry you? It just doesn't make much sense to me. Kinda screwed up to let his own kids get down and dirty, don't you think? I mean, he's fucked in the head alright. Damn. The guy must have some morals, right?" He throws his question out but it's like he already knows the answer to that question.

"Ya think?" My hands go up. "Cause I think the guy doesn't even know ass from tail if it sat on his face."

Rick just stares at me for the longest time, unsure what to say or how to proceed. One look in Zack's eyes to know the remark about Frankie D. wanting his son to marry me bothered him. Let's just hope the words 'down and dirty' skipped his ears. The only thing that keeps him glued to his spot is the fact that I'm wearing his ring.

"Let's do this. Just so we can rule this out." Frederick takes a step closer to me.

He stops as soon as he hears Zack's voice. "Just so we're clear, slick, that's my soon to be wife. If you'd check her hand, she's wearing my ring. So you can rule out the down and dirty and the getting married joke."

I hear Lynn gasp. Frederick grimaced when he heard Zack's statement and his eyes went to the ring on my finger. I feel a small pain in my chest. I always felt comfortable with him, I considered him a friend. His face went sad but when his eyes met mine his face softened.

With a small smile he says, "Then with all my heart I do hope you're my half-sister. Just so I can keep you in my life and annoy the shit out of that soon to be husband of yours."

Dams chuckles next to Zack, earning him a smack on the back of the head.

"Alright, let's go. I've managed to pull a few strings, so the both of us can get our bloodwork done. We'll just have to wait a few days to get the results," I inform them.

Zack walks up to me and places his hands on each side of my face.

His forehead resting against mine. "I need you on the back of my bike, yeah?"

I give him a soft kiss on his lips as an agreement, knowing I freaked him out the last time I raced off when I was on my own bike. Either that or he still feels like he needs to show Frederick my place is on the back of his bike.

He puts his lips near my ear and whispers, "Now don't freak out on me, yeah?"

Again I give him a soft kiss and I smile, I'm good that way. At least for the time being. He turns but keeps one arm around my waist.

He stares up at Frederick and shocks the hell out of me. "Did you know your father placed the order to grab her?"

By the look on Frederick's face and the string of curses that leave his mouth, we are all sure that the answer to that question would be 'hell no'.

Even more when he replies to Zack. "I need to reach out to Deeds, he needs to know she's hands off."

Frederick's concern spreads a little spike of warmth in my chest. I knew he would always be there for me. The guy has a good heart, although he wouldn't show it to anyone, I know it's buried deep.

"Deeds knows she's hands off." With those words leaving his mouth, Zack's arm tightens a bit more around my waist pulling me even more against his hard body.

My hand reaches his back, stroking up and down. His face turns to me as he strokes his knuckles of his other hand against my cheek.

"Hands the fuck off, and step away from each other," Dams bellows as Frederick's face turns into a question and Lynn's laughter fills the room.

Zack's murmur of curses doesn't stop until he's a few feet away from me. He turns and gives me a wink.

"We need to take care of my father, one way or the other. If he gave the order to Deeds, and Deeds doesn't follow up or takes his time? Well, he's been known to take matters into his own hands. What did the order say? Detain or destroy?" Frederick questions.

Holy freaking shitballs. Did he just say what I thought he said? Those exact words? Destroy as in take out, end things, no more breathing, bye bye world? Destroy, destroy?

"Breathe, Honeybump," Zack's voice fills the room. "We're all here for you. Nothing's gonna happen. I won't allow it."

Won't fucking allow it? That fucking alpha piece of shit statement doesn't help. Fuck. What if I'm on the wrong side of a gun or in a car hitting a concrete wall? What the hell?

"He's right you know, I won't allow it either," Frederick agrees. "I'd rather take my own father out for good myself, if it would come to that."

Now that did sound a bit more settling, but fucking hell. It's still alpha male shit, except for the different mouth it spilled from.

"Alrighty then. We need ice cream. You guys need Alpha male shit, talk and blow steam and show dicks. So Blue and me? We will be in the kitchen. Eating ice cream. And discussing your dicks. Exclusively." Lynn walks up to me, wraps her hand around my wrist and guides me into the kitchen.

******

A few hours later with my ears still ringing from talking to the old lady who saw my mom getting killed, I walk back into Lynn's house. Zack needed to handle some stuff. He left me with C.Rash and a prospect named Tony that I hadn't met before.

They are both sitting in a chair at the dining room table. Lynn gestures for me to come into the kitchen. Looking at the two guys talking to each other I walk behind Lynn into the kitchen.

"What's up?" I question.

"Spill, girl!" Lynn says. "What's on your mind? What are you thinking about all of this?"

"About what? The fact that Frankie D. has it in for me? Your brilliant suggestion that Frederick's my half-brother? Or the fact that I'm marrying your brother so we'll be sisters-in-law?"

She jumps up and down and grabs me around the neck, hugging me so hard I can't get any oxygen into my brain. With the strangled noise coming out of my mouth, that thank fuck is next to her ear, she lets go of me.

"Sorry about that, I just kinda forgot about the getting married. I'm so happy." She grabs my hand and takes a good look at the ring. "That's one badass ring."

"Your brother has extremely good taste." My smile is huge.

"Yeah, yeah. He must have since he's marrying you. Now spill before this kitchen begins to stink with all your ego shit." I chuckle, Lynn always cracks me up with those silly ass remarks of her.

"Dunno what to say." I shrug. "Kinda hope I have a brother, Frederick is a good guy. We'll just have to wait and see. You know, I think I'd rather…"

Lynn's phone starts to buzz with what sounds like an incoming message.

"You wanna get that?" I nod in the direction of her cell.

"Nah." She waves her hand. "Go on, you were saying?"

"I think I'd rather not know. I mean, I would love for him to be my half-brother. Might just be the only option to hold onto the friendship I have with him. I don't see Zack letting him get close to me if he isn't related to me."

"Yeah, you have a good point there. That kinda blows," Lynn agrees.

We nod in silence as Lynn's phone gives another buzz. Annoyed, she reaches for the phone inside her pocket and pulls it out.

Smiling, I ask. "Mr. TakeAMessage, I presume? Hey, did you ever ask for his name?"

"Nope, he just calls me Hotlips and I refer to him as Dick. Works juuuust fine." She nods to her phone.

"How could you send messages back and forth for days now and not have a name, a picture, or even know who the hell he is? You two are weird."

Shrugging one shoulder, Lynn throws back. "Nah, not weird. I annoy him. He annoys me. Kind of like a daily distraction. It's fun."

"Yeah, like I said. Weird. Let's go watch a movie while we wait for your brother to come and pick me up," I suggest.

We walk to the couch as Lynn grabs the remote in the hand that's not texting. She turns on the TV and flips some channels. After thirty minutes my eyes start to feel heavy and I hear Lynn snoring next to me.

I push myself off the couch and walk to C.Rash. "Could you follow me home? I'm tired, Lynn's asleep and I want to sleep in my own bed. It's been one hell of a day."

"Lemme just check in with Zack, Darlin'." Putting his phone to his ear the conversation only lasts a few seconds. "He's just about ten minutes out. We'll ride and he'll either catch up or meet us at your apartment."

I'm relieved I'm going home. My bike is still here so I can drive myself home with C.Rash and Tony, the cute prospect, behind me. I promised Zack I'd behave, so I'm not driving that fast and won't try to get away from his two guys.

Seeing the traffic light turn red, I lessen my speed. When I'm almost to a stop, I hear tires shriek. My head turns just in time to see a black Chevy slam into my front tire. The bike twists underneath me and I fall to the ground, hard. The heavy weight of the bike lands on top of me.

I turn to look behind me, ignoring the pain in my leg where the bike is pressing on me. I hear a car door open as I look at C.Rash. His eyes switch from me to the car and he reaches for his back. I see his body jerk as gunshots echo in my ears. One shot hits him in the left shoulder and another in his right arm as he falls. My head whips around to the car and I see Frankie D. with his arm outstretched and a gun in his hand.

His arm shifts slightly and I see the gun go off again.

My eyes follow and I see the prospect get hit in the belly. Another shot sounds and I see a hole appear in his forehead right above his left eye. Tony falls down like a sack of potatoes taking his bike with him to the ground. I can't help but scream at the top of my lungs. This can't be happening.

Pulling at my leg while shoving the bike off, I get on my hands and knees. Ignoring the stinging pain in my right leg, I crawl toward C.Rash, hoping he's still alive.

"Stop right there, daughter of a whore." I freeze at the tone of Frankie D.'s voice.

Still on hands and knees I turn my head to look up to him. It feels like I'm moving in slow motion as I look straight into the barrel of his gun. This fucker killed my mother. Killed my father and my brother. There is no more fucking doubt in my mind. Hell, I bet he plans to finish me too. Pushing my hands off the asphalt I stand up.

He takes a step back and waves the gun. "Get in."

My eyes go to the car. I'm dead either way so why the fuck should I get in. That shit never ends well in movies.

So I take my chances and decide to answer politely. "Fuck no."

"Get in or I'll shoot you right now and you will never know the reason your mother is dead." My eyes must have given me away since his next reply comes fast after that. "That got your attention, right? Now get in so we can go. You have my word I will tell you everything before I kill you."

Well fuck me, at least he was being honest about one thing. He steps closer to the car as he walks backwards, keeping the gun pointed right at me. He opens the passenger door and waves the gun, signaling me to get in.

I sit down into the passenger seat, my head turns to see Frankie D. standing next to the door. Except, I never get to see him completely. All I manage is a flash of the gun before it hits me over the head. Pain flashes hot waves though my body. After that, I only register darkness.

******

Somebody should shoot that fucking elephant. Really, just nail that sucker down. Or throw some bananas at him, so he'd stop moving his damn feet. Fuck. My head is pounding in a rhythm that needs to stop fast. Like right freaking now.

I groan and try to pull my hands to my face. And apparently my hands are tied at the wrists, so I smack both hands hard into my face. Pain explodes in my face.

"Fuck, that was stupid," I mumble and rub both my hands over my face.

"You don't say. I thought it was quite hilarious to watch. You mind doing it again?" Frankie D. chuckles.

"Go stick a gun up your ass and pull the trigger would you?" I growl.

The fucker clicks his tongue. "Now, is that any way for a young lady to talk?"

"What? I can do anything I want to anyone I want. You're not my father, I don't owe you shit," I sneer.

He has a glint in his eyes. The evil man knows I'm trying to draw him out. "What makes you so sure? You look just like her, you know?"

"I know." Yeah, I know. I'm throwing the daddy card out there. I also know I look like my mom. Let him fucking pick the one he wants to have a conversation over.

My eyes go around the room. It's small. I'm sitting on a wooden chair and Frankie D. is sitting with just half his ass on a wooden table. There's a bed in the corner and that's pretty much it. There's just one tiny window in the wall on the left of me. One door leading out on the right.

"So you know all about your mother being a whore then? She was a lying cunt, that's what she was. Sweet-talking me into signing that property over to her. Promising she'd leave your father this time. In the meantime, fucking me over. Just like your father. No fucking loyalty." At this point Frankie D. is yelling and right in my face too.

His spittle is landing on my cheek as I turn my head and suck my lips in. Gross.

"You're gonna sign everything over to me. That's why you're here. I'm finally getting back what was mine in the first place," he growls.

"That's what this shit's about? Fucking property?" I shake my head in disbelief. "Besides, you dumb fuck, that will never work. No one will believe that shit."

"No? Why not? You sign it all over to me, then leave for Japan. I make sure someone that looks like you boards the plane... Bye, bye Jazzebelle. Just like your daddy ran away from here. It's all too much, it hurts to breathe here. Everyone will believe it. While you of course won't be breathing anywhere ever again. Rotting away in the ground while I suck on a cigar and sip my wine," he sneers.

His words make me snort. "Like Zack would ever let that happen, you fucking piece of shit. Let me just burst your bubble before you have a chance to blow that sucker. I ain't signing shit."

The back of his hand hits me hard in the face. I can feel the sting and taste the metallic tang of blood as it flows into my mouth and down my chin.

Zack

Guiding my bike around the corner, I see blue lights flashing at the end of the street. I look toward my right, my eyes connect with Dams. We both speed up as the scene in front of us get closer by the second. Stopping my bike, I jump off and run forward to the scene in front of me. There are three bikes on the road. My eyes go to the bike closest to me and I see an EMT covering up a body.

Just before the cover settles, I see Tony's face. One cheek to the asphalt, eyes open. A bullet hole just above his eye. Fuck, no. My eyes go to the other bikes. I see three EMTs working hard on a body next to the bike. My blood freezes in my veins as I step closer.

I hear Dams talking to people around me, who try to keep me at a distance. C.Rash is covered in blood. They've cut away his shirt and are working on him to stop the bleeding. Fuck. This is bad. It looks like he's been shot in the fucking chest. The EMT that is working with his back to me stands up. Fucking hell, he's got another large bandage on his arm too. What the fuck happened here?

I glance back to the third bike. That's when panic hits me. Seeing the fluffy unicorn on the keys in the bike my chest tightens and I roar with fury.

Both of my hands go into my hair as I bellow out the words. "Where is she? Fuck! Is she dead? Where. Is. She?"

The EMT who was working on C.Rash is near me so I grab him by the throat. "Where the fuck is my woman?"

"Wha what, are you, you talking about sir? There wwas nnno woman, sir," he stutters.

"What the fuck do you mean there was no woman?" I seethe. "The third bike, you fuckhead. Can't you fucking count? Two bodies, three bikes!"

I feel Dams pull me away as I give a hard push against the guy's chest throwing him to the ground. I fucking know it's stupid and that he needs to work on C.Rash. But I can't fucking help myself. I failed her. I need her back. I need her safe. I need her. Most of all, she needs me. She. She is the one who doesn't fucking deserve this. Fuck.

"Get all the brothers into church. We need to find Blue." I look back at Dams. "He fucking got to her. He has her."

"I know, brother. We'll get her back," Dams states. "We'll put him into the ground in twelve pieces."

I nod as we both reach for our phones. I hear Dams give out orders to the brothers standing behind us. They all get on their phone to call in all our brothers.

I dial Deeds, who picks up at the third ring. "Frankie D. took Blue. I got one dead and one down...Yeah... Good. Meet me at the clubhouse, we'll be there in ten."

Some of my brothers are still calling around, making sure word is spread. We'll be at full force the moment we get back at the clubhouse. We need to know where to look. Deeds has good intel. I look at Dams who is pumping his phone up and down in his hand. He's either jerking off his phone or thinking. Let's fucking hope he's thinking.

"I'm calling Nerd," Dams tells me.

"What the fuck, brother, calling pussy? 'Cause we already got everything she could find on him," I growl.

Dams holds his hand up. "Yeah, I know but maybe when I explain she'll know some weird back trail or property that doesn't fucking smell right. We need anything here right, anything that might help."

"Fuck. Yeah, sorry. I can't think," I grumble.

Dams nods. "No prob, we all have your back. You need to think clear, brother. We'll get your ol'lady back. She's a tough one, you know that. Hell, if one bitch could hang on, it's her."

When I have her in my arms, I'm gonna punch Dams in the face for calling her bitch. I can't do that now since he's already on the fucking phone.

Shit, I need to make a call. "Ask Nerd for Frederick's number. I need it, now."

Dams rattles off the numbers he's hearing in his ear.

I punch them in and with the first ring I hear that slick's voice. "Shut up and listen. That son of a bitch took Blue. Killed one of my guys and I got one in the hospital.

Doesn't look good. I need to know where he might have taken her."

All I hear through the phone is fucking cursing. This shit isn't helping and I can't deal with him flipping out right now.

I need to get to the clubhouse to get things rolling. "Get your shit together, I'm gonna be calling you back in five and I'll need a list of places he could have her locked up in. Yeah?"

Another curse hits my ear as I end the call and put the phone away. "Tyler."

"Yeah, Prez?"

"Follow that ambulance and stay with C.Rash. I wanna know every fucking thing the moment they know. Got it?"

"On it, Prez!" The prospect guides his bike around the others and speeds up to follow the ambulance.

Throwing my leg over my bike, I roar it to life and ride like hell to get to the clubhouse. Driving into the lot there are brothers everywhere. Not only our MC, but also what seems to be the entire chapter of Broken Deeds MC.

I climb off my bike as Deeds walks up to me. "Sorry, brother. This shit's fucked up. I knew he would step up himself if it took us too long."

I slap him on the back as we both walk into the clubhouse. It's crowded and the door is open since we can't fit everyone in there.

Dams walks in with what seems to be a long list of places. "Nerd e-mailed this. We need to nail things down 'cause this list is fucking long and it would take all night and fucking day to find Blue."

Deeds grabs the piece of paper. My phone rings and I reach for it, hoping it's Blue. My heart falters when I see it's not. I growl into the phone for them to speak.

Frederick's voice enters my ear. "Zack, I might have nailed it down to a few places. I'll text them to you as soon as I end this call. One is about a thirty minute drive, the other is barely fifteen. These are my best guess since he's never used them before. There is one other option, but the deal hasn't been made yet, he doesn't own that property but I saw it on the bottom of the dossiers he had on his desk. And Zack?"

"Yeah."

"The property is owned by Jazzebelle." Frederick releases his breath.

"Anything else, Frederick?" I snap.

His voice is weary. "Need anything? Anything I can help with?"

"No," I state. "You've done enough."

"Zack, I... Never mind, I'm going to check the property that hasn't been bought yet."

"Leave it to us, Frederick."

"She means a lot to me too, you know," Frederick grumbles.

I can barely manage to hold my phone in my hand, instead of throwing it into the wall. How dare this fucker talk about her now? Right at this fucking moment?

"Zack."

"Yeah," I sigh.

"Get our girl back."

"I will." My voice is as firm as the promise I just gave him.

Ending the call, I look at my phone when it signals I've received a text message. Pulling it up I see the places Frederick talked about. Grabbing the list out of Deeds' hands, I go over every single one. Deeds has circled five places he thinks might be an option. Frederick was right, those two might be our best option. The one whose deal hasn't been closed yet is at the very bottom. Nerd put a few stars in front of it.

"Dams, get Nerd back on the phone and ask her about this property. It's not in his hands yet, Blue is the owner. I want to know every fucking detail about it. Yeah?" I wait for his nod.

Dams gives it to me as he gets to work. Deeds and I agree to send teams to the places that might have her. Twelve of my guys and eight of Deeds' will be heading over to Blue's property.

My gut is telling me there's a reason the file was on his desk and Blue's the owner. It's about twenty minutes away from the city. My head fills with fear as I think about how isolated it is. If she's in pain and screams? No one would hear her for miles. Fuck. I can't lose her.

Belle

"Shall I start with cutting off one of those pretty little fingers?" Frankie D.'s slimy voice flows through the room.

I keep my breath shallow as my anger ignites inside me. Fuck him. I'm not showing any signs of fear. He's holding my bound wrists to the table and flattened one hand with my fingers splayed. He has a knife in his hand and keeps stroking my fingers with it. I look him straight in the eyes, his arm holding the knife lifts up.

"Well, let me just skip right to the good part then," he croons.

I close my eyes and brace myself for the pain. A deep slash of pain hits my hand then flashes up my arm and spreads throughout my body. It feels like flames inside my veins. I force myself to open my eyes. The knife is standing up. Straight up, through my hand and into the table.

I turn my head away as my stomach turns. When there is nothing left in my stomach, I dry heave a few more times before my stomach settles down. I can't even wipe my fucking mouth because my hands are tied together. Oh yeah, and let's not forget the knife that's lodged in one.

"Isn't that just… dandy," Frankie sneers. "You're disgusting. Did you know that, you little cunt?"

I want to kill this asshole so bad, it's not even funny anymore. If my hands weren't tied I'd bash his head in. Fuck. My anger rises as my hand starts to throb like crazy. The only way to kick his ass now is with words. That stupid fuck.

"Oh you're the genius in the room. The puke for brains idiot who wants me to sign something then stabs me in the very hand I need to sign with? Brilliant dude. Fucking brilliant. Not." That motherfucker doesn't need to know I'm not a lefty.

Let him fucking suck on it. Damn, my hand hurts. I hear a door open in the other room. My eyes flash to the door as Frankie D. stands up and grabs his gun, pointing it in that direction. The door slowly opens and a guy in a suit walks in.

"It took you long enough." Frankie D. tucks the gun away as he walks up to the guy and grabs a stack of papers from him.

"The lawyer's fault, not mine," the guy in the suit states. "What's that awful smell in here?"

His eyes go to the table. He looks at the knife, that's still in my fucking hand I must add, then his eyes go to the floor.

Shock and disgust hits his face. "Oh that's just great. Why did the bitch have to puke on the floor?"

Fuck me. The knife in my hand should rule out the need for an explanation but apparently not. Mr. ImWearingAsuit gets his panties in a twist that I puked on the fucking floor. Yeah, because people do that without *any* reason.

"Fuck you, dickhead," I growl.

"Do we need to hose her down? Her mouth's still dirty by the sounds of it." The suit guy chuckles.

Frankie D. laughs at the fucker. He makes my skin crawl. I look at the knife and think what might happen if I raise my hand fast up and then down. Will the knife come out? Can I do it? If so, fast enough for me to grab and slice the fucker? Would I have any strength left in my hand? Shit, even the thought of it is fucked up.

Out of the corner of my eye, I think I see movement through the window. My head turns to look, but it's gone. Maybe it was just wishful thinking. A new jolt of pain brings my attention back to the table. Frankie D. has his hand on the knife and wiggles it back and forth while keeping it in place. I swallow hard, bile rising in my throat. I close my eyes and take a deep breath through my nose. Holding it, I try to block the pain away.

Yet again, I hear a door on the outside of the room. My eyes open and I see Frankie D. reach for his gun. I mentally thank the person on the outside of the room for drawing the attention away from the knife in my hand. The suit guy takes the same position as Frankie D. and two guns are now pointed at the door.

Because there's nothing more I can do with my hand still pinned to the table, I turn my head to look. The door opens slowly and I see Frederick walk into the room. Frankie D. lowers his gun.

He puts his hand on the sleeve of the guy in the suit, giving a slight push so he too lowers the gun. "What are you doing here, son?"

Rick's eyes go to me and they widen when he sees how my hands are pinned in front of me. He rushes forward to stand next to me, his eyes flicking between the knife and his dad and back. One of his hands goes into his hair, while the other one scrubs down his face.

"What have you done?" Fredericks voice is filled with anger.

"What needs to be done." Frankie D. shrugs.

"You can't…this never…Fuck. I love her. How could you do this?" Frederick growls.

"You can't love her," Frankie throws out in disgust. "You just fucking met her a few weeks ago. Besides, you told me yourself she's in love with that biker. Take it from me, son, never trust a woman who leads two men into her bed."

Frederick shakes his head. "She never led me to her bed. She led me to her heart."

He reaches forward, wraps his hands around the knife and pulls it out in one swift motion. The knife clatters on the table as it falls out of his hands. Pulling my hands to my chest, I hold on to the wound and put pressure on it with my thumb on one side and my fingers on the other.

Luckily, it's not a hard thing to do with my wrists still tied. There is plenty of blood but it's not pumping like it would if he'd nicked an artery and for that I am thankful.

Frederick pulls his shirt from his pants and takes it up to his mouth, ripping a piece of it off with his hands after his teeth gave it a start. He takes my hand in his and wraps the piece of shirt tightly around the wound.

I wiggle my fingers painfully to see if they still work. Frederick gives me a look as if to say I need to cut that shit out. Believe me, it's just to know if everything still works for now. Strapping it tightly he lets go of my hand and I bring it back up to my chest.

"Get her to sign these documents, Frederick." Frankie D. waves the papers in front of his son.

Frederick's eyes go from my hands to his father's face. If one look could slice a man's throat, Frankie D.'s blood would be all over this floor right now.

"I told you to leave her alone," Frederick growls out.

"And I told you I'd handle my own business. This doesn't concern you. If you're not going to get her to sign, you need to leave. Seeing you're all softhearted for this cunt you'd better leave anyway. Leave. Now. Before I have Ken here throw you out."

I look at Ken and back to Rick. Is Frankie D. kidding? I mean, if Frederick pushed one finger into Ken's chest he would fall back on his head and never get up. The guy is a twig! I can't help the laughter escaping me. Shit! I must be losing it. Heads turn to me as I cradle my hands in my chest while I try to shut the hell up.

"I'm leaving, alright. But I will be taking her with me." Determination laces Frederick's voice.

"No you're not." Frankie D. raises his gun in the direction of his son and waves it a bit. "Step away from her. Now."

Frederick never takes his eyes off his father but steps a few feet away from me. His father moves forward and grabs me by the arm. He pulls me up hard and I bite my lip trying to stay quiet.

He maneuvers us toward the door backwards, keeping an eye on Frederick. "Let's go, Ken."

Ken walks out the door behind us and locks Frederick in. The moment we walk out of the house, I hear glass shatter and know Frederick just smashed the window. Frankie D. pushes me into the front seat of the car and puts the seat belt over my arms. He gets in the car himself and slams the door.

I look out the side window and hear shots being fired. Ken is running, taking cover behind the car as I feel the car shake. With the shake comes a person stepping up onto the hood of the car. Gun drawn and pointed right at Frankie D. I look over at Frankie D. and he's got both hands on the steering wheel and is staring right in front of him. Seeing no gun in his hands I look down to see it's tucked into the waistband of his pants.

My eyes go back to the guy standing on the hood, pointing a gun. All I see is from the waist down but I know it's Zack before I even hear his voice.

His voice is hard and filled with authority. "Get the fuck out of the car with your hands in sight. I'm gonna count to one." And then he shoots.

The window doesn't shatter on impact but it does have a hole in it with cracks all over. I hear Frankie D. scream and his hand goes to the left side of his head.

Very slowly he steps out of the car. "You fucking idiot! You better aim to kill next time 'cause I sure as hell am going to slice your throat for this."

Zack shuts him up with a punch to the face. Frankie D. falls to his knees and stays down. Zack grabs the gun out of Frankie D's waistband and tucks it into his own.

With my hands still holding onto each other, keeping pressure on the wound, I manage to unlock my seat belt. My hand is throbbing like crazy. The piece of shirt Frederick tied around it is drenched with blood and it is dripping everywhere.

Climbing out of the car I hear Tyler murmur something to Dams. "Can't he count? I mean, when someone says I'm gonna count. People expect to hear at least a 2 and a 3. Right?"

"Element of surprise, fucker. Man, you really lack more than a few brain cells, don't you?" Dams shakes his head and walks up to me. "You okay there, Darlin?" His eyes go to my hands that I'm cradling in my chest. "We're gonna have that looked at as soon as possible, yeah?"

I nod and take a step forward to lean against him but back away fast. Remembering the puking I whisper to the ground. "Do you have gum? I need gum."

He chuckles and reaches in his back pocket. "The girl gets taken, is hurt and bleeding, guns pointing and bullets flying and the first thing she asks for is gum."

I keep my voice low so only Dams can hear me. "Yeah, well, you would too if you puked. And fuck my hand hurts! The idiot stuck a knife right through it."

I hear Dams suck in a breath as he holds out the gum package. "Here you go, Darlin."

"Do you mind?" I hold up my hands indicating I can't grab and pick one.

The guy next to Dams laughs. My eyes go to his cut as I see he's not one of ours. His cut says Broken Deeds MC. Just like Zack he also has the word President on his chest. He looks slightly familiar, but I can't place him.

Dams curses himself and gets one out and delicately places it into my mouth. The mint gives me a slight jolt through my nose as I take a deep breath. I hear Frederick call out when he comes up from around the house. Smart, since the guys in front of the house might shoot his ass.

As we all look toward Frederick, I hear footsteps behind me. Before I can turn around I feel an arm around the front of my shoulders and I'm pressed against a chest. A long arm comes up beside me and is now pointing a gun at Dams.

I look over at Zack. As his eyes meet mine, he steps closer to me, forgetting Frankie D. on the ground in front of him. The other guys behind Zack are looking right at me and follow Zack.

"Don't move!" His hand is shaking and he keeps shouting right next to my ear. "Nobody fucking move, or the girl gets it!"

The girl gets it? What the fuck is that supposed to mean? I pop my gum furiously, getting very annoyed by this fucked up situation that seems to get better and better every fucking second.

My eyes land on Dams and he wiggles his eyebrows. What the fuck? "Wish you'd pop like you used to do, Blue, back in the glory days."

It takes a second for me to process what Dams might mean and then it hits me, or at least, I hit Ken. With the back of my head right in the nose.

Dams reaches for the gun as he guides the hand away from him. Two shots ring out and I feel the body behind me drop to the ground. I look over to see Ken with the back of his head blown away. Swallowing hard, desperately trying not to puke again, I look away from the gross mess of what was once Ken's head.

My eyes land on the president of Broken Deeds MC who is quietly studying me. My eyes lower to his hand and see that he's holding a gun. So he was the one who shot the fucker.

Commotion next to the house draws my attention. I see Zack running and more guys shouting and running. Then I see him. Frederick is on the ground. Blood is soaking the front of his shirt. Oh fuck, no.

Ken must have pulled the trigger when Dams went for the gun. My feet are moving to him on their own.

I quickly drop to my knees next to him. "Help him! Do something."

Zack keeps pressure on the wound on Rick's lower abdomen. I can't fucking believe I'm about to lose another one I care about. Fuck. I can't lose anybody else.

My hands reach his face as I stroke his cheek with the back of my right hand. "Don't you dare leave me, Rick. Do you hear me? Don't go into the fucking light. You're my friend, I need you with me."

His eyes close as he moans in pain. I hear somebody say the ambulance is only a few minutes out. I hear sirens, faint in the background. Or is it wishful thinking? Fuck. My mother died this way, people fighting, innocent people getting shot. History fucking repeating itself. My mind flips to Frankie D., yet again he's to blame. But he's not getting away this time. I'm going to fucking kill him.

Looking up to the spot where Zack knocked him out, I bellow, "Where the fuck is he?" as I stand up on my feet by placing my elbows on my knee.

Zack's hands don't move from keeping pressure on Rick's wound. But his eyes tell me he knows exactly what I mean. "Deeds. Where's Frankie D.?"

I turn to see Deeds move in the direction where Frankie D. was standing. The guy is nowhere to be seen.

"Spread out, find him," Deeds barks orders at his men, and Zack's men also listen. Everybody spreads out, guns aimed in front of them.

"Kill the bastard on sight! On. Fucking. Sight. Are we clear?" Some look back at me for screaming at the top of my lungs but I don't fucking care.

That guy doesn't deserve his next breath. I don't even fucking care if I get to kill him. He just needs to die. My eyes find Deeds, he smiles and nods before he runs off. It's a few long dragging moments before the ambulance comes and the EMTs push us away. We step back, so they can work on Frederick.

What chance does he have? None. My family tends to die on me. Dammit. He might be my half-brother. Apparently being related to me is a curse, or so it might seem. He's better off not being my half-brother. I haven't even gotten the results back, that might just give him a chance to live.

Chapter 17
Belle

I fucking hate hospitals. Ironic, right? I turn my head so I don't have to look at the big ass needle the doctor is shoving into my hand. The time spent waiting in the emergency room, the testing and all that shit was more time than they needed to fix my hand.

Luckily, the knife didn't hit any tendons, due to the angle it went in or something. Shit, my mind is still foggy. I didn't pay attention to the details. I could wiggle my freaking fingers. My medical background has abandoned me. Something snaps when it happens to yourself, or so it seems for me. The almost doctor becomes a patient and loses all sanity and interest in the details.

What I did want to know was how Frederick was doing. Nobody would give me any information, dammit. 'Are you family?' Fucking hell. That fucking nurse sure knew what buttons to push. Talk about a loaded question. I could have very well hit her with my fist. The right one. You know... the one that wasn't stabbed. Luckily Zack grabbed me just in time to prevent it from happening.

"There, all done. We need you back next week. Be sure to make an appointment up front," the doctor tells me.

I thank the doc, even manage to give him a smile. Bet he sees right through it, but at least I try to be polite.

Stepping out of the room, I feel Zack's hand on my lower back as the president of Broken Deeds MC steps up to us. He gives me a slight nod and leans in close to give Zack some information. Stepping back, he slaps his hand three times on Zack's shoulder, gives me another nod and walks off.

"What was that all about?" I question.

Zack kisses the top of my head and pushes me slightly forward, immediately removing his hand. "We still can't find any trace of Frankie D."

I spin around and look him in the eyes. "He can't disappear like that. He needs to be found and killed. And found. Then killed again."

"Shush, Honeybump. He will, trust me. All chapters of the two MC's nationwide have their eyes open. He won't get very far," Zack assures me.

Taking a deep breath, I turn and start to walk toward the desk. I need to make an appointment. After that I need to know if I still have a chance to find out I might have a half-brother walking this earth.

******

It's been two weeks. Fourteen freaking days without any information on Frankie D. Zack assures me he's on top of things. As hard as it is, I need to leave it to him. This is something I will get into the moment they find his ass.

My phone on the table indicates I have a message. I check to see who it's from and smile when I see Frederick's name on the screen. I'm so glad he pulled through. He's still in the hospital, but he will recover. That's what counts.

They even moved C.Rash into the same room. Rick likes to complain about this fact, but I'm sure they enjoy each other's company. A few more days and they can both leave the hospital.

This reminds me again of the envelope that holds our test results. It's in the drawer next to my bed. I haven't opened it yet. To be honest, I don't want to know the results. He's close to me, a friend. I need him in my life, brother or not, it doesn't matter. To me he feels like family. That's all I need to know.

Besides, with him helping out. Choosing our side instead of his own father's. Yeah, he's earned the respect from Zack and the rest of the MC.

Pulling up my workout pants and fastening my sneakers, I walk downstairs. Lynn is meeting me at the gym so we can workout together. She's already at the bottom of the stairs punching into her phone.

"Hey, texting Mr. TakeAMessage again are we?" I chuckle.

She shakes her head. "Nah, haven't heard from him in over an hour."

"Wow, over an hour!" I fake a gasp. "Well, there might be something wrong with his phone then right? Or he's dying in a corner or something."

She gives me a shove as we both start to laugh and walk toward the treadmills. Lynn stops dead in her tracks and stretches her arm so I run into it. I look at her face and practically see her drool. I follow her line of sight.

The hot guy with the training mask is working out again. Dumbbells in his hands, punching the air in front of him. My head turns back to look at Lynn.

"Mmmmmm my dream man. He's here, not just a picture this time. Re-fucking-ality. Now him. His cum, I'd swallow," she murmurs dreamily.

I can't help but snort. "Yeah? No burping or gagging?"

"Oh fuck no," Lynn states. "Look at his skin, slick with sweat and muscle. Oh God! That ink. Oh look at that, even his bare feet are covered. That mask…"

He turns as he stops his workout and steps closer to us. He sets the dumbbells back in the rack and he takes off his mask. I hear Lynn whisper next to me that he's hot as hell, with and without the mask. Without the mask though, I now recognize him.

His eyes go to me and gives a slight nod, dismissing me as his eyes go and stay hooked on Lynn. "Hello, lovely ladies. You enjoyed watching me."

It is more of a statement than a question. I feel arms go around my waist and soft lips kiss my neck. The smell and warmth I love the most surrounds me... Zack.

One hand leaves me and reaches forward. They grab each other's hands and pump once before letting go. "Deeds, good to see you my man. You've already met Blue. This here is my sister Lynn. Lynn, meet the president of Broken Deeds MC."

He takes a step closer while his eyes stay focused on Lynn, looking up and down until his eyes land on her lips.

Recognition sets in. "Hotlips."

He smiles and his eyes fill with hunger and satisfaction. Like a dog who just found his favorite bone.

"Fuck. I need to throw up," Lynn mutters as my head turns to her and I think things through.

So two minutes ago you felt the need to swallow his cum without burping or gagging, but now you know who your dream man is you need to puke? You're funny...and he should put the mask back on.

"Blue!" Lynn snaps.

"Oh fuck, I said that out loud again didn't I?" I mutter.

"You need to learn the difference, that shit ain't funny!" Lynn is furious with me.

Deeds and also Dams, who is standing behind Zack, both chuckle. Zack's hands tighten around me.

"I disagree with you there, Hotlips. And you need to put your mouth where your words are." Deeds' voice is husky as

297

he throws out those words.

"You back the fuck off, Deeds, that's my sister you're talking to and about. Off-limits. Not. Gonna. Happen. Pal," Zack growls.

"That's where you're wrong, Zack." Deeds lifts his chin. "She was mine the moment she answered my call for a sit-down with you. That was your request, you're the one who hooked us up in the first place. So…. Thanks, I guess."

Oh shit, Zack is going to… I look back and see the moment the words register. Zack is going to fucking flip. My hands go to his shirt as he pushes forward. His shirt tears and my eyes go to the blue ink on his chest. One of my hands glides over it and Zack sucks in a breath when I touch the ink because it's still tender.

Our eyes meet. It's beautiful. Tears start to burn in my eyes as a lump grows in my throat. My finger strokes the name that has been freshly inked into his skin right above his heart. Entangled with his old tattoos is the name "Sallybelle" along with a tiny blue orchid.

I smile as he wipes away a tear from my cheek. His lips touch mine as my hands move to his neck. Zack's hands find my ass and he pulls me in tight against his body. I wrap my legs around his waist.

Very faint in the background I hear Dams' voice as Zack deepens the kiss. "Everybody out, out, right the fuck now. Fuck. One of these days I ain't gonna be around for this shit. Fucking bunnies I tell ya."

Continue to the next page to read an excerpt of
"Deeds" Broken Deeds MC #1

Broken Deeds MC is a whole new series and a
spin-off from Areion Fury MC.

"Deeds" Broken Deeds MC #1

CHAPTER ONE

Lynn

A cold blast of air conditioning greets me as I stroll out of the locker room. For a weekend, it isn't too busy, and the sound of metal clanking against metal mixes with the occasional grunt. I make my way to the stairs to wait for my best friend to come downstairs so we can workout together.

To kill time, I scroll through my phone and click on the last text message I received. Smiling when I re-read it. The dick that sent it is so freaking funny. Annoying, but funny. I have no clue who he is, that's why I call him dick. He, on the other hand, calls me Hotlips.

"Hey! Texting Mr. TakeAMessage again, are we?"

I turn and see Blue coming down the stairs. Her apartment is attached to the gym that she co-owns with Areion Fury MC, the motorcycle club my brother, Zack, is the president of.

Smiling at her, I give her the truth. "Nah, haven't heard from him in over an hour."

"Wow, over an hour! Well, there might be something wrong with his phone then, right? Or he's dying in a corner or something."

Giving her a shove to the shoulder, we both burst out in a fit of laughter while we start toward the treadmills. My head turns away from Blue and my eyes meet the most perfect man I've seen in my whole life. Coming to an abrupt halt, I put my arm up to stop Blue. I'm sure when she looks at me she sees drool coming from my mouth.

I just can't help myself. Just a few weeks ago, Blue was at the gym late at night. There was a hot guy training there. Or so she said, so I made her send me a picture to prove it. One look at that picture and I baptized him my dream man. That same hot guy is here, right now! Working out again with a training mask on. Looks like he's boxing except there are dumbbells in his hands, and he's just punching into the air in front of him. It doesn't matter that I can't see part of his face, because it's hidden behind that mask. For me, that just adds to the hotness of the complete image.

I can't help myself when I say. "Mmmmmm my dream man! He's here, not just a picture this time! Re-fucking-ality. Now him. His cum, I'd swallow."

Blue gives a snort and asks. "Yeah? No burping or gagging?"

"Oh, fuck no! Look at his skin, slick with sweat and muscle. Oh God! That ink. Even his legs are covered and disappear right into his shoes, I bet even his feet are covered. That mask…"

He turns as he stops his workout and steps closer to us.

301

He sets the dumbbells back on the rack and takes off his mask. I whisper to Blue. "He's hot as hell, with and without the mask."

He gives Blue a slight nod. That's when our eyes meet and lock. Just one look in his eyes and heat flows through my body, making it flame up inside.

"Hello, lovely ladies. You enjoyed watching me." It was more of a statement than a question.

My brother comes up from behind and grabs Blue in a tight hug. He sticks one hand out in front of him, towards the hot guy. They grab each other's hands and pump once before letting go.

"Deeds, good to see you, my man. You've already met Blue. This here is my sister Lynn. Lynn, meet the president of Broken Deeds MC."

He keeps looking into my eyes while he takes a step closer to me. Slowly, his eyes slide down my body and back up again, landing on my lips. That's when I see recognition flash in his eyes. Fuck, no. A memory flashes through my mind of a picture I send that dick that's been texting me. A close-up of my middle finger in my mouth. Yeah, I send him that picture to flip him off after he asked me to send a picture showing my tits.

"Hotlips." He smiles brightly while his eyes now fill with hunger and satisfaction. Like a freaking dog who just found his favorite bone.

The heat flowing through my body now turns to ice. This can't be happening. He can't be the dick who's been texting me all this time. My stomach twists into a knot.

"Fuck! I need to throw up," I mutter as Blue's head turns to me and I can see her thinking things through.

"So two minutes ago you felt the need to swallow his cum without burping or gagging, but now you know who your dream man is you need to puke? You're funny…and he should put the mask back on."

"Blue!" That freaking bitch has a nasty habit of thinking out loud.

"Oh fuck, I said that out loud again, didn't I?"

"You need to learn the difference. That shit ain't funny!"

I'm furious while Deeds, the fucker chuckles. "I disagree with you there, Hotlips. And you need to put your mouth where your words are."

Zack's booming voice fills the gym. "Back the fuck off Deeds. That's my sister you're talking to and about. Off-limits. Not. Gonna. Happen. Pal."

Deeds' body language gets defensive as he throws back his shoulders and draws up to his full height. Making a visible stand against my brothers threat. "That's where you're wrong Zack. She was mine the moment she answered my call for a sit-down with you. That was your request; you're the one who hooked us up in the first place. So…. thanks, I guess."

I can't take this shit. This is so not happening. Turning on my heels, I practically run toward the women's locker room. I cannot believe the guy who's been texting me for the past several weeks is the president of a fucking MC. Christ, I'm so stupid. How could I not have known?

Sure, I knew he was a biker. An arrogant, filthy-mouthed dick, calling for a sit-down with my brother, the president of Areion Fury MC. Fuck! The president of Broken Deeds MC, himself! Why the fuck would he text me all day, every day, for weeks? What the hell was my friend Blue thinking when she gave a random guy my cell number? I shouldn't have let her answer the phone after I hung up on the rude asshole. Calling me a cunt. Mother fucker. I gave him hell after the first few words he said to me over the phone.

Oh, how I hate that word. Cunt. I don't care who says it, just don't ever call me one. Fuck! Me and my big mouth. Okay, so I might have enjoyed his messages. Just a fun distraction, that's all it was, right? Me calling him Dick, him calling me Hotlips. On. My. Phone. Fucking hell! Why did I have to run into him?

And to discover who he was when my brother introduced us? Shit. For him to know who I am? That… that… dick! A Prez. No wonder I've been calling him dick, he really is one. I mean, doesn't he have ho's all over his dick? I mean clubhouse. Ho's that keep him and his dick occupied? I am so, so fucked. God, how could I be so, so…

"Stupid!"

With a grunt, I shove open the door to the locker room. Two girls gasp when I burst my way inside. I mumble an apology and they both tie their shoes and walk out. Taking a deep breath, I'm thankful that the locker room is now completely empty. Enough with the humiliation. I need to change and get the fuck out of here.

Heading over to my locker, I grab my bag. Kicking off my sneakers, I strip off my workout pants so I'm down to my lime green thong and black sports bra. I toss the pants back into my bag and as I reach for my shorts and tank top, I hear the door slam shut and the snick of a lock. Shit, that can't be good.

Turning around to face the door, I see Deeds standing right there. I have no control of how my body reacts to him. Though I keep my breath steady, my heart is pounding in my chest. There's no way around him, no escape. He's slowly walking toward me while his eyes scan my body, from my face to my bare feet. They linger way too long on my thong before moving up to my tits. I drop the bag and cross my arms in front of my chest. Pushing up my tits, I act like I'm fully dressed. I refuse to be intimidated by him.

It's fucking over. I could have been texting with anyone for that matter. Just like those social media scams. You think it's a hot guy, but in reality it's just a tiny old wrinkled man wanting naked pictures.

Except in my case it is a freaking hottie. Ink all over, cut muscles, gorgeous face, solid chest. I mean this guy is built but moves with so much fluidity. And he's freaking flexible. Yeah, I noticed all of that when my eyes locked on his body for that shortest of moments watching him train. So hot! That is, until my brother introduced us and we both realized who the fuck we were.

It was just words from one phone to another, right? There was nothing between us to begin with. I sure as fuck ain't getting involved with anyone from another chapter of Areion Fury, let alone someone from another MC. I'm sure as fuck not hopping into bed with the president. My father was a president and a huge dick. Pure alpha caveman, just like his son is now. I grew up in a house full of bad boy alphas and they're annoying as fucking hell. Besides, my brother would rather lock me in a barn way out in the country than let me date this guy. Oh, who am I kidding? These guys don't date. They grab your hair and fuck you till you're screaming and...

"What are you thinking? I like the sounds coming from those sexy-as-fuck lips."

Fuck, how embarrassing. Was I moaning at the thought of him grabbing my... Stop! I need to stop and focus. "What the fuck are you doing here? Deeds, was it?"

"Yeah, babe, Deeds." He steps closer and his chest bumps against my arms.

Pushing my shoulders back, I straighten my spine, lifting my chin as my gaze locks with his.

"Don't fucking call me babe. You dicks always call pussy those bullshit names. Babe, Sweetheart, Darlin', Sugar. You know what? Don't call me, period. Not. At. All. No need to text, call, email… Hell, don't even send smoke signals. Nothing. Just fucking leave and get back to the ho's you guys like to stick it in and be all happy and shit."

I sidestep him and grab my bag off the floor. But before I can even take one step, my back is up against the lockers. My bag hits the ground and my hands are pinned on each side of my head by his hands.

His face is already close to mine and he inches even closer. "Such a mouth on you. Do you know that was the first thing that turned me on? The moment I heard your voice utter those filthy words. So rattle on, Hotlips, stroke my ears as if you're stroking my cock."

He grinds his hips into me and I feel his hard length. Holy shit, he's huge! He licks my lower lip and with the tip of his tongue, flips the metal stud from my snake bite piercing. I have one on each side of my bottom lip, near the corners of my mouth.

Starting on the right, his tongue traces my upper lip to the other side as he now gives my other piercing the same attention. Sucking in a breath, my mouth opens slightly, and I'm surprised by the jolt of desire that runs through me. This is a very bad fucking idea, but I can't help being extremely turned on by him right now.

He takes advantage and licks into my mouth, tracing my teeth with his tongue. Giving in to temptation, I let my tongue meet his. He moans loud and long when he discovers my tongue piercing as he pushes his body into mine. He slides my arms above my head and switches his grip, placing both of my wrists in one of his huge hands. He strokes his free hand down my neck, over my collarbone, brushing my nipple, past my belly and over my hip to grasp my ass.

His grip tightens as he pulls me forward and grinds his hips at the same time. The friction sends a jolt through my clit and I gasp in his mouth. A rumble of satisfaction vibrates from deep within his chest. He leaves me no time to react as his hand slides from my ass to the edge of my thong, tracing it down to the lips of my pussy.

His fingers slide up and down as I feel myself getting wet. His actions shoot jolts of pleasure through my body. I'm sure my thong is drenched by the time he pushes two fingers inside me.

"So wet and ready. All this for me?"

I can't seem to think of any words. I don't even think I can find my voice right now. Fuck, what's he doing with me? My body seems to react automatically. I want him. Can't think of anything else. Well, except for the fact that this is a very bad fucking idea. Oh, what the hell! Just once and then he's done. It's a fucking fantasy that's been built from all those fucking texts back and forth. We just have to fuck it out of our system and be done with it. Somehow he's managed to free his cock and enters me with one hard push. Fuck. Me. That feels so fucking good. I'm so damn full I'm stretched like a rubber band ready to pop.

"Fucking tight, Hotlips."

His hips stay still as his mouth moves to my ear. He bites down on my earlobe and releases a deep breath.

"I knew you'd feel this good. Just fucking knew it. The kind of cunt that's a special edition. No, make that a fucking limited edition, created just for my cock."

I squeeze my inner muscles at the sound of his words. He bites my neck in response and pulls out half way and slams back in. Each time he thrusts he grinds himself deeper. I need to grab him, touch him, get my nails into his skin. Pulling at my trapped hands, I let out a frustrated sound.

"Not the one in charge here. I am. "

He keeps pounding as fire starts to grow inside me. I'm about to come when he bends slightly with his knees and pushes harder upward. Hitting me at just the right angle, my head slams back into the lockers and I scream his name. I'm lost.

"Deeds! Fuck. Move that ass. Oh! YES!"

He pumps a few more times before biting down hard on my neck and sucking my skin into his mouth. His hand on my ass holds me still as his body freezes and it feels like he's showering my insides with his cum.

He moves his hips slowly as if he's pumping the last of his seed. Making sure every last drop is gone. At last, he releases my neck and his tongue laps a few more times at the sensitive spot. By the feel of it, I'm pretty sure he left the imprint of his teeth on my fucking neck.

"So fucking good, Hotlips, so fucking good. Remember now. This…"

He pushes his hips forward, and his cock that's going from soft to half erect twitches inside my pussy.

"…is my cunt. You're not even allowed to look at another cock. You hear me, Hotlips?"

Who the fuck died and made him king of my pussycastle?

"Seeing as this cunt is attached to me, it would be my own fucking choice if I let a cock, any cock in there. And seriously, stop calling it a cunt! It's fucking degrading."

He chuckles as he pumps his hips a few more times.

"Wish I had more time; then we'd go for round two. Your mouth sets my dick on fire. You'd best to remember that."

"Just pull out, dick. Leave so I can go to work. You're not the only one who needs to be somewhere."

He chuckles as he pulls out, steps away from me, and releases my wrists. I feel his cum sliding down the inside of my leg as realization hits home. Again the blood in my veins chills to ice, making my heart stop for a few seconds.

"You fucked me bare? What the hell, fuckhead? Now I need to get tested and take a morning after pill." Holding my breath as I rub a hand down my face. I shake my head at the thought of getting pregnant or catching an STD.

"Fuck! I'm so fucked right now."

The asshole has the nerve to act offended. "Shut those hot lips for a few seconds, would you? First, I'm clean. I always have my dick wrapped in rubber."

"Yeah, I feel ya, brother. Thanks so much for wrapping it in a rubber. Oh, no, wait. You didn't fucking use one. So excuse me while I don't trust your ass. Or dick for that matter."

"Hotlips."

That fucking nickname. That fucking phone call! Demanding to speak to the president instead of some stupid cunt. I cursed him to hell and back the moment he called me that and voila, Hotlips was born. The way he says that nickname now, though? All low and husky? It begs my traitorous mouth to reply. "What?"

"What did I tell you about your mouth?"

My eyes go to his cock as it stands up proud, jumping to get back inside me. I huff as I cross my arms in front of my chest again. "He's not getting back in, so you might as well lock him the fuck back up."

He chuckles again as he stuffs his dick back into his pants. Stepping closer, he grabs my chin with one hand while he looks into my eyes. "Leave my cum where it is, you get me?"

"Fuck off, dickhead."

He smiles before he kisses me hard and fast. Making my pussy flame up while I try very hard to ignore the feeling and instead try to push him away. He pulls back but grabs a hold of my bottom lip with his teeth and gives it a slight pull. Backing up, he releases me completely.

"Get dressed, Hotlips."

He turns and leaves the locker room. Standing there, unable to move, the only sound I hear is the pounding of my heartbeat in my ears and my breath that seems to pick up. What the hell just happened and what the hell am I doing? Oh yeah right, I was fucked. Am fucked. Oh shit this is just, fuck! Damn, I need to stop using my favorite word. Stopping myself from freaking out, I stalk to the bathroom and clean up.

Getting dressed quickly, I step into my jeans shorts. I made them myself, so they might be a bit too short and show a little ass cheek, but I like them. I pull my tank over my sports bra and adjust my tits, then grab my Harley boots and slide them on. I pick my bag up from the floor and walk out, glad to see Deeds isn't waiting for me outside the locker room.

I push open the door to leave the gym but come to an abrupt stop when I see Deeds leaning against his bike. On his left and right are two other motorcycles, with bikers sitting on them. One is a very freaky tiny dude with lots of ink. And when I say lots of ink, I mean even his face is covered in that shit. The other guy could be a cover model for a fitness magazine. He looks a lot like Deeds, except this one has a 5 o'clock shadow. He has blue eyes and...

"Get your fucking eyes off my brother."

Shit! No wonder I was drawn to the hot guy. He really does look just like Deeds, well, not completely. This guy doesn't seem to have any ink, while Deeds is covered in it. Deeds has dark, long spiky hair while his brother's hair is just a few inches long and seems a bit lighter. Deeds has more muscle too. I bet…

"Hotlips!"

"What?"

"Stop eye-fucking Broke."

"Well, get him out of my sight then! Not my fucking fault he's standing there asking to be eye-fucked when he looks like that!"

"Hotlips."

Fuck, the hairs on my arms stand up at the way he says that stupid nickname. It's threatening, yet very seductive. Taking a deep breath I close my eyes.

"Fine."

I turn to walk to the shop.

"Where are you going?"

"Work."

"I'll take you there, hop on."

"I ain't getting on the back of no man's bike, dickhead. Besides, it's not that far."

As I walk away from his bike, the other two chuckle. He tells them to wait right there as he walks up to me and slides his hand in the back pocket of my jeans shorts and falls in step beside me. After a few seconds, I come to a stop.

"Why are ya stopping?" He asks as he steps in front of me.

"I'm here." I nod toward the shop that is right next to the gym.

He takes it all in and shakes his head. "What do you do for a living?"

"I pierce and sometimes ink."

The left corner of his mouth comes up in a smile while his eyes give away a hint of shock. "Well, fuck me, ain't you just full of surprises."

"Yeah, well, here's another surprise for ya. We're not doing it again. The fucking or the texting. Or the meeting or walking me to work. None of it. Done. Not happening."

A lazy smile forms on his face as he leans in. One hand circles my waist as the other grabs my neck. He crushes his lips down on mine and pushes his tongue inside. He finds my piercing and plays with it. With the hand around my waist, he pulls me into his body and I can't help feeling a little annoyed by the fact my body responds to him. The fucking heat is back, flashing through my veins and fueling desire that's shooting straight to my clit.

"Feel that? We're doing all of that again."

"I don't feel anything, dickhead."

His hand slides down my ass as he grips it hard and pushes his hips forward. He is hard as fuck and his cock tries to leave an imprint on my body. I refuse to give him the satisfaction of knowing he's getting to me. My body might

314

betray me, so for that very reason I'm telling him the opposite of what I feel.

"Nope, still nothing. Maybe I need to pierce that sucker so it adds something."

Fisting his hand deep into my hair, he pulls my head back to look into my eyes. "I'm perfectly fine with the holes in my body I was born with. No fucking way in hell am I adding more."

I smile at his tone of voice. Deep and throaty, almost a growl. And I just love the way I get to him that fast. Might as well add more fuel to the fire. "Well, isn't that just disappointing?"

"Didn't hear you complaining a moment ago."

Before I can give another reply, his mouth is on me again. He kisses me deep and hard for just a few seconds. Then his lips leave mine and go to my ear.

"I'll be back for round two soon." The hand on my ass slides to the edge of my very short shorts and slips beneath. Yet again, his fingers push my thong to the side, stroking the lips of my pussy. "Keep it wet and ready for me."

Leaving with a soft brush of his lips on mine, he steps away and saunters to his bike, leaving my body to vibrate with desire at the promise for round two. I am truly fucked. I know it's better if this stops right here, but with what just happened? My body craves more. Never have I felt so much desire and pleasure in all my freaking life. He made me feel wanted, needed, like I was solely alive to be with him.

Right, like that's the biker way.

Shaking my head, I turn and open the shop. Stepping inside while leaving the door open, I check my watch. Just ten more minutes before the shop opens. Lee and Blue will be here soon.

Lee, as in Brandlee. My partner in crime. We own this shop. We can both pierce and ink. He's a good friend of mine and is very good at what he does. I look at the agenda on the counter. Lee's only got three hours scheduled this morning. Blue, on the other hand, has a full day.

Since she returned from Japan, I talked her into working with us in the shop. She's one hell of an artist and everybody loves her work. I, on the other hand, have never liked giving anybody ink. I'm good at it, don't get me wrong, but I'd rather just do the piercings. Oh, who am I kidding? I don't like ink at all. Funny, right? Owning a tattoo shop and not liking ink should be blasphemy!

I don't know why I don't like it, but I just don't. Well that was until a few weeks ago, when Blue send me a picture of my dream man. Inked muscles slick with sweat, oh shit. Then seeing him again, just now in the gym. Punching the air in front of him while he's holding dumbbells in his hands. And wearing a training mask. It covers his nose and mouth so all you can see are his eyes. I know it's used for strengthening the lungs but for me, it strengthens the need to fuck him.

Fuck! I still can't believe that was the guy who was texting me all this time. Holy shit, I need to focus. I don't like ink. I need to remember this. No ink, no Deeds. I should blame Blue, for throwing Deeds at me, but I don't. She's been my best friend my whole life. We used to live right next door to each other. I'm so happy she's back and reunited with my brother. Those two are literally made for each other. I also like the fact she's taken over my load of ink appointments. But mostly, I just like having my best friend back in the same town.

.....The story continues in "Deeds" Broken Deeds MC #1

Visit Esther E. Schmidt online:

Website:

www.esthereschmidt.nl

Facebook - AuthorEstherESchmidt

Twitter - @esthereschmidt

Instagram - @esthereschmidt

Pinterest - @esthereschmidt

Signup for Esther's newsletter:

http://esthereschmidt.nl/newsletter

Join Esther's fan group on Facebook:

https://www.facebook.com/groups/estherselite

MORE BOOKS & SERIES:

LOST VALKYRIES

PEACOCK
THE FAULTS OF OUR SINS

319

Made in the USA
Middletown, DE
05 January 2022

57680309R10179